Unlocked

MARGO KELLY

Author of Merit Press's *Who R U Really?*

MeritPress

Published by
Merit Press
an imprint of F+W Media, Inc.
10151 Carver Road, Suite 200
Blue Ash, OH 45242. U.S.A.
www.meritpressbooks.com

ISBN 10: 1-4405-9359-0
ISBN 13: 978-1-4405-9359-8
eISBN 10: 1-4405-9360-4
eISBN 13: 978-1-4405-9360-4

Printed in the United States of America.

10 9 8 7 6 5 4 3 2 1

This is a work of fiction. Names, characters, corporations, institutions, organizations,
events, or locales in this novel are either the product of the author's imagination or, if
real, used fictitiously. The resemblance of any character to actual persons (living or dead)
is entirely coincidental.

Many of the designations used by manufacturers and sellers to distinguish their products
are claimed as trademarks. Where those designations appear in this book and F+W
Media, Inc. was aware of a trademark claim, the designations have been printed with
initial capital letters.

Cover design by Frank Rivera.
Cover images © iStockphoto.com/joshuaraineyphotography; iStockphoto.com/
Timothy Hughes; iStockphoto.com/imagoRB.

This book is available at quantity discounts for bulk purchases.
For information, please call 1-800-289-0963.

Acknowledgments

I hereby declare my gratitude to the people who directly influenced the publication of this story.

Brianne Johnson: You are the best agent in the industry! You've been a crucial advocate, and your support means the world to me. Thank you.

Jacquelyn Mitchard: You helped me break into the publishing world with my debut novel, *Who R U Really?*, and your continued generosity with *Unlocked* has brought me great joy. Thank you.

Merit Press: You have terrific people like Frank Rivera, who created an amazing cover, Lisa Laing, who refined this manuscript with proper punctuation and grammar, and Bethany Carland-Adams, who managed the publicity efforts with persistence and patience. Thank you.

Early readers: Your insights on character development and plot points were essential to improving this story. When I asked you to read it just one more time, you did. Michele Yancey, Shelby Engstrom, Mary Buersmeyer, Holly Barnes, Artemis Grey, Christi Corbett, and Melissa Dean. Thank you.

My family: You people are the biggest blessings in my life. Katherine, Jacob, Mitchell, Sarah, and Chris. For your daily unconditional love, I thank you.

BOOK ONE

Chaos

A peculiar sort of chaos looms beneath the pretense of peace.

FRIDAY
AUGUST 23

Crimson lights flashed beneath the darkening Idaho sky, and swarms of people screamed as they plummeted on roller coaster rails. My friends and I passed unshaven men who blew whistles and offered the world, if you'd only play their game—toss their rings, shoot their balls, throw their darts—for a small price, of course. The tempting aroma of fried foods made my empty stomach tighten. Funnel cakes. Corn dogs. Fried Twinkies.

"Hannah, there it is!" Lily motioned toward a massive white tent. A throng of people near the opening pointed and laughed at the show inside. Lily snatched my wrist and yanked me forward, but Manny tugged me back.

"Food first." He patted his stomach.

"No. Hypnotist first," Lily said. "He's the whole reason we came tonight." She pulled, and her tan shoulders hunched. But Manny held on, and together, the three of us blocked the crowd trying to move down the fairway. A tall blond lady grunted and hedged around us. Then Lily's long-time love, Jordan, laughed at our spectacle, which was the last thing I wanted. I wrenched free from my friends and took a step away.

"Let's work this out," I said.

"Oh, Hannah . . ." Lily adjusted her golden tank top. "You're crazy if you think Manny and I will ever agree on anything."

"Then we'll flip a coin," I said.

Jordan plucked a quarter from his pocket. "Who wants to call it?"

Lily clapped. "Heads!"

Jordan tossed the quarter high into the evening sky. We craned our necks, and the evening breeze blew my hair across my face. I smoothed it back into place as the coin crested and began to fall. Jordan reached for it, but a burly man—too busy laughing to watch where he was walking—bumped into Jordan before he caught the coin.

"Dude! Watch out!" Manny yelled at the stranger. I wrapped my fingers around Manny's arm, and he relaxed. The offending guy held his hands up in apology and wandered away.

Manny raked his fingers through his thick chestnut hair. "Let's get the hypnotist over with so we can enjoy the rest of the night."

Lily beamed, and her hazel eyes sparkled. "We need to hurry and get our seats. The next show starts in ten minutes." She grabbed Jordan's hand, and they darted toward the white tent, but the crowd from the previous performance flooded out and blocked their path.

"Thanks," I said to Manny. "I just want everyone to get along and have fun tonight."

Manny laced his fingers through mine, and my heart fluttered. Would tonight be the night we finally kissed? We'd been friends for years, but we just officially started dating last week. He was the best thing in my life, and I wanted to be with him forever. He squeezed my hand, and we meandered over to the tent to wait with Jordan and Lily.

Jordan fiddled with the gold hoop dangling from Lily's ear, and she fussed over the spikes in his sun-bleached hair. They were the poster children for cute couples. Lily had even bought Jordan a plaid shirt with golden lines through it to coordinate with her tank top, and they both wore faded denim shorts and Converse sneakers.

The crowd of people cleared, and we ducked inside the mammoth structure. Spotlights illuminated the entire space and rock music blasted from corner speakers. Stands of bleachers spanned two-thirds of the perimeter, and a stage filled the remainder. Men, like a colony of worker ants, moved around, sweeping and rearranging chairs for the next show.

Lily claimed a spot near the middle front of the bleachers, and I perched next to her. A shiver ran up my spine when the cold metal touched the backs of my thighs. I wedged my fingers beneath my legs, and my silver bracelets clanked against the steel.

"Why do you want to sit so close?" I raised my voice over the blaring song.

"To get picked for the show." Lily bugged out her eyes, as if it should've been obvious.

My throat tightened at the idea of making a fool of myself in front of everyone. I wished we could move further back, but all around us, the stands were filling fast.

Over the noise, a familiar hee-haw laugh split the arena: Chelsea. She and her date, Mark, bounded toward us, her long tan legs accentuated by her short shorts. Her single blond braid swished back and forth as she moved. She was a starting center for volleyball and towered five inches over Mark, who was a second-string tight end for the football team. He had to move twice as fast to keep up with her, but he had pursued her ever since she moved here last fall.

"You didn't save us seats?" Chelsea asked.

"It flooded with people too fast," Lily said. We hopped up and exchanged hugs with her.

Jordan stepped in front of Chelsea and fingered the collar of my white blouse. "You'd be hilarious hypnotized," he said.

"No, I wouldn't." I swatted his hand away and straightened my collar. "Besides, it's only entertainment. A gimmick."

"Jordan's right," Chelsea said. "You would be funny onstage, but you're way too uptight to be submissive to anyone." My jaw dropped, and Chelsea laughed.

"I'm not uptight," I said, but my words faded into the deafening music. I just never wanted to be disorderly like my dad. He embarrassed Mom so many times in public. She would flush beet red as she worked to quiet his outbursts. One evening back in New Jersey, when I was eleven, Dad refused to get into the car. Mom started the engine and threatened to leave him in that crowded mall parking lot. I loved him too much to abandon him there. I pleaded with him, and when I reached for his arm, he backhanded me. My head flung to the side, and the pain seared through my cheek. Less than twenty feet away, a trio of girls from the popular clique gawked at my family's debacle. Their ringleader cocked an eyebrow. Then the girls snickered and scurried away. I fought back my tears and turned toward Dad. I opened his door and waited—keeping my hands to myself. Several minutes passed before he relented and sank into the passenger seat. He never touched me again. He died three months later.

The music in the arena suddenly changed from blaring rock to a peppier pop song at half the volume.

Chelsea edged around me and took my seat. "Well if you're too chicken to be in the show, Lily and I can volunteer."

"Go ahead," I said.

"No!" Lily said. "She's just teasing."

Chelsea shrugged and surrendered my seat. "Fine, just make sure you entertain us." She grabbed Mark's hand, and they ran off to claim spots at the top of the bleachers.

"Don't let them badger you into doing it, if it's something you don't want to do," Manny said. His towering six-foot frame shaded me from the arena's spotlights.

"Trust me," I said. "I'll choose for myself."

His brown eyes widened, and he caressed my cheek with his smooth fingertips.

10

"Oh gag." Jordan pretended to barf. "It's a good thing we haven't eaten yet; otherwise I'd be blowing chunks all over you two."

Manny whacked Jordan's chest.

"Dude!" Jordan lifted his hands.

"Stop." Lily pulled him toward her, and he sat to her right. I sat to her left, and when Manny took the spot next to me, he wrapped his arm around my waist.

He whispered in my ear, "You're amazing." His breath made my skin quiver.

A guy on the stage thumped the microphone.

"Ladies and gentlemen," the announcer said, and the song changed to an anthem of drums and guitars, building the excitement. "Tonight, I have the honor of introducing the mystical Master Gira." The guy swept his arm to the side of the stage, the drums beat at a maddening level, and the crowd applauded as a man stepped onto the stage. He wore powder-blue sneakers, worn-out jeans, and a white button-up collared shirt beneath a black blazer. His face, too tan. His hair, too white. He clapped his huge hands together, and his bleached teeth glowed under the glare of the spotlights.

Lily whacked my knee. "Volunteer with me." She twisted several strands of her long brown locks around her finger. "Take a risk with me. Life is meant to be lived. Please?"

I glanced up at the stage and back at Lily. "I'll do it, but only because we're friends."

"Yes!" Lily threw her arms around my neck. "Best friends."

"Welcome to my Mystical Madness!" Master Gira swung the microphone stand out of his way and clutched the mike with his other hand. The crowd cheered.

He spread his arms wide and asked, "Who's been hypnotized before?" Half the crowd thrust their hands into the air. They clearly thought this was no big deal. Maybe I *was* too uptight.

"Who thinks it's all a giant hoax?" he asked. Lily clutched my wrist and raised it high. I yanked it back down, but the master mystic had already locked eyes with me. He raised his bushy white eyebrows and strutted to the left side of the stage.

"Who's afraid of appearing foolish tonight?" A majority lifted their hands. "I'll tell you what"—he pointed, and the music in the background softened—"everyone shake your hands high in the air." Everyone did, including me. "Shake them faster. Higher. Lower. In front of your face. Turn to your neighbor. Who seems foolish now?" The volume of the music increased, and everyone burst into raucous laughter. "And we haven't even started the show yet!" Master Gira shouted into the microphone.

He moved back to center stage, directly in front of me, but he looked beyond me—higher up into the stands. "Grab the hand of your neighbor and extend your arms out straight." Both Manny and Lily linked fingers with me. The animated hypnotist lifted his arms up and down, and everyone in the crowd followed without hesitation. We all looked ridiculous, but the merriment was contagious.

"Who's ready to have the most amazing time of their life?" The crowd shouted their approval. "Well, the best seats in the house are right up here." He pointed toward the row of chairs on the stage. "If you want to let go of your fears and feel more relaxed than you ever have, join the show tonight. I have fifteen chairs, and I need them filled boy, girl, boy, girl. Who wants to help?"

Lily tugged me to my feet, and with her other hand, she reached for Jordan. I reminded myself that I was doing this for her. I was nothing like my dad. I could have fun and keep my composure.

Manny hopped up with us. "I'll go, too. When it's over we can do whatever you want."

"Eat funnel cakes," I said.

"Funnel cakes it is."

I gave a quick nod, and all four of us ran up onstage with eleven other suckers. Several stage assistants showed us which seats to take. Manny and I sat next to each other, but they positioned Lily and Jordan at the other end of the row. She gave me an enthusiastic thumbs-up, and he winked at me.

Gira explained to the audience that they needed to be very quiet while he hypnotized us. "Not everyone can be hypnotized," he said. "If I or my assistants see someone is not fully under, we will excuse them from the show to return to the bleachers. And likewise, if a member of the audience falls under, we may bring him or her to join us up here."

The lights over the bleachers dimmed, and the spotlights aimed at the stage brightened. I squinted at the harsh beams. The hypnotist stepped in front of the row of chairs and touched each person on the shoulder. His jeans brushed my bare knees, and he paused in front of me with his index finger on my shoulder. I focused on the blacks of his pupils, and goose bumps popped out on my arms. My instincts told me to get off the stage. But the show had already begun. Lily would kill me if I left now. I could just pretend to be hypnotized.

Master Gira shifted his hand in front of me and offered it to shake. He didn't do that with anyone else, and so I hesitated at first, but then I relented and extended my own hand. Without warning, he clutched my wrist and jerked it upward, nearly lifting me out of my chair. He held my palm so close to his face, his breath warmed my skin. He lowered his voice and spoke in a rapid monotone.

"From the tips of your fingers relax your muscles." He released my wrist and touched my fingertips. Then he trailed his hand down toward my elbow. I was uncertain about how I should react. "Feel an overwhelming sense of peace. Let go of your worries. When I count to three you will slip into a deep resting place of serenity and comfort. One. Two. Three. Sleep!"

He snapped, and my chin fell to my chest.

But I wasn't asleep.

I wasn't snoring. I wasn't dreaming. My eyes were open, and I was aware of everything around me, but my head felt heavy. I played along, and even with my chin down, I could see the hypnotist step to the person next to me. On my other side, Manny tugged at the hem of his tan shorts and bounced his knee. He leaned forward and whispered, "Are you okay?"

"Yes," I whispered without moving a muscle.

A stage assistant said to Manny, "Please return to the audience."

I needed him to stay.

Manny's hand tightened into a fist on his thigh. "I want to continue," he said.

"No." The stage assistant nudged his arm.

Manny flexed his fingers and plucked at his blue polo shirt. The assistant led him away, and another assistant guided someone else to Manny's chair. The stranger's chin sank to his chest. My eyes throbbed from straining, but before I closed them to rest, a shadow crept across the stage floor. I took a deep breath and listened to the hypnotist tell more people to sleep. Were they all faking like I was?

"Open your minds," Master Gira said with a cadence. "Open your minds and listen to my voice. I'm going to count and when I reach ten, you will be in a deep restful sleep, but you will still hear my voice and respond to my directions. As I count, visualize yourself moving down a plush staircase. Each step down brings you closer to true relaxation. Each step doubles your sense of peace. One, you're on the first step moving down."

I'm doing this for Lily.

"Two. Three."

I hope Manny is okay.

"Four. Five."

I am not like my dad. I can stay in control.

"Six. Seven."

I wish I could see Lily and Jordan.

"Eight. Nine."

An ant crawled across the stage. It was out of my reach; otherwise, I would have squished it under my flip-flop. I hated those pests.

"I only want you to experience an overwhelming sense of serenity and comfort. Relax . . . Ten. Accept the feeling of immense satisfaction. Gradually lift your heads and open your eyes."

I lifted my chin, thrilled my neck didn't ache from being in the same position for so long. I stretched from side to side and scanned the audience for Manny, but the bright spotlights kept me from making out the faces. They seemed like distant ghosts instead of living people. I glanced down to the end of the row, expecting to see Lily and Jordan, but they were gone.

"Slowly inhale, expand your diaphragm, and hold it." I followed Master Gira's instructions, but I faced straight ahead and avoided eye contact with him as he paced the stage. I wanted him to assume I was under his spell. "Gently release the breath out through your mouth."

The music changed again. A familiar tune, but a few seconds passed before I recognized the anthem of "La Bamba."

"We're listening to one of your favorite songs," Gira said. "You love it so much; you want to be a part of it, right?"

Not really, but I was willing to join in for the show.

"Imagine your favorite musical instrument: drums, trumpet, guitar, anything that makes you happy. On the count of three pick up your favorite instrument from your lap and play along with the music. The more you participate, the more relaxed you'll feel."

I could do that. One. Two. Three. Trumpet up. Lips puckered. Fingers moving. We played our instruments for a few seconds.

Then Master Gira quickly said, "One. Two. Three. Sleep." My body drooped, and my chin sank to my chest. I relaxed.

The hypnotist called on other participants to do random silly things on the stage: pretend to be a duck, pretend to juggle fire sticks, pretend to be naked. Then he had a group of five lying center stage sunbathing. He told them the temperature dropped below freezing. While they reacted and the audience laughed, the hypnotist stood in front of me. He gave more monotonous instructions to the group of sunbathers and told them to cuddle together. The crowd clapped and whistled.

Master Gira swung the microphone behind his back, leaned in close to me, and whispered, "Open your mind and allow your subconscious to hear me. I want only goodness for you. Open your mind and let my voice in. Experience this peace."

His breath, moist against my ear, smelled of cigarettes. Part of me worried about his intentions, but a larger part of me sensed an overwhelming degree of comfort. I took a deep breath and released the remaining tension from my muscles.

Gira moved back to center stage and suggested to the group that the temperature had become warm again. He counted to three, and an Irish dance song replaced the previous melody.

The hypnotist spoke rapidly with the cadence of the Celtic music and told us how much we wanted to move to it. I had been sitting a long time. I was ready to stand up and stretch. He counted to three, and everyone onstage popped out of their chairs at the same time, including me, glad to do it. We stepped around a bit, and as he suggested, we kept our arms glued to our sides and moved our feet to the music like Irish dancers. It felt energizing to prance around. I grinned and sent a mental message to Lily: This one's for you, sister. I tapped my feet to the rhythm.

Lily's voice rang out from the crowd, "Yay! Hannah!" My smile grew.

Master Gira counted in a smooth-textured voice, and the music changed to a harp.

"You are so relaxed after dancing, the only thing you want to do now is rest. So, float like a leaf, to your chair on the stage, and go to sleep."

I drifted across the stage, and then I sank into my seat, delighted to rest. The guy to my right leaned into me. I wanted to push him off, but it was too much effort.

"Remain asleep," the hypnotist said, "but sit up straight and open your eyes." I followed his instructions and sat taller in my chair.

Gira summoned a guy to center stage. "You're a famous exotic male dancer, highly paid and highly sought after for your perfect physique."

The music changed to a darker jazz sound with an accentuated beat.

The guy flexed his muscles. The crowd cheered him on, and he shifted from pose to pose.

Master Gira turned to us. "Ladies, you're excited to have this famous performer here tonight. Pull your wallets from your purses and take out all your dollar bills."

I went along with the fantasy and pretended to find my purse under the chair and pull money from the make-believe wallet.

"The more cash you find in your wallet, the more relaxed you feel. One. Two. Three. Four . . ." He continued counting and moved closer to our chairs. Then he swept his arm forward. "Come on ladies! Show your gratitude for the performer. Tuck the dollars into his shorts."

We swarmed the guy, and the other girls tucked imaginary money into the waistband of his shorts. One of the girls even offered me some of her pretend cash and encouraged me to participate. In my peripheral vision, the hypnotist watched, so I reached out and tucked the bills into the back pocket of the guy's shorts. Then I clapped and cheered to display my appreciation for his performance. He tugged his shirt up and over his head and flung it out toward the crowd. They rewarded him with whistles and cheers.

But when he unbuttoned his shorts and showed some hip, the hypnotist reined everyone back in. The music changed to a softer melody, and the hypnotist counted everyone down.

"Relax and float back to your seats," he said.

I glided across the stage, relieved to sit. The guy to my right leaned into me again. After a few seconds, his mountain of a body shifted my balance, and I pressed into the guy on my other side. His posture gave way, and we slid lower on the chairs. Embarrassing. But surely the show was almost over. I could go along with it for a few more minutes. I kept my eyes closed.

"When I count to three, you're going to experience more relaxation than you've ever felt in your life, as if you've had a five-hour massage and an eight-hour nap. When I touch your forehead and say, 'Awake,' you will be fully conscious and feel amazing. One. Two. Three." His feet shuffled along the stage. The crowd gasped as he said "Awake" to each participant. The guy next to me lifted his own weight and sat upright when the mystic told him to awake. But when Master Gira reached me, instead of touching my forehead and saying "Awake," he leaned in close to my ear and whispered, "Open your eyes, Hannah."

I hadn't deceived him. He moved to the next person, touched his forehead, and told him to awake. I stretched and wondered how he knew my name.

"A big round of applause for our amazing participants!" Master Gira yelled to the crowd. Everyone burst into cheers, and the lights evened out, illuminating the entire tent interior. Rock music, once again, blasted from the speakers. My friends rushed up onto the stage and started talking all at once, but the song was too loud for me to understand a thing they said. Manny looped his arm through mine, and we maneuvered toward the exit.

Once outside with the music behind us, Manny asked, "Funnel cakes?"

"Yes, please." I took a deep breath, rejuvenated.

We walked toward the fairway and the food alley. Lily chattered on about my hilarious performance and how she felt jilted for getting pulled off the stage.

"Robbed. Just robbed," she said.

We lingered in line at the funnel cake trailer, and Lily rocked from foot to foot.

"Did the deep fryer spring a leak?" Jordan stepped to the side and gawked.

"I'm starving to death." Lily kicked the dirt.

"You guys can go get your food," I said, "and then we can meet over there." I pointed across the fairway to a covered area with picnic tables.

"I'll wait with you," Manny said.

"What?" Lily asked. "Are you so codependent you can't let her stand in line by herself?"

Manny narrowed his eyes.

Before he could get into another argument with her, I said, "I'm fine. Go get your food."

He glanced at Lily, then back to me. "You're sure?"

"Go," I said. He snaked through the crowded fairway, and a shadow fell across him. I lifted my head skyward to see the cause, but only the moon filled the heavens and the fairway lights blocked out any sign of the stars. I faced forward again and studied the menu: scones, donkey droppings, Indian fry bread, and funnel cakes.

I reached the front of the line and recognized Eugene, a boy from school, working inside the food trailer. He wore penny-sized plugs in his earlobes, a silver ring in his lower lip, and more trinkets on his fingers, in his nose, and in his eyebrows. The pits of his gray V-neck T-shirt were wet, and his cropped black hair glistened in the heat and humidity of the trailer.

"What can I get for you, Hannah?"

"Funnel cakes."

"Hmm." He leaned forward and drummed his fingers against the countertop. "You'd rather have one of my Indian fry breads."

"You think you know what I'm craving?"

"Best fried food at the Western Idaho State Fair."

I couldn't help but smile. "What makes it the best?"

"Secret family recipe." He peered to his left. "Right, Grandma?"

An elderly woman, with thick gray braids extending to her waist, peeked up. "Stop flirting. Just work."

I laughed and couldn't resist him. "I'll try it."

"All right!" He patted the counter and turned toward a coworker.

I pulled a $10 bill from my pocket to pay, but when I lifted it, two ants darted across its edge and onto my wrist. I gasped, dropped the cash, and shook off the ants.

"Three dollars," Eugene said.

I bent to grab the money from the ground, but a man's hand reached it first. I shrieked and straightened up, but there were no men anywhere near me. And no one had picked up the $10 bill. My chest tightened, and when I snatched the cash from the ground, another ant fell from it. I stomped on the bug and twisted my foot into the dirt.

"Hannah?" Eugene said.

The women and kids waiting in line gawked at me. I turned away from them and slid the money across the counter to Eugene.

"You okay?" he asked and then bit down on his lip ring.

I nodded.

He gave me my change and passed me the large, round fried bread.

"Enjoy!" he said.

"Thanks." I drizzled honey over the bread.

Manny called from across the fairway, "Hannah!" He waved a corn dog smothered in mustard. I took one step along the side of the trailer, expecting to see a man standing there, but instead a family laughed and posed for a picture. I shook off the strange feeling and hurried over to the picnic table where Manny waited.

"Why did you go behind the funnel cake trailer?" Manny asked.

I swung my legs over the bench just as Lily and Jordan joined us with an onion blossom and chili cheese fries.

"I didn't—"

"Carnival food is to die for!" Lily clapped her hands.

"It certainly is." Jordan dug into his fries.

Manny rubbed his shoulder against mine and scooted closer. I wiped mustard from the corner of his mouth, and he pointed toward my fry bread.

"What happened to funnel cakes?" he asked.

"Eugene talked me into—"

"Who?" Manny asked.

"You know," Jordan said. "That dude with all the piercings."

"Oh." Manny studied me for a few seconds. Then he moved a drink toward me. "I got your usual."

"Dr. Pepper!" I took a long relaxing pull on the straw. Then I covered my mouth and let out a burp.

"Really?" Lily asked. "Were you raised in a barn?"

"Hey," Jordan said, "at least a nervous belch is better than a nervous bladder."

"Speaking from experience?" Manny asked.

"I don't have nervous burps," I said. "I have a recurring reaction to soda."

"Mmm. Hmm," Lily said.

"So, Hannah"—Jordan had chili covering his fingers—"what was it like to be hypnotized? Do you remember the stupid stuff you did?"

"What stupid stuff?"

"You don't remember?" Lily said.

"Of course I remember. I was awake the entire time."

"You were under his influence," Lily said. "Your green eyes were frozen in an empty stare, and yet you were totally absorbed with everything he told you to do. Especially when you were lusting after that naked hottie!" Lily dunked her onion into some fry sauce and popped it into her mouth.

"He wasn't naked," Manny said, but when Lily waggled her eyebrows he blushed.

"Whatever helps you sleep at night," Jordan said, "but Hannah can tuck money into my shorts any—"

"Stop." Manny pointed at Jordan. "Don't talk to her like—"

"Chill," Lily said. "It's not like she was going to actually do anything with the guy."

I clutched Manny's extended hand and pulled him closer.

Then Lily winked at me and continued, "Hannah's holding out for a special someone."

Jordan laughed.

I sighed and let go of Manny's hand. "I played along to give you a good show," I said to Lily.

"They would've known if you were faking," she said. "They made us leave the stage. Besides, you did everything he told you to."

I wanted her to know I was awake the whole time, but I also didn't want her to be disappointed that the magical mystic of a hypnotist was a fraud.

"You were hypnotized." Jordan scooped more fries into his mouth.

"Let's enjoy our last night of freedom," I said. "School starts Monday."

"I can't believe we're seniors!" Lily said.

"I can." Manny tilted his head toward me. "We have to get into the same college."

"We will," I said. "Princeton would be nuts to reject you." I used the last piece of bread to wipe up the honey from my plate. Eugene was right; it was the best fried food at the fair.

"Maybe we could go to a local college and stay closer to our families," Manny said.

"Where's the adventure in that?" Lily asked. "I know I won't get into some fancy East Coast school with my grades, but I definitely want to get out of Idaho and see the world before I die."

Unlike Lily, it wasn't about adventure for me. I had goals and a plan to achieve them.

"Hannah, why do you want to break the bank with such an expensive school anyway?" Lily asked.

"My dad went there."

"Is that where your parents met and fell in love?" Lily giggled. Then she leaned over and planted a kiss on Jordan. "Mmm. Chili." She licked her lips and turned back to me.

"Uh, no," I said. "My parents had been married for years before my dad decided to go back for his master's degree in psychology."

"Did your mom go there?" Manny asked.

"No, she earned a business degree from a college in Atlantic City."

"You know," Lily said, "Chelsea wants to go to Princeton, too."

"Did I hear my name?" Chelsea said from behind me, and I twisted around.

"You want to go to Princeton?" I asked.

"Yup." Chelsea took a few steps and then perched on the end of the table. Mark wrapped his arm around her shoulders.

"Why?" I asked.

"Because it's the ultimate, and only the best students are accepted." Chelsea smirked.

Manny whispered to me, "What if my SAT score is too low?"

"Stop worrying," I said. "We will be together." I reached for his hand, but a small black ant crawled across the tabletop. I flicked it away.

"Hannah?" Manny's eyes darted between the table and me.

"Just getting an ant off—"

"Ants! What ants?" Lily jumped up.

"Calm down, freakazoid," Manny said. She leaned over and smacked his shoulder, leaving a smear of fry sauce on his polo shirt.

"Don't tell me to calm down! I do not want to get stung!" Lily said.

"No chance—"

"How do you know?" Lily asked.

"Red fire ants infest southern states. Idaho is a northern state."

"So? Maybe it was a biting carpenter ant," Lily insisted. She licked her fingers and dabbed a napkin against her lips.

"Unlikely," Manny said.

"Whatever," Lily said. "Let's go. We'd better start with an easy ride like the Ferris wheel until our food settles." She turned to Chelsea and Mark. "Are you joining us?"

Chelsea, apparently lost in her own thoughts, stared out at the people moving down the fairway. Mark drew his finger along Chelsea's cheek and said, "We're cruising over to the tunnel of love." He did a little spin and mimicked the "exotic male dancer" from the hypnotism show. Then he struck a pose and flexed his biceps for everyone. We all laughed. Chelsea clutched his hand, and they sauntered away.

Manny collected our trash from the table and threw it into a nearby can. A breeze blew across the fairway and goose bumps popped out on my legs, which was odd, considering it was an August night in the high mountain desert. It had to be at least ninety degrees. I linked my arm through Manny's to steal some of his body heat.

Jordan and Lily climbed into a car on the big wheel first. I was content to be separated from them for a while. Manny and I settled into the next car, and the wheel rotated, sending us backward. We crested and spotted Jordan and Lily in front of us. He combed his fingers through her long hair, leaned in, and kissed her. A deep, mouthy one. When he finished, he peered back at us and grinned.

"He creeps me out." I realized I had said the words aloud and tried to recant. "I mean—"

"No, I agree," Manny said. "I've never liked him. Just because he's senior class president, he thinks he's God's gift to women. He's supposed to be dating Lily, but he's always watching you. I'd like to punch—"

"No you wouldn't," I said. "Hurting him is not going to fix anything."

"You're right," Manny said.

We reached the apex of the Ferris wheel, and soon after, Jordan and Lily's car dropped out of sight. The wheel stopped in place, and we had the best view ever. We gazed out across the fairgrounds, being cautious not to rock our seat.

"The flashing lights and crowds seem so far away," I said. When Manny said nothing in response, I turned toward him. He fidgeted with his collar, and then his dark brown eyes burrowed straight to my heart. He fingered the ends of my hair and leaned in toward me. He paused a few inches from my face, and my breath caught. He closed the distance between us and pressed his lips to mine. He smelled like corn dogs and a hint of shaving cream. His fingers enclosed the back of my neck and shivers ran up and down my spine.

He drew back slightly. "Do you want me to stop?"

"No," I whispered.

He leaned in, and the car jerked forward. I shrieked and grabbed the safety bar. We stopped again.

"Sheesh!" I squinted at the ground below. "Good thing I'm not scared of falling from here."

"I've already fallen . . . for you," Manny said with a goofy expression on his face.

"Oh my gosh—" I started to tease him, but before I finished, he leaned in and kissed me. This could become a wonderful habit. The wheel started to rotate. Manny's lips brushed against my ear, and I relaxed into him.

"I've waited so long to kiss you," he said. "This makes everything perfect. I never want any of it to change."

"I agree." It was perfect. Lily always teased me for not making a move on Manny sooner, but I appreciated that he wanted to go slow. He wrapped his arm around me and pulled me close. We watched the sights stirring below us.

A dark mist moved over the nearby kiddie roller coaster and blocked out the flashing lights. "Look at that," I said.

"Where?" Manny asked.

"That black cloud, blotting out the coaster." I made sure his eyes tracked where I pointed.

"I don't see it." He shook his head.

The cloud of darkness disappeared.

The Ferris wheel swung us to the bottom of the circle, and lifted us backward, putting Jordan and Lily behind us and moving up.

"Plant one on her!" Jordan yelled.

"Don't even," I said to Manny.

"Ignore him. We're having a nice time."

"Agreed." I rested my head against his shoulder, but when we reached the top of the wheel, I scanned the area for that ominous black cloud.

Manny leaned forward and rocked the car. "What are you—"

"Be careful." I pulled him back.

"Jordan and Lily are out of view." Manny stroked my cheek. "I love your long dark hair. I love the curve of your neck. I love the way you smell." He leaned in and kissed me, and we got lost in the moment.

The wheel swung around and before we knew it, Lily hollered out. "It's about time!"

"Give her some tongue!" Jordan taunted us.

Uggh. I jerked away from Manny.

"Don't let them ruin this," Manny said.

"I won't. I never want to kiss in front of them, or anyone. I want it to be something special that you and I share."

"No problem." He squeezed my hand.

The ride ended, and we walked toward the Twister.

Lily dragged me aside and whispered, "So? Details! How was it?"

"Perfect. Until you and Jordan started yelling." I fake punched her shoulder.

"We were just teasing."

"I know, but please, stop."

"Okay," she said. "I'm sorry."

I wrapped my arm around her. "Come on, let's hit the rides."

After several trips around the coasters and more fried food, we played a few of the carnival games. Manny won a large pink elephant for me by showing off his mad water gun skills. Jordan won a small monkey for Lily.

"The game was rigged," Jordan said.

"Right," Manny said.

We paused at a booth full of velvet paintings and half admired, half mocked the framed pieces. Some depicted tigers and elephants, but others were totally cheesy with clowns and dogs playing poker. Paintings on fuzzy fabric seemed pointless to me, but Jordan shelled out money for one of the eerie clowns.

We piled into my small blue Mazda around midnight. I settled behind the steering wheel and started the engine.

"Pop the hatch," Manny said. Apparently, the pink elephant was too big to hold on his lap. He hopped out, and Lily and Jordan started making out in the back seat.

When Manny slammed down the hatchback, he startled the lovers. Jordan caught my eye in the rearview mirror, and I looked away. Manny returned to the front seat.

"Buckle up," I said to everyone. In the mirror, Jordan still gawked at me. "Buckle up."

"What if I don't?" Jordan lifted his hands. "Are you going to climb back here and—"

Lily smacked his leg.

"Your funeral, Dude," Manny said and clicked his own belt into place.

I'd had enough of Jordan tonight, and I wanted to be rid of him. I shifted into reverse and pulled out of the parking space.

"Something smells funny," I said. Everyone started sniffing the air like a pack of beagles.

"I just smell your dirty old car," Lily said.

"Like smoke," I prodded.

"Let in some fresh air. That'll help." Manny rolled down his window, and I rolled down mine. But the odor lingered.

I drove north and followed the stream of vehicles leaving the fairgrounds. Traffic thinned as people went their separate ways, and once we hit the road winding through the Boise foothills, we were alone. I switched the headlights to high beam and sped up. The dazzling full moon spotlighted the many sagebrushes and few trees bordering the road.

A dark mist danced along the blacktop like a mischievous imp. I swerved and repositioned the car in the lane. I checked my rearview mirror to determine what I'd almost hit.

Jordan glared back at me.

"Are you okay?" Manny asked.

"Fine." I tightened my grip on the wheel. "I thought I saw something." I was just tired. But then an ant scampered across the top of the steering wheel and across my knuckles. I jerked and swatted it away.

"Do you want me to drive?" Manny leaned closer.

"No! I'm fine."

I straightened in my seat and refocused on the road, but my fingers tingled. The dashboard backlit dozens of ants trailing across the wheel and over my skin. I flung the ants loose and then wrung my hands together, embarrassed by my reaction to the little bugs.

"Hannah!" Manny reached for the abandoned steering wheel.

Lily shrieked.

I shifted my foot to the brake pedal, but the edge of my flip-flop snagged. When I jerked it free, my foot smashed back down against the gas pedal. My eyes widened as the needle of the speedometer topped ninety miles per hour.

In front of us, black smoke churned on the roadway, and we slammed into something hidden within it. The car flipped.

And we all screamed.

A loud bang precipitated the abrupt explosion of the airbags. They receded just as suddenly. A fine white powder filled the scorched air. The Mazda's frame groaned as it rolled again and again until it landed against a large hackberry tree. Leaves fluttered down in front of the car, illuminated by the headlights.

Everything went silent.

I hung upside down, held in place by my seat belt. Manny hung limply. Blood spotted his shirt and dripped from his face.

"Manny." I clutched his hand. "Manny!" I shook him, but he didn't respond. I looked over my shoulder. Lily drooped unconscious in her seat belt. Jordan's body lay against the inside of the roof. A bone protruded from his sleeve. His shoe was wedged beneath his neck. A terrible odor like a rotten outhouse filled the interior of the car. I gagged, my body convulsed, and I vomited. Hanging upside down. I wiped the puke from my face, but it was in my nose, on my eyelids, and in my hair.

I glanced toward the back seat. "Lily!" No reaction at all. Black smoke billowed in through Lily's open window and blew into her mouth, as if she'd pulled in a breath of air. More smoke swirled in and out of Jordan's mouth. At first I assumed it was from the smoldering engine, but then little demon-like eyes took shape from the swelling smoke. I started screaming. The cloud of darkness came closer to me, and I covered my mouth and closed my eyes. A tickle scratched across my skin, and my hair danced against my face. Tears flooded my eyes and ran down my forehead into my hair. I bit my lips together. And then I peed myself. The warm, fragrant urine spread across my shorts, and I realized in that moment I'd lost control of everything. Nothing would ever be the same again.

After an eternity of crying, I heard muffled voices outside. They came closer and yelled to each other.

"Call for an ambulance!"

"She's alive!"

"We have to get them out before they burn!"

And a man said, "This one's already dead."

Someone touched me through my open window. A woman's voice said, "It's going be okay. We're going get you out." She slipped her fingers under my hand, which still covered my mouth, and clutched it in hers. I relaxed my rigid muscles and stared at her. She was upside down. Everything was. "My name is Laura. Can you tell me yours?"

"Hannah," I whispered.

"We're going to help you, Hannah. Do you hurt anywhere?"

Everywhere. But before I answered someone pushed her out of the way and reached toward me with long, slender, hairy arms. He used a pocketknife to cut my seat belt, and I fell to the ceiling. My head and shoulder took the brunt of the fall. I heard Laura in the distance tell him to be careful.

"We have to hurry if we want to save any of them. When that fire reaches the gas tank, this whole thing will explode," he yelled back to her. Someone on the other side cut Lily's belt.

"Is Lily okay?" I whispered. No one answered. I tried to yell, but my voice failed me. What about Manny? He was my best friend in the world. What about Jordan?

The man tugged me through the window, lifted me, and hauled me away. He propped me on the side of the road against a truck, and then he ran back to the Mazda.

The driver's side was dented and contorted. Flames licked out from the engine, and the mangled blue hood dangled to the side. Black smoke rolled out and up. A breeze fanned the smoke into the main part of the car. The hatchback lid hung open, and the pink elephant lay on its side several feet away from the bumper.

The three strangers coughed and covered their faces with their shirts. Another man ran over to me, clutching Lily. He set her next to me and returned to the burning car.

"I can't get him out," one man hollered. "His leg is pinned."

The breeze shifted, and the black smoke blew away from the fire. I saw through the driver's side window that Manny was still in the front seat. The flames shot higher into the sky. They left Manny and worked to rescue Jordan.

Tears blurred my vision. "Help Manny!" I tried to yell, but my coarse voice came out as a whisper. "Help Manny!" I pleaded. With great effort, I lifted myself up, and stumbled toward them. An explosion from the engine rocked the car. The fire doubled in size. The people staggered away from the blast.

"Help Manny!" I yelled.

Laura turned around. "Stay back!" She ran to me, grabbed my arm, and angled me away from the accident. I strained against her, but I was too weak.

"Manny," I said. "He's in the front seat." I peered over my shoulder. The two men tugged Jordan out and dragged him a few feet away. I jerked away from Laura and ran back toward them. "Manny!" I yelled.

And the car exploded.

The concussion of the blast threw us all backward. I floated through the air, until I hit the asphalt. My head struck twice, and the black smoke overtook me.

SATURDAY
AUGUST 24

I jerked upright and gasped for air.

"Manny!"

My breaths came faster. I was no longer on the asphalt in the dark of night, but on a bed in a bright hospital room. Time had passed without me.

"Manny!"

I pounded the soft white sheets with my fists. And then I screamed.

A woman in blue scrubs with a stethoscope dangling from her neck rushed into the room and right to my bedside. "You're safe now," she said and gripped my hand.

"What day is it?" I asked.

"Saturday. You were in a serious car accident, and you've been admitted to the hospital for observation." Her intense hazel eyes locked onto me, and I remembered the sparkle in Lily's hazel eyes before the hypnotism show. Before she hung unconscious in the back seat.

"My name is Audrey," the woman said. "I'm your nurse, and I'll be taking care of you today."

"Where's Lily?" I asked.

A uniformed police officer stepped into the room, but he stayed near the door and scanned the room. His graying hair was neatly trimmed above his ears, but several wild strands stuck out from his eyebrows. He hooked his thumbs into his duty belt and waited.

"That's Officer Stephens," Audrey said. "He has a few questions for you, but I need to check your vitals first. Okay?"

I nodded.

Audrey lowered the bedrail and pressed her fingers against my wrist. Her lips moved while she counted and focused on her wristwatch. Her blond hair was cut in a cute pixie style, she wore little makeup, and she smelled like Ivory soap. Clean and fresh. Unlike the putrid stench from the car. I gagged, and she snatched a barf bag from the side table. She held it under my chin, and I gagged again. But the gut-wrenching agony only produced shuddering dry heaves. I pushed back my hair and found clumps of stiffened vomit from the accident, which made me remember the blood on Manny's forehead. Had it crusted in his hair?

"Where's Manny?" I asked, panic bubbling within me.

"Manuel Santos?" Audrey adjusted my IV line.

"Yes."

She repositioned my blood pressure cuff, and I wanted to scream again. I needed an answer.

"Is he dead?" I whispered.

Audrey patted my arm. "He has a concussion and cracked ribs, but he will be fine."

"I need to see him." I swung my legs over the side of the bed and winced. The edges of my vision blurred, but if Manny was alive I had to find him. The police officer took a step forward.

"Not yet," Audrey said. "The doctor hasn't cleared you." She lifted my feet back up, and then she raised the bedrail.

"I don't hurt," I said.

She pursed her lips.

"Not much." But I did. I peeked beneath the neckline of the gray dotted hospital gown. A purple bruise marked where my seat belt had been, and even the cotton fabric made it sting.

"You received pain meds when you arrived, but I can give you more if you need them."

"No, thank you." I wanted to be alert, unhindered by pain medicine, if they decided to let me see Manny. "I really need to see him."

"His doctors need to finish with him first." Audrey tugged the bedcovers over me, and I used the sheet to wipe away my tears.

Officer Stephens moved to the foot of my bed and pulled a notepad and pen from his pocket. He glanced at Audrey and raised his wiry eyebrows. "May I now?" he asked her.

"Yes, go ahead," she said.

"Manuel had his wallet in his pocket," Officer Stephens said, "and we've already spoken with his parents. They told us your name is either Lily Sloane or Hannah O'Leary."

"Hannah," I said.

"Hannah, we need to phone your parents. Where can we reach them?"

"My mom's at work."

"How about your dad?"

"My dad?" More tears rolled down my cheeks. He was dead, and the last time Mom had been in a hospital was back in Princeton, New Jersey, when it happened. She'd received a phone call then, too, telling her he'd "passed away" . . . as if vague words would lessen the pain. It had been almost six years, and the wound was still fresh in my heart. Maybe it would never heal.

"Hannah?" the officer asked again. "Can we call your dad?"

I shook my head. "He's dead."

The officer fixed his eyes on me. "And your mother works at four in the morning?"

"Four?" Out of habit, I reached for my cell to check the time, but it wasn't with me. Nothing in this room belonged to me. My phone most likely lay in a million bits on the side of the road. My heart hammered inside my chest. Four in the morning. Mom had to be worried out of her mind. I'd never missed a curfew before. She probably left work and sped home to search for me when I didn't answer my cell or the house phone. She'd think something had happened to me. Which it had.

"Hannah?" Officer Stephens asked again. "Does your mother usually work overnight?"

"Sometimes. She's the general manager of the Main Street Hotel."

"The large one here in downtown Boise?"

"Yes."

"What's the number?" he asked.

"Excuse me," Audrey said, "but maybe Mrs. O'Leary would react better if she heard Hannah's voice first. To know she's okay."

She read my mind.

The officer agreed, and Audrey passed me a phone. I dialed Mom's cell number, and she answered immediately.

"Hello?" she said.

I wanted to sound calm, but my breath caught in my throat.

"Hello?" Mom said again. "Hannah?"

"I'm okay," I said, but my voice trembled.

"I've been looking for you," Mom said. "Where are you? You're supposed to be here at home. What's happened?"

"I'm sorry—"

I gasped and covered my mouth and sobbed. I was sorry. For everything. For losing control of the car. For hurting my friends. For scaring Mom.

Her voice softened. "Oh, honey—"

The phone slipped from my grasp, and the officer recovered it.

"This is Police Officer Stephens," he said to my mom. "There was an accident. Yes, she's at Gracen Hospital, but she's fine. Yes, we'll give you more details once you arrive. Yes." He ended the call and returned the phone to the nurse. He jotted something in his notepad, and then he stared at me.

"Hannah, did you have anything to drink last night before you got behind the wheel?"

"No."

"Drugs?"

"No."

"What caused the accident?" he asked.

"There was this awful smell, and there were these ants . . ." As soon as I uttered the words, I knew I sounded foolish, but I needed to explain what happened. I replayed the events in my mind and tried again.

"There were these beady eyes . . ."

Audrey's jaw dropped, but Officer Stephens kept his disciplined composure.

"Are you saying there was an animal in the road?" he asked.

"I don't know what it was, but we hit something."

He took notes and said, "Hannah, there's no evidence the vehicle hit anything."

"But it flipped."

"And we're investigating that," he said. "What were you doing out so late?"

"We were at the fair."

"Did anything unusual happen?"

"No."

The officer stopped writing.

"We ate, played games, rode the coasters, and went to the hypnotist show."

"Were you hypnotized?" he asked.

"I took part in the show, but I wasn't actually hypnotized."

There was a knock at the door.

"Am I interrupting?" Mrs. Santos—Manny's mom—didn't wait for an answer. She swooped in and wrapped her large, soft arms around me. "Oh, child, are you all right?"

I bawled into her shoulder.

"I'm so sorry," I whispered.

Mrs. Santos leaned back slightly. Her red lipstick trailed into the tiny wrinkles around her full lips. She squeezed my shoulders and said, "It was an accident."

"How can you so easily forgive me?"

She locked her gaze on me. "Anyone could have been driving."

"Do you know if Lily is okay?" I asked Mrs. Santos, but Audrey stepped closer and answered.

"She's still in surgery."

"And Jordan?" I asked.

Audrey twisted the stethoscope between her fingers. "I'm sorry, Hannah, but Jordan died."

"What?" The word came out as a faint whisper. "But they pulled him from the car."

"We're still gathering the facts," Officer Stephens said. "However, it does appear Jordan died on impact."

Mrs. Santos squeezed my hand, and a tear slipped down her cheek. She pulled a tattered tissue from the sleeve of her plum-colored blouse and dabbed her face.

"We'll give you some time alone," Officer Stephens said and left with Audrey.

"Lily loves Jordan," I said. They were a couple. He was senior class president, and she was vice president. We're all in student council together. We had plans. My chin quivered. Mrs. Santos drew me in closer, and I wept again.

She stroked my hair. "Oh, child, have faith. Everything's going to be okay."

"Jordan's dead," I whispered, "and I was driving. Everything's not okay."

Mrs. Santos's chest heaved, and more tears flooded down her cheeks. She clutched my hands and offered a prayer. I stifled my sobs while she spoke the words, and then I added an "amen" along with hers. The Santos family prayed over everything. Manny had probably even offered a silent prayer before eating his mustard-smothered corn dog.

"Are you sure Manny will be okay?" I asked.

"Yes, I promise."

"He has to be," I said. "I can't imagine life without him."

"Me either. You children are the most important thing in the world to me." Mrs. Santos rocked me in her arms, as if I was her baby. She hummed a tune to ease my crying.

A tap at the door made Mrs. Santos release me to glance in that direction.

"Hello, Hannah." A tall, slender man in a long white coat moved to the edge of my bed. He smoothed his solid black tie, which matched his shirt . . . and his hair. He extended his hand to me. "I'm Dr. James."

I shook his hand.

Mrs. Santos introduced herself also. "Would you like me to stay?"

"Actually," the doctor said, "this needs to be a private consult."

"Why?" I asked.

"Since you were hypnotized last night I've been asked to perform an evaluation."

I scooted up in the bed and sat taller.

Mrs. Santos said to him, "Shouldn't you wait for this child's mother to arrive before asking—"

"This is not a police interrogation." Dr. James pinched the bridge of his nose, and when he pulled his fingers away, the crook was pinker than the rest of his pale skin. "I'm a psychiatrist, and a seventeen-year-old does not need her parents present for a medical examination. Hannah has a right to privacy."

Mrs. Santos cupped my face. "If you need anything, I'll be right down the hall."

"Thank you," I said, and my vision blurred around the edges. Mrs. Santos seemed to walk down an endless narrow tunnel toward the door. I massaged my temples, hoping to clear my head.

"Can you tell me what you remember about last night, before the accident?" Dr. James asked.

I hesitated and stared at the white sheets covering my legs. Maybe this was all a bad dream. Surely, Jordan was still alive, but then Manny's words popped into my head: *Your funeral, Dude.* I pulled my knees up to my chest and wrapped my arms around them.

"Hannah?"

If I told this man what I saw, would he believe me?

Dr. James moved toward the bed and tucked a tissue under my fingers.

I wiped my eyes and blew my nose. Maybe he could help me. I told him everything, from the hypnotism show to the smoky demon eyes. He remained expressionless, and he listened without interrupting me. When I finished the story, I blew out a long breath.

"What do you think caused the accident?" he asked.

"Ants."

"Why do you think that?"

"Ants crawled across my hands, and I let go of the steering wheel."

He relaxed his stance, and his wristwatch clanked against the bedrail. "Can you tell me more?"

I narrowed my eyes at him. "No. I can't. For some reason those ants really freaked me out. And now, I've killed someone. Manny and Lily are both injured. I would never intentionally hurt anyone. None of it makes any sense!" I chomped down on my cheek and hoped the pain would quash my impending hysteria.

Dr. James remained unruffled. "Did you have any mood-altering substances like alcohol or drugs of any sort before the accident?"

"No."

"Tell me again how the hypnosis session ended," Dr. James said. I told him what I remembered.

"The smoky images started appearing during the show?" he asked.

"A shadow moved across the stage, but that could have been anything." I rubbed my sweating palms against the bed sheets. "Later, I saw weird pockets of darkness from the top of the Ferris wheel. They blocked out some of the lights."

"It's possible," Dr. James said, "that you're still under the influence of the hypnosis." He pulled a penlight from his pocket and shined the beam into my eyes. I squinted.

"Keep your eyes here," he said and wiggled the fingers on his left hand. Then, with his right, he snapped the light back and forth across my eyes. I blinked several times but tried to stay focused. Dr. James put away the penlight and checked my pulse.

"Well?" I asked.

"You're not hypnotized. Your eyes are reactive, and your pulse is normal."

"Is there something else wrong with me then?" I asked.

"It's too early to say . . ."

"But?"

"But sometimes hypnosis can bring an underlying psychosis to the surface."

"I do not have a psychosis."

"You can be hypnotized, and even if the hypnosis was unsuccessful, the process can still unlock a door to a buried mental illness—"

"I don't have a mental illness."

"Hannah, you saw things and smelled things that weren't actually there."

"The ants were real," I said.

"How do you know?"

"Lily jumped up from the picnic table when she saw them."

"Did she say she saw them? Or was she merely responding to what you said you saw?"

"Is that a riddle?" I asked.

"No."

"So you're saying the hypnosis triggered something in my brain, and now I'm seeing weird things?" I disagreed, but making him angry wasn't going to help me either.

"Possibly."

"If hypnosis caused this," I said, "just reverse the process."

"I wish it were that simple. And yes, we may use more hypnosis to help you. Or we may find other techniques are better. But we're getting ahead of ourselves. We need more tests for a diagnosis. Have you had any more hallucinations since you've been in the hospital?"

"No." But I assumed everything last night was real.

"Don't worry, Hannah, I'm here to help you, and we'll figure this out," Dr. James said.

"Before someone else dies?"

He shook his head. "No one else is going to die."

But Lily was still in surgery, and Manny was still with the doctors. I needed my friends to pull through this. They were my world, and I'd be lost without them. I swiped away my tears and took a deep breath.

"Hannah, is there any history of depression or other mental—"

"Hannah!" My mom blew through the doorway and ran to my side. A large tote bag slipped off her shoulder and wedged between us when she hugged me. "Are you okay?" She checked my face, checked my hands, and checked my arms. She heaved a sigh of relief and dropped her purse and tote to the floor.

She tucked her thick brown hair behind her ears, fastened the top button of her blazer, and then stuck out her hand to the doctor.

"I'm Beth O'Leary." Even in the middle of the night, she was ready to conduct business and take charge. Her hair, always tidy. Her makeup, always perfect.

"Dr. James." He shook her hand.

"So, how is she?"

"Physically, she's fine."

Mom's forehead creased.

"Mrs. O'Leary, is there any family history of mental illness?"

Mom stepped around the tote on the floor and asked, "Why?"

"A detailed medical history will help me make an accurate diagnosis." He raised his eyebrows at Mom and waited for her response. But Mom merely twisted the rings on her fingers.

"Mrs. O'Leary," he said, "I'm willing to release Hannah later this afternoon but with the condition you make a follow-up appointment for Friday at my office."

Mom avoided his gaze.

Dr. James tapped the bedrail. "Hannah, if you have any more hallucinations—"

Mom gasped at his words.

He turned back to my mom. "Mrs. O'Leary?"

She covered her mouth, and the color drained from her face.

"We'll do some tests," he said in a calming tone. "Then we can evaluate Hannah more thoroughly on Friday"—Dr. James cleared his throat—"but Mrs. O'Leary, can you tell me more about your family? Are there any accounts of depression or schizophrenia?"

"Let's discuss this outside." She gripped his elbow and urged him toward the hallway. Just outside the doorway, with her back to me, Mom spoke to Dr. James. The door was still open, and Mom had no idea how easily voices carried in this rigid hospital.

"Hannah's father . . ." Mom shifted her weight from one foot to the other.

"Yes?" Dr. James said.

"He was . . ." Mom lowered her voice to a whisper, and I missed the words in the middle, but I caught the end: ". . . committed suicide."

I must've heard her wrong.

Dr. James glanced toward me and then back to my mom. "When?"

"Six years ago," Mom said.

Suicide.

I wanted to yell and let her know I heard what she'd said, but instead I rocked back and forth as the anxiety buzzed in my ears.

Suicide.

I pressed my temples and tried to silence the word repeating over and over in my mind. Dr. James returned to my bedside. His lips formed my name, but the buzzing increased. Mom sidestepped him and reached for me, but I yanked away and flattened my palms against my ears.

Suicide.

The pressure mounted in my head, and I pushed harder. Dr. James and my mom gawked at me. I must've looked ridiculous. I pulled my hands away, and my ears popped, as if suction cups had been plucked from my head. After a moment of pain, my hearing returned. The machines in the room beeped. The blood pressure monitor hummed; the cuff expanded, squeezing my arm.

"You told me"—I whispered each word carefully—"he had an aneurysm." All of these years, she'd told me it was no one's fault. That there was nothing we could've done.

"Hannah—"

"Why would he kill himself?" I asked.

"Schizophrenia." Mom stepped back and snatched a tissue from the bedside table to wipe her eyes.

I clutched my gut and tried to hold myself together as I digested the information. I hated the idea of Dad having a mental disorder, but it made sense. It explained his irrational behavior. But it also changed everything. A few minutes ago I wanted the truth behind my hallucinations, but now . . . maybe I'd rather not know. Because maybe schizophrenia was hereditary. Maybe suicide was hereditary. And maybe Mom would end up despising me the way she had Dad.

"Hannah," Dr. James said, "take a breath."

I met his gaze and realized I'd stopped breathing. I pulled in a lungful of air.

"Hannah," Mom said, "your—"

"What else have you lied about?" I asked, exhaling.

"Please," Mom said. "Your dad was—"

"My dad was schizophrenic. My dad was helpless. My dad was someone I didn't even know."

"Hannah, this is a lot for you to absorb," Dr. James said. He scrutinized my mom for a moment. Then he reached forward and pushed the call button on the side of my bed. "For now, a long shower and some fresh clothes will—"

"Seriously?" I asked. "A shower and change of clothes will fix the fact that my mother has lied to me about my father's death for years?"

"No, Hannah," Dr. James said, "but it's a place for you to start. Counseling sessions will help you process all that's happened, and I will guide you through this."

The nurse came into the room, and Dr. James asked her to remove my IV. She worked on it, and Dr. James motioned for my mom to step away from my bedside. Once they were on the other side of the room, he lowered his voice. But I still heard nearly every word.

"Mrs. O'Leary, can you tell me more? When was your husband diagnosed?"

"Shortly before he died."

"Did he claim to see things or hear things that were unusual?" Dr. James asked.

"Do we really need to discuss this right now? Right here?" Mom asked

"This information changes everything," he said.

Mom wiped away a tear.

"For now, just one more question," Dr. James said. "Were any other relatives diagnosed with mental illness?"

"No," Mom said. "No one on either side of our families had issues. Just him."

"All right," Dr. James said. "This gives us a starting point."

"Do I have schizophrenia?" I asked.

Dr. James and my mom returned to my bedside.

"Not necessarily," he said. "Let's do some tests and evaluate everything. Okay?"

I nodded.

"Another physician will be in later this afternoon to sign your final release from the hospital, and I'll see you both on Friday." Dr. James squeezed my shoulder. "We will work through this, Hannah."

The nurse finished removing the IV and then followed Dr. James out of the room. The door closed behind them, and the click echoed through the silence of the sterile room.

"I'm sorry, Hannah."

"Right." I struggled to unlock and release the bedrail. Mom lowered it for me. I scooted to the edge of the bed and swung my legs over, but before my feet hit the floor, Mom grabbed my arms.

"I never meant to tell you like this," she said.

"You never meant to tell me at all."

"Your father was a good man. I wanted you to remember that—"

"I remember how he backhanded me." I wiped my nose with the worn-out tissue and swallowed my anguish.

"That happened once," she said.

"Mom, I always thought we moved to Idaho because you hated the memory of Dad," I said. "You even changed our last name. Why would you do that unless you detested everything about him?"

"Hannah, I didn't hate—"

"I don't believe you," I said. "I can't handle more—"

"Hannah—"

"Mom, I was just in a car accident. Jordan died because of me. The last thing I need right now is you confusing me with more lies." I grabbed the tote bag and headed for the adjoining bathroom. I tried to slam the bathroom door behind me, but the stupid hydraulic closure thwarted my intentions.

I set the bag on the toilet lid and sank to the floor on my knees. Silent tears ran down my face, and I let them fall. I tried to picture Dad in my mind, but I couldn't form the details. Was his nose crooked like Dr. James's? Was his hair neatly trimmed around the ears like Officer Stephens's? If I could recall his exact features from when he laughed and chased me on the beach, then maybe he wouldn't seem so lost to me.

Instead, images of Jordan's contorted expression came to mind: his gaping mouth, his empty, glaring eyes, and his blood-spattered blond spikes.

Jordan had been a jerk about the seat belt. I hated him for it, and now his life was over, and I still hated him for it. If only he'd strapped in. If only I'd let Manny drive. If only we'd not gone to the fair at all. Then Jordan would still be alive. My body shivered against the cold tiles. I rubbed my arms, but the motion barely warmed me.

I stood, and my head spun. I steadied myself at the sink and stared at myself in the mirror until the dizziness passed. My eyes were a darker shade of green than normal. Probably from crying. My eyelids were pink and swollen. I blew out a breath and reached into the tote.

Mom had brought my favorite things from home. I lifted the items out one by one. Jasmine-scented shampoo and conditioner, shower gel, and body spray. My loofah scrub, my toothbrush and toothpaste, and my old treasured pearl-handled hairbrush. I left the clean clothes in the tote and selected from the items I'd set along the sink. I held the bristles of the toothbrush under scalding hot water. Then, with a generous squeeze of Crest, I scrubbed the residual sour flavor from my mouth. I rinsed with hot water and then brushed again.

I tore off the hospital gown, gathered my supplies, and stepped into the shower stall. The hot water sprayed my face and obscured my tears. Dad committed suicide. What did that mean? Did it change anything? Jordan died in the car accident. And that changed everything. I slapped the wall and a sliver of pain shot through my wrist. I shook it out. Then I studied the bruise left by the seat belt. It was too tender to touch, and the spray from the water pricked it, but I only had bruises and sore muscles. I couldn't say the same for my friends.

I shampooed my hair several times until the snarls and knots disappeared. Then I covered the loofah with a generous amount of shower gel and scrubbed every inch of my body. I wanted to wash away the last twenty-four hours. I leaned against the shower wall and let the water pelt my back. I held my breath and imagined all my troubles flowing down the drain. My muscles relaxed, and I stayed there a while longer. I loved the solitude of the shower.

Mom rapped at the door and opened it. "Hannah?"

I stiffened. "Almost done."

Mom left and closed the door behind her.

I dried off and wrapped the towel around me. I took another towel and mopped the steam off the mirror, but my reflection faded as the mirror fogged over again. I spritzed myself with the jasmine body spray and reached into the tote for clean clothes.

Something pricked my finger.

I jerked my hand away, and in the process, the tote tumbled to the floor. A three-inch hairy wolf spider scampered across the white tiled floor. I screamed and jumped up, perching on the sink. The neatly lined supplies hammered against the floor, and my hairbrush landed near the spider. He paused, but then darted toward the shower stall.

The bathroom door flew open.

"What's the matter?" Mom yelled.

I clutched the towel to my chest and pointed to the shower.

Mom touched my knee. "What?"

"A freaking monster-sized spider!" I hopped down from the sink and examined the shower stall. "It must have gone down the drain," I said.

"I'm sure you scared it more than it scared you." She picked up the items from the floor and set the bag back on the toilet.

"It was real." I held out my finger and showed Mom the tiny red welt at the tip. She kissed it and drew me into a hug.

"Couldn't you have told me the truth sooner?" I whispered.

Mom drew back from me. "I didn't want the suicide looming in your mind."

"Why did we move to Idaho?" I asked.

"I was trying to protect you." She gripped my hands in hers.

"From the truth?" I asked.

"We'll work through this, Hannah, but it won't happen in an instant."

I tried to summon the courage to reach into the bag, but my hand trembled. Mom stepped forward and plucked a pair of white ruffled shorts from the bag. Before passing them to me, she shook them. No spiders. She did the same with a white camisole, underwear, and a sheer lavender blouse.

Mom had always had a flair for selecting outfits. Throughout my life, she had said to me, "You never get a second chance to make a good first impression." My temples throbbed, and images of my family's parking lot fiasco in New Jersey came to mind. That outburst had repercussions. The next day, those three irritating girls had told everyone at school about it. I had never been a part of any clique back then, and so it didn't really matter when they all snubbed me. I already knew what loneliness felt like, because I usually sat by myself at lunch anyhow. When we moved to Idaho, Mom was determined to help change things. She bought me all the right clothes, shoes, and accessories. My debut as the new girl was still awkward, even with the best jeans. But after a few days, and a few great outfits, the popular crowd invited me into their world. Lily and I had been friends ever since.

Mom lifted a pair of leather sandals from the bag and dropped them on the floor in front of me.

"No spiders," she said and moved to the door.

"Leave it open a little," I said. She nodded and left me alone to dress.

I dropped my towel and reached for the underwear. My skin itched. I positioned myself next to the sink to keep an eye on the shower stall while I dressed. If that creature crawled back out of the drain, I wanted to see it before it saw me.

⊰ • ⊱

Several hours later, Mom dozed in the corner armchair, and I sat in the bed, tapping my fingers against the bedrail. I pushed the call button.

Audrey came into the room. "Yes? What can I do for you, Hannah?"

"I need to see Manny."

"I'll let you as soon as possible, but right now I'm pretty sure he's still down in radiology." She checked my vitals and left.

A few minutes later, I pressed the call button again.

Audrey returned, but she paused at the doorway.

"Can I see Lily?" I asked.

"She's still in recovery. Later they'll move her to ICU, but I doubt you'll get to see her today."

I pressed the call button a few more times over the next couple of hours, but Audrey always had an excuse why I couldn't see them yet. Meanwhile, Mom had woken from her nap and was replying to messages on her phone.

"Please find out what rooms they're in," I said to Mom.

"Sure, honey." She stepped out to the hallway to talk to the nurses, but then returned when another doctor came in to examine me.

"You're a lucky girl," he said. "You're the only one who came out of that accident unscathed." Right. Lucky. He discharged me, but before we left, Officer Stephens came into the room.

"Based on the information I've gathered from you, the doctors, and your friend, I need to suspend your driver's license." He lifted one unkempt eyebrow and passed me a citation to sign.

My hand trembled, and the pen wobbled. Mom reached out and stroked my arm. Shudders ran through my body, and I began to cry again.

Officer Stephens stepped forward and patted my shoulder. "You can request a re-examination when Dr. James writes a letter to the judge on your behalf. Plus, if the doctor clears you to drive, the judge may simply put an expiration date on your suspension. But Hannah, you drove recklessly last night, and it resulted in a fatality."

I breathed deeply through my nose, signed the form, and returned it to him.

"She's a good kid," Mom said.

"I can see that." He tore off the back copy of the citation and gave it to Mom.

I wiped my face and shook out my hands.

"Ready to go?" Mom asked.

"I need to see Manny and Lily first," I said.

"The nurse said we can't see Lily today," Mom said.

We stepped into the hall and spotted Mrs. Santos coming our way. "Manny is asking for you."

She led us to Manny's room, and my spirits lifted as I stepped over the threshold. Sunshine flooded through the window, and the fragrance of flowers overwhelmed me. Bouquets and balloons adorned the room. Manny's mom probably brought them to cheer him up. Manny propped himself up in bed, and a smile lit across his face when we made eye contact. I ran and threw my arms around him.

"Careful!" Manny said. His body clenched. "Two cracked ribs." I leaned back, and he flushed red with pain.

"Sorry." I perched next to him and tried to hold back my emotions, but the thought of hurting Manny yet again was too much to bear. He reached up with his thumb and wiped the tears from my face.

"We'll give you a few minutes," Mrs. Santos said. She set her hand on my mom's back and guided her from the room.

"It's not your fault," Manny whispered.

"Jordan is dead, Lily's in ICU, and you're all broken up."

Manny's eyes welled. "I'll be fine." He lifted his chin, refusing to cry. "Lily will be fine." He tucked my hair behind my ear.

"Jordan is dead," I said.

Manny pointed at me. "You told him to put his seat belt on." The heart rate monitor beeped faster.

I laced my fingers with his.

"I let go of the steering wheel." I lowered my gaze and lowered my voice and spoke as fast as possible. "Ants crawled across my skin, and I freaked. I saw this crazy black smoke. A doctor did a consult. He thinks I might be nuts. He thinks the hypnosis may have triggered an underlying psychosis."

"What?"

Surely he didn't expect me to say it all again.

"You are not nuts." He drew me in closer, and I carefully embraced him.

"Things won't ever be the same," I said.

"Maybe not, but we don't have to change."

"When will you get out of the hospital?" I asked.

"They said they want to monitor me for a day or two to make sure there's no internal bleeding."

"Days?" My breath caught.

"It'll be okay," Manny said.

I drew my finger along his jaw where plum-colored bruises had already formed. I cautiously leaned in and kissed him. When I pulled back, our eyes locked.

"Manny, I love you." I blurted out the words, which had been in my heart for years. The accident made me realize I couldn't wait another day to tell him . . . even if he felt differently. I needed him to know I loved him more than anything.

"I've loved you longer," he said. My heart lifted. Hearing those words, I believed anything was possible.

He caressed my neck and inhaled. "You still smell like flowers. That hasn't changed." He pulled me close for a long kiss, and I melted. Before we said anything else to each other, Mrs. Santos and my mom came back into the room.

"We need to go." Mom motioned toward the door.

"We'll be okay." Manny squeezed my hand. "Remember what I said."

I nodded.

Mom touched my elbow and ushered me from the room.

Book Two

Authority

A lingering grain of inefficacy
capitulates to the arrogance of authority.

SUNDAY
AUGUST 25

I sat at my bedroom desk and smoothed out a new sheet of coral stationery. Two hours had passed since I first sat here, and I still struggled to find the right words to convey my sorrow to Jordan's parents. I needed to do this. I reconsidered my words and wrote in my best penmanship:

> *Dear Mr. & Mrs. Hilaman,*
> *I am so very sorry for your loss.*

My fingers twitched. I clutched the pen and gouged out the words. The tip of the pen tore through the paper and left scratches in the walnut desktop. I groaned, crumpled the paper, and threw it across the room toward my bed. It landed on the carpet next to the other wads of paper.

I turned back to my desk and glanced at the wall above it where three pictures hung: a family photo from when I was eight on the New Jersey shoreline, a snapshot of my friends at last year's homecoming, and a Disney World caricature of me.

I lifted the family portrait from its hook and cradled it in my hands. My dad's behavior wasn't always irrational and unpredictable. Several times, he took me on long walks through the zoo and taught me about the animals and named the trees— elm, redwood, sycamore, chestnut, and more. He was strong and stable then, just like the trees, and I idolized him. When he hugged me, he smelled of Old Spice after-shave lotion. When he started having outbursts in public, I began to fear him. To know, now, that he committed suicide because he had schizophrenia terrified me, and more than ever, I wished I could go back in time and do something to help him.

With the picture still in hand, I hurried to my closet. I set the framed picture on a shelf next to my shoe collection. Then I reached up to the top shelf and nudged a box closer to the edge. I lost my grip on it, and the dusty box fell to the floor with a thud. Snapshots and an old family album spilled out across the carpet. I sank to my knees, and I flipped the album open to the first page, which displayed a picture of Mom and Dad on their wedding day. She wore a long, full white dress with puffy sleeves, and he wore a black tuxedo with a pointy collar. I studied his face: a straight nose proportioned just right for his head, green eyes that resembled mine, dark, thick hair neatly trimmed around his ears, and a broad smile that lifted the corners of his eyes.

He was happy.

And I longed to keep that image of him in my mind.

I returned everything to the box and tucked it on a lower shelf behind some shoes. Before we'd left New Jersey, I'd hidden these pictures away. Mom had thrown out nearly everything else that reminded her of Dad. She knew I had the one family picture hanging on my bedroom wall, and she avoided looking at it whenever she came into my room. I left my closet and rehung that portrait above my desk. My hand traveled from its frame to the next one: the caricature from Disney World. The artist had distorted my head and exaggerated my eyes. The cartoon pictured me sitting on a red-and-white-checkered blanket with a picnic basket next to me. Ants dotted the edges of the blanket.

Ants.

How had I never noticed that before?

I grabbed the framed drawing from the wall and examined it. The artist had drawn the small black pests in a uniformed line, creeping along the edge of the blanket and into the picnic basket. I opened the bottom desk drawer and dropped the picture inside, face-down, and then I slammed the drawer closed.

In one sweeping motion, I shoved everything off my desktop, plunked my head down on the bare surface, and cried.

When the phone rang, I jumped from my chair, wiped my eyes, and tried to focus. The cordless house phone—buried next to my stapler under a pile of stationery on the floor—stopped ringing before I could click the talk button. It didn't matter; the caller ID showed it was one of Mom's friends.

I stood there and stared out my bedroom window at the giant oak. There were few trees in the foothills, but our neighborhood had planted a variety for shade and privacy. Even with the large cottonwoods and maples, we still had a great view of downtown Boise in the distance, but Mom didn't buy this house for the view. She bought it because it was less than a ten-minute drive to her hotel. While people swarmed downtown Boise with their clatter and commotion, families retreated to their homes in the foothills for peace and quiet. Nothing ever happened up here. No crime. No traffic. No noise.

Finally, the screen on the phone showed the line was free. I dialed the hospital's number. When the automated system prompted me, I typed in Manny's room number. Mrs. Santos answered.

"Can I speak with Manny?" I asked

"They've taken him for a CT scan."

"Another one?" When I called earlier, she'd said the same thing.

"Patience, child," Mrs. Santos said. "It was an x-ray before. They need to make sure everything is fine before they release him."

"Today?" My heart raced.

"Tomorrow at the earliest. I'll have him call you as soon as he can."

We said goodbye, and I dialed again. This time I typed in Lily's room number.

"ICU nurses' station," a woman said.

"Oh. I wanted Lily Sloane's room."

"Her calls are being directed here."

"How is she doing?" I asked.

"Are you family?"

"I'm her best friend."

"I'm sorry, but we're only able to give information to family members."

I disconnected the call.

I flopped face-down onto my bed and dropped the phone. Mom knocked on my door, but I remained on the bed. She knocked again and came right on in. She knelt next to my bed.

"Oh, Hannah." She stroked my hair.

I lifted up and met her gaze. "Never lie to me about anything, ever again."

She sat next to me on the bed. "I promise. I'm sorry for not telling you about your father sooner."

My stomach twisted. I wanted everyone to forgive me for the accident, but I was unsure that I could forgive her for lying to me about Dad.

"Will you accept my apology?" she asked.

"I'm working on it," I said.

"That's all I ask." After a few seconds of awkward silence, she patted my knee. "Let's go to the mall."

"Are you kidding me?"

She smiled a crooked, halfhearted smile. "Mall therapy is just what we need. We can get you a new phone, a new pair of shoes, a new purse."

"And that will make everything all right?" I asked.

"No." Her smile disappeared. "But it will be better than sitting here alone in your room. And we can pick up gifts for Manny and Lily."

I wanted to see Manny, and I wanted to find out how Lily was doing. So, I conceded to Mom's plan. I took a shower and changed into an embellished silver tank top and faded denim shorts. My bruise from the seat belt peeked out at the neckline of my tank, and I felt a pang of guilt for going to the mall when Manny and Lily were still in the hospital. I changed into a ruby-red blouse that covered my bruise and headed out with Mom. Some people went to church on Sundays; we went to the mall—my mother's favorite place of worship.

⊰ • ⊱

Manny's extended family—who'd probably come straight from church, because they were all decked out in their best Sunday attire—crowded his hospital room. They teased Manny about his hospital gown.

"Are you going to get some shiny heels to finish the outfit?" his brother asked. Everyone laughed. The spirited gathering filled the room with love. They noticed me in the doorway and welcomed me as if I was one of them. When Manny saw me, he smiled, and my heart warmed, but it was then that I realized no one had visited me. Unlike Manny, I had a small family. Both of my parents were only children, and my grandparents still lived in New Jersey. But none of our friends from school had even called to check on me. And in this crowded room, I felt very alone.

I plastered on a smile and told myself it was fine, because Manny was the only community I needed. I moved toward him and extended the gift sack.

"What's this?" he asked.

"Open, open," his family chanted.

Manny tossed the tissue paper to the floor, and his brothers leaned in closer. Manny lifted out the iPod and held it high for everyone to see. They cheered. I grinned. Their energy was contagious.

"Why'd you get me another iPod?" Manny asked.

"I figured yours was lost in the accident." I bit my lower lip. A lot of things were lost in the accident. He motioned me forward, and I sat next to him on the bed.

"Actually, it wasn't," he said. "Chelsea had it. She brought it by earlier today." He pointed to the side table.

"How did Chelsea get your iPod?"

"During the hypnotist show, she joined us for a better view, and she asked if she could borrow it."

"And she visited you today?"

"She came with the student council gang. I was surprised you didn't come with them, but Chelsea said you weren't feeling well."

"I haven't even talked to Chelsea today."

"Oh. She called you at home this morning to check on you."

"What else did she tell you?"

"She said you were pretty out of it. Maybe that's why you don't remember."

"I'd remember if she called."

Mrs. Santos set her hand on my shoulder. "It's okay, child. Just a misunderstanding."

I struggled to catch my breath and calm myself. Why would Chelsea lie? We were friends. It made no sense for her to invent a story for Manny, but I didn't want to cause a spectacle in front of his relatives . . . so I let it go.

Manny introduced me to his extended family, and one by one, they told me embarrassing stories about him. After a while, my mom announced we needed to head out.

"Please, let me stay," I said. "You could come back later and pick me up."

"No. Plus, we still need to give Lily her gift."

"Right." I squeezed Manny's fingers and said goodbye to his family.

We took the elevator to the ICU and followed the signs to Lily's room. My heart beat faster at the idea of seeing her, but when we got to her room, my heart sank. We stood in the hallway and stared through the sliding glass doors. A gloomy pallor masked her vibrant, tan face. Gauze wrapped around her head where her long brown locks should have been. Ashen lids cloaked her hazel eyes. Hoses and tubes connected Lily to machines and pumps and drains. A ventilator helped her breathe. A gray blanket covered her seemingly lifeless form. This was not the Lily I knew. Her dream was to leave Idaho and explore the world. She had to recover.

"May I help you?" a nurse asked.

"We're here to see Lily," my mom said.

"I'm sorry, only family members can visit," the nurse said. "However, Mrs. Sloane is just down the hall in the waiting area if you want to speak with her."

"Thank you," Mom said, and we moved in that direction.

Mrs. Sloane sat with another woman. I smiled when she looked up. The other woman's face turned bright red, and Mrs. Sloane glanced nervously between her and me. We approached, and they stood. I wanted to give Mrs. Sloane a hug and talk with her, but my body tensed the closer I got to the two women.

"Hi, Mrs. Sloane," I said. "How's Lily doing?"

She wrung her hands together. "She's still unconscious."

"I'm so sorry—"

"You should be," the other woman said. Tears tore down her face.

Mrs. Sloane cleared her throat and motioned toward her. "This is Jordan's mother."

"Oh," I said. I'd never met Mrs. Hilaman before. I swallowed and tried to find the right words. "Mrs. Hilaman, I am—"

Jordan's mom thrust her finger into my face. "Do. Not. Patronize. Me."

"I wasn't."

She stepped closer to me, and I took a step back.

"How can you even justify being here?" She turned from me to my mother. "Either of you?"

"I brought a gift for Lily." I lifted the glittered pink sack. As soon as I said it, I realized it was a stupid thing to say, but in the tense moment, I couldn't think straight. Jordan's and Lily's moms needed to know how sorry I was, but I said, "We went to the mall—"

And Jordan's mom slapped me across the cheek.

I dropped the gift to the floor and covered my face. It was the second time in my life I'd been hit by someone. I didn't deserve it the first time, but maybe I did this time.

Mom stepped in front of me, and in a low, restrained tone she said, "I understand you're grieving, but don't ever touch my daughter again. It was a car accident, and Hannah never intended to harm anyone."

"Leave!" Jordan's mom pointed toward the elevators. A bead of sweat rolled down her forehead.

Mrs. Sloane covered her mouth and sobbed. I hated myself for causing this grief. I'd give anything to bring Jordan back and make Lily whole again. If only I could.

Mom looped her arm through mine, and we walked away, trembling. The gift sack was left abandoned on the floor.

⊱ • ⊰

I ran up the stairs to my room, slammed the door behind me, and threw myself on the bed. I buried my face in my pillows and cried myself to sleep.

Sometime during the night I awoke, still fully dressed and on top of my covers. The light of the waning full moon shone through my window and cast strange patterns along the upper edges of my walls. The hairs on my forearms stood, and a menacing gloom came over me. The shapes grew and changed, elongated toward the center of the ceiling. Then they descended like murky vapors.

I twisted over and flipped on the bedside lamp. Then I bolted from the bed and yanked the drapes across the window, blocking out the strange silhouettes cast by the moonlight. My eyes darted around the room and toward the ceiling. No more scary apparitions danced overhead, but something was still wrong.

My heart thumped. I tiptoed around my room, and then I shuddered. No more piles of wadded stationary spotted the floor. The stapler, pencil sharpener, and other items had been returned to my desktop.

Maybe Mom came in and picked up things while I slept.

But then my back stiffened.

The Disney World caricature was back on the wall. Mom would not have searched through my desk drawers for that cartoon. I snatched it off the wall and opened the bottom desk drawer, but before I dropped the picture in, I gasped. The picture slipped from my fingers and fell to the carpet.

I knelt next to the drawer and peered inside. All my botched attempts at writing a letter to Jordan's parents had been smoothed out and stacked together. The top letter read:

Dear Mr. & Mrs. Hilaman,
*   It's not my fault that Jordan didn't wear his seat belt. He*
was a jerk.

Sincerely,
Hannah O'Leary

My hands began to shake. I never wrote that letter, and yet, it was my penmanship. Yes, Jordan was a jerk, but I would never say that to his parents. Never. The accident happened because of me, whether Jordan wore a seat belt or not.

I lifted the letter out and methodically tore it into a million tiny bits, letting the pieces fall back into the drawer. Then I grabbed the other failed letters and ripped them all to shreds. When I finished, I placed the framed caricature on top of the mess and closed the drawer. I sat at my desk and pulled out an unspotted piece of stationery. With deliberate strokes, I wrote:

Dear Mr. & Mrs. Hilaman,
*   I am so sorry for the accident. No words can ever convey my*
sorrow. I will understand if you never forgive me.

Sincerely,
Hannah O'Leary

MONDAY
AUGUST 26

I dabbed more concealer onto my chin and said to myself in the bathroom mirror, "You can do this." I lifted the flat iron and pulled it through my hair, again, section by section. The hot enamel intensified the fragrance of my jasmine conditioner.

First day of our senior year.

Last week, Lily, Chelsea, and I had been so excited we bought coordinating outfits for today: new jeans with rhinestones on the front and back pockets and shirts in school colors. Mine was an emerald-green blouse with ruffles down the front. Lily's was a simple sleeveless marigold knit top. Chelsea's was a green-striped polo with a white collar. As student council members at Peregrine High, we planned to start the year with spirit. But now, Lily clung to life in a hospital bed, and Chelsea ignored my texts.

I slid an emerald sequined headband in place and smoothed my dark hair. A tear slipped down, and I swiped it away. Manny had bruises on his face, the least of his injuries. I felt guilty for wanting to look good, but today was my first time anchoring the morning broadcast at school. I had worked hard to earn that position, and Mr. Arnold expected me to show up and do my part. I touched up my mascara and promised myself: no more waterworks today. I spritzed myself with my jasmine body spray and returned to my room.

I finished putting my supplies into my backpack, but hesitated when I noticed the letter I'd written last night still sitting on the desktop. No tears, I reminded myself. I slid the letter inside a spiral notebook and added it to my bag.

I straightened the quilt on my bed and considered kicking off my shoes and climbing back under the covers. But if I ignored the world today, I'd still have to face it tomorrow, and it wouldn't be any easier. I'd still have to go to school alone. Hopefully, Manny would return soon. I grabbed my backpack and headed downstairs. In the kitchen, Mom rinsed a cup in the sink.

"You're up early," she said.

"I need to get to school. Student council is passing out class schedules."

She picked up her purse and then kissed me on the forehead. "Try and have a good day, sweetheart."

"Wait," I said. "I need you to take me."

She checked her watch. "I need you to ride the bus."

"Mom, I haven't ridden the bus since freshman year. And I just told you, I have to get there early."

"Hurry up then. I can't be late for work."

I grabbed a Pop-Tart from the cupboard. "I'm ready. Let's go." I hoisted my backpack over one shoulder and followed Mom out the door. I bit off a large chunk from the strawberry pastry. Crumbs sprinkled down my blouse and onto the pristine floor mat of Mom's Toyota Prius. She narrowed her eyes at me and drove out of the neighborhood.

"Thanks for picking up my room last night," I said.

Mom glanced toward me. "I didn't."

"Oh."

"Did something unusual happen?" Mom asked. "Should we call Dr. James?"

Now that I hovered in the shadow of Dad's mental illness, I needed to be more careful; otherwise, Mom would worry. And even though Dr. James was the expert to help me, he also held clout with the judge.

"Hannah?"

I doubted my ability to ease her mind, but I tried. "I'm fine. My room was just cleaner than I remembered. No big deal."

She kept her eyes on the road. "You're sure?"

"Yup."

She dropped me off at school, and I walked straight to the Commons. Chelsea's laugh rang out before I even spotted her. My pace slowed when I discovered football and volleyball players had already manned the tables. Chelsea and her teammates were all decked out in their matching game jerseys.

"Hannah!" The principal patted my back. "We weren't sure you'd make it today, what with the accident and all. How are you?"

"The student council is supposed to—"

"Don't fret about it. We changed things around, and we've got it covered. Take it easy, and let me know if you need anything." He shuffled across the giant green-and-gold mosaic of our mascot—a falcon—and headed toward his office. I didn't want to take it easy. I wanted to hand out schedules with the student council members as we'd planned, but they'd changed things without me.

The tables were labeled with letters based on last names, and I stepped over to the O table, where Chelsea sat with two other girls. Their chatter stopped. Chelsea went stone-faced and avoided my gaze. I stood straighter and concealed my disappointment.

"Hi, Chelsea," I said.

The other girls gawked at me. I blinked, again and again, to keep my imminent tears at bay.

"Did you get my texts?" I asked Chelsea. No response. My throat tightened, and heat rose from the pit of my gut. I waved my hand in front of her, and she locked eyes with me in a terrifying stare. She leaned forward, thumbed through her stack of papers, and then slid my class schedule across the table.

"You're just going to ignore me?" I found myself swaying back and forth between anger and aching.

She leaned back and batted her eyelashes. If she'd used any more mascara, those tarantula legs would have scampered right off her face. She was publicly snubbing me.

I snatched up the paper and stormed away. Chelsea spoke to the girls behind me. I only caught snippets: *Can you believe she came? Shouldn't she be in jail or something?* I clenched my jaw. No tears. Not here. I kept walking, shocked by her rebuke. Chelsea had been one of my closest friends since she'd moved here last fall, and I'd hoped she'd help me through this. If only I'd gone back to bed this morning. I should've waited for Manny, and we could have returned together. But silly me, I thought I was needed here today.

I plopped down on a bench in front of the school. A tear slipped and fell onto my schedule: Broadcasting III, AP Literature, an open period before lunch, Leadership, AP Statistics, Spanish II, and Introduction to Creative Writing.

The other upperclassmen on the student council and I had planned it out perfectly. We figured an open period before lunch gave us plenty of time to leave school grounds and go somewhere fun to eat. We'd be back in time for our leadership class together, but even if we returned late, our advisors would cut us slack. They usually did.

I lingered in a daze until other students began to arrive. They whispered and wandered by me. The pit in my stomach grew. I grabbed my backpack and headed off for broadcasting. Maybe Mr. Arnold needed help setting up the studio equipment.

Upstairs in the broadcasting studio, I found Chelsea rehearsing behind the anchor's desk. Mr. Arnold interrupted her and gave her pointers. Mark leaned against the wall, watching. There was also a guy working the camera, and through a side window, I spotted Eugene working in the equipment booth.

"What is Chelsea doing here?" I asked.

Everyone twisted in my direction. My backpack dropped to the floor with a thud.

"Chelsea," I said, "a second ago, you were giving out schedules. Now you're here—"

"Oh, Hannah!" Mr. Arnold said and adjusted his brown spectacles. "We're so glad to see you. We assumed you'd be home recovering from the accident."

Heat rose from my chest to my face. My voice cracked when I asked, "Why is Chelsea in my chair?"

Mr. Arnold tugged at his tan plaid shirt around his generous midriff. "She offered to fill in for you as anchor today."

I glared at Chelsea. "You knew I was here."

"You left." Chelsea smiled like an angel. "I figured you went home. You're probably too emotional to stay the whole day. What with the accident and all."

I lunged across the desk and swung at her. She ducked before my fist connected, but she screamed as though it had. And she kept screaming. Mr. Arnold seized me around the waist with one of his large fleshy arms and pulled me back from the desk. I wrestled free from him.

"You're a freaking psycho!" Chelsea popped up from behind the desk and swept her long blond hair from her face.

"Forget your meds this morning?" Mark turned against me and slunk around the desk to help Chelsea.

Mr. Arnold grabbed my backpack, and with his other hand, he gripped my wrist and led me out of the studio.

"I wasn't really going to hit her," I said.

"Are you sure you're ready to come back to school?" Mr. Arnold wiped perspiration from the bridge of his nose with his thumb and forefinger. Then he repositioned his glasses.

"I'm the morning anchor."

"I know," he said, "but maybe it's too soon. Emotions are running high. Maybe you should go hang out in the library this period, and we'll try again tomorrow." He handed me my backpack. I let it thump to the floor. Then I dragged it behind me as I walked away.

In the library, students gawked at me.

"What?" I said. No one responded, except for the librarian, who shushed me. I feigned self-discipline, propped my backpack against a table, and repositioned my hairband.

I could barely breathe. I texted Mom and begged her to come and get me, but she had to stay at work.

She texted back: Hang in there!

I texted Manny, but he didn't respond. He was probably still at the hospital.

"Hannah?"

I glanced up. Eugene stood next to me.

"You okay?" he asked.

"Aren't you supposed to be in the control booth, helping with the morning broadcast?"

He held up the ginormous three-by-ten-inch wooden bathroom pass that Mr. Arnold made people carry. It had the words I NEED TO PEE painted on it. Mr. Arnold thought it was funny. I thought it was humiliating.

"I wanted to make sure you're all right," Eugene said.

I suddenly recalled how Eugene had said those exact words to me over five years ago on my first day of school in Idaho. I had been eating lunch by myself when he joined me. He was kind and said that my eyes reminded him of his mother's eyes, full of legendary strength. Later, I got caught up in the excitement of being accepted by the popular group, and I only ever said hello to Eugene in passing after that.

"Are you all right?" Eugene asked again.

"You mean after my ridiculous outburst?"

He nodded.

"I'm fine," I said. "Is Chelsea okay?"

"Only a bruised ego."

"Thanks for checking on me," I said.

"Don't let Chelsea's antics mess with your mind." Eugene tapped his forehead, and then he strolled out of the library.

If only it were that easy. I rested my head on the table and waited for the bell.

⊱ • ⊰

When first period ended, I tromped back down the stairs to my literature class. Chelsea sat in the back row. I chewed on the inside of my cheek and debated what to do. I could apologize and work it out with her, or I could continue as an outcast all day.

I took a seat next to her.

"Sorry," I said. "I'm really embarrassed I took a swing at you. This weekend's been bad, and I'm not—"

Chelsea took in a slow breath, stood, and then moved to the front row.

I flashed back to a time in the park when Mom walked away from Dad in the middle of an apology. My throat tightened as I considered Dad's perspective. He had sat alone on that park bench. At the time, instead of following Mom, I chose to sit and wait with Dad. After an hour we walked home together in continued silence.

And now no one sat on either side of me or in front of me.

Chelsea leaned across the aisle and whispered something to the girl next to her. She cocked an eyebrow at me. I bit down on my tongue and steeled myself against more tears. Not here. When the teacher started class, I faced straight ahead and used every ounce of energy to keep my composure. I needed the clock to move faster. Finally, the bell rang and everyone herded out.

Last week, at our end-of-summer party, the student council had agreed to meet in the Commons for our open period and carpool to lunch. I needed to patch things up with my friends.

"Chelsea, wait!" I hollered down the hall to her, but she kept going. I jogged to catch up to her. When I touched her back, she whipped around.

"Go home, Hannah!" Her spittle hit me in the face. "At least you still can. Jordan can never go home again. His mom will never see him again. You drove like an idiot, and you killed him—"

"I told him to wear his seat belt!"

Chelsea shook her head. The disgust in her eyes made me cringe.

"You hated Jordan all along. I don't know what's possessed you, but we want you off the student council. Drop off. And back off. Go rot in your own miserable little nightmare."

Stunned, I let her leave.

After a minute of standing alone in the hallway, I made my way to the Commons, hoping the rest of the student council felt differently. But when I arrived, they were already heading out to the parking lot. No one even glanced back for me.

My phone vibrated with an incoming text. I pulled it from my pocket and clicked on a message from Chelsea: Jordan's dead because of you. I hope you rot a slow and painful death while evil minions pick your flesh to the bone. That's what you deserve. Stop bothering me.

Tears fell onto my phone. I wiped them away and slipped my phone back into my pocket. I would give anything to go back to Friday and make different choices, but that was impossible.

The tardy bell rang, and the principal came up to me. "Hannah? Are you okay?"

I nodded.

"All right, then you need to get to class."

I had an open period but no car and no friends. So I went to the school counselor's office to change my schedule. Five other students waited in line before me. Apparently, they had problems today, too.

When my name was finally called, I sat next to Mr. Turney's desk and passed him my class schedule.

"What can I do for you, Hannah?" he asked, and his thick brown mustache twitched.

"I'm resigning as senior class secretary," I said, "so, I need to replace my leadership class that's after lunch." Because only student council members took that class.

"Hannah," Mr. Turney said, "why would you want to quit?"

I'd worked so hard to win the student council office with the posters, the promises, and the parties. A part of me wanted to keep the position, but the idea of continuing on when Lily lay in a hospital bed, and Jordan lay dead, wrenched my heart right out of my chest. We were supposed to all be in student council leadership together, and I couldn't do it without them, especially when Chelsea blamed me for the accident. I might not be able to control everything, but I could control my resignation. I didn't trust myself around Chelsea. Maybe she and the others would criticize me less if I stepped down from my position. Plus, that would be one less class period I'd have to endure with her, and I needed some semblance of peace.

"Hannah?" Mr. Turney smoothed his mustache with his thumb and forefinger.

"Thanks, Mr. Turney, but I've already decided."

"If you're sure," he said.

"I am."

He tapped his keyboard. "To replace leadership, how about art?"

I knew nothing about art. I'd always been too busy with student council and broadcasting to even consider an art class.

"What are my other choices?"

"Well, most of the classes after lunch are already full. You could do first-year French, Physics, Choir, or Advanced Art." He leaned back in his chair and clasped his hands.

"Can I have another open period?"

He squinted at the computer monitor. "Not if you still want to graduate this year. You need to meet the required number of class credits."

"How can I take Advanced Art when I haven't taken the prerequisites?"

"Under the circumstances . . . what with the accident and all . . ."

My heart beat faster, and my hands began to sweat. I imagined lunging at Mr. Turney the way I had at Chelsea in broadcasting, but even more, I saw my fingers wrap around his throat. His face reddening. A voice behind me whispered, "Do it."

I spun around to see who had said it, but no one was there. I held my breath, afraid to look at Mr. Turney. I needed to regain my composure, but I felt completely unnerved. I gasped for air and tried to picture Manny. His lips moved as he told me he loved me. I drew in a deep breath and swiveled back around in my chair.

Mr. Turney's jaw hung slack as he stared at me.

"Art sounds fine, thank you," I said. I plucked a tissue from the box on Mr. Turney's desk and wiped the perspiration from my face.

He made the corrections on my class schedule and returned it to me. I rose, hesitated, and with reluctance I plopped back down and passed my schedule back to him. "What's available during this class period?"

"Auto Mechanics, Latin, Law Enforcement I, or Introduction to Psychology."

"Psychology."

He made the changes and suggested I go to lunch and attend psychology tomorrow since the bell would ring soon. I agreed. I moved through the lunch line, and with my tray in hand I debated where to sit. Since the cafeteria was the land of underclassmen, I walked out to the barren soccer field and for the first time in years, I ate lunch by myself. I considered the art class instead of leadership with my friends. Former friends. Advanced Art was for the students who'd taken an art class every year in high school. I would be a finger painter among the Rembrandts and Monets.

I strolled back to the Commons and threw my trash into a bin. Right then, the student council members clambered in from another door, laughing and joking with one another. I shuddered and turned in the other direction. We all had such great plans for this year. And now I'd be alone in Advanced Art. I headed down the hall, but had to stop and pull out my schedule to find the room number . . . M193. I'd never even set foot in that part of the building before.

I arrived at M193 and hovered outside the room. Could I do this? Leave my old life behind and move forward on my own? I set my hand on my chest and tried to calm myself, but my heart rate escalated anyhow. I lifted my foot and stepped across the threshold.

Colorful artwork blanketed the walls of the bright room, and the fragrance of flowers filled the air. I took another step inside, and the students in the room hushed. Tables filled the space instead of desks. About twelve students huddled around three separate tables in the center of the room. I searched their faces and recognized one.

A short, plump teacher approached me. "Are you lost?"

I gave her my class schedule. She lifted her reading glasses to her nose, and the long string of beads attached to the frames sparkled in the light. She noted the counselor's signature on my schedule. "Oh. You're Hannah?" She peered over the rims of her glasses at me.

I gritted my teeth and silently begged her not to reference the accident.

She didn't. Instead, she wrapped her arm around me and led me to a group of students at one of the tables. "Kyla, this is Hannah. Please introduce her around." The teacher smiled at me. "I'm Rose, and I'm glad to have you in our class."

I sat next to Kyla, who was slender with clear skin and vivid blue eyes. She sported a brilliant red hairdo. Not auburn but stop-sign, fire-engine, clown-nose red. And it was made even more dramatic by her sheer turquoise blouse and matching camisole.

She introduced me to the other two people at her table: Nick and Plug. I must have heard her incorrectly, because across from me was the one face I recognized: Eugene. He lifted his ring-laden fingers and waved. Next to him a bald-headed guy wore a navy T-shirt with large white words: LAST CLEAN T-SHIRT.

The rest of the art students appeared normal compared to these three. But if I took anyone from this class and propped them next to a student council member, there'd be a distinct difference. I scrutinized my manicured nails and mall-bought clothes and realized with clarity, I was the outcast here. But none of them moved away from me; none of them referenced the accident; and none of them ignored me. Unlike the student council members.

Eugene opened his mouth, as if he was about to say something to me, but then Rose began class, and he said nothing.

Rose had everyone pull out their summer portfolios and hand them to their neighbors. Kyla reached past me and gave her portfolio to the bald guy in his last clean T-shirt, and then she shared Eugene's portfolio with me. Rose gave out assessment forms for us to critique each other's artwork. Kyla flipped open the portfolio, and my eyes widened.

An incredible painting of a sky full of thunderclouds over a golden field seemed to lift off the page.

"That's amazing." I reached out to feel the texture of the paint, but Kyla pulled my hand back.

"No touching," she said.

"Why?"

"It's someone's original art. We only observe it."

"Oh," I said, still confused. "It's amazing." I repeated myself like a dork, because I had no other words to describe it.

"It captures van Gogh's vast fields under the savage sky," Kyla said.

I stared at her, dumbfounded.

"Have you ever taken an art class?" she asked in a curious, nonchalant way.

"Never," I said. Everyone at the table lifted their heads.

"How did you register for this class?" Bald-Boy asked.

"The counselor said I could take this class or physics."

"What were you in before?" Kyla asked.

"Leadership."

"Oh," they chimed in unison, as if I'd just committed blasphemy in the middle of a Bible study class.

"You." Bald-Boy pointed his pencil at me. I sat on my hands so I wouldn't be tempted to lunge across the table if he announced to everyone I'd killed Jordan. "You took a massive swing at Chelsea this morning in broadcasting. I thought you were going to pummel her for weaseling into your anchor position."

"Were you there?" I asked, unable to place his face.

He reached into his bag and pulled out a knit cap, tugged it onto his head, and slipped on a pair of black horn-rimmed glasses.

He made air quotes with his fingers and said, "My cameraman disguise." He thumped his pencil against the table before pointing at Eugene. "And Plug works in the equipment booth."

As Eugene beamed at me his silver lip ring caught the light. His cropped black hair framed his face.

"Plug?" I asked.

He pointed at his ears. "Gauge piercings. Nick envies my fine body candy." He toyed with the ring in his lower lip. Then he pushed up the long sleeves of his gray V-neck T-shirt and rested his elbows against the table.

I focused back on Nick and pointed at the knit cap. "Your cameraman disguise?" I laughed. "It works, because I didn't even recognize you."

"Our secret identities," Nick said. "We only tell you because you tried to chop down Tall-Tree-Chelsea."

I grinned at the moniker and imagined long birch tree trunks in place of her legs. "She is freakishly tall, even for a volleyball player," I said.

Nick pursed his lips and nodded. He removed his cap and glasses, and then he smiled, revealing straight white teeth.

I asked Kyla, "What's your secret identity?"

Nick spoke up before Kyla. "She's a chameleon. Today she's Crimson. Tomorrow she might be Cerulean. It's always a surprise." Nick reached across the table and touched Kyla's red hair. She held his gaze for a few seconds until Rose came over and asked how the critiques were coming along.

"Back to work," Eugene, also known as Plug, said. And everyone's heads bowed back down to the portfolios.

Kyla flipped to the next painting, and my heart stopped.

I covered my mouth.

Kyla remained calm. "The use of white chalk on the black paper to create the illusion of screaming skulls takes my breath away, too," she said.

I leaned in. At first glance, the swirling black mist along the edges of the drawing had caught my attention, but when I re-examined it, I distinguished shapes of hollowed-out skulls. And they silently screamed out in horror.

"Who drew this?" I whispered.

"Plug," Kyla said and jerked her thumb toward him.

"Why?" I asked him.

He fidgeted with his ear and said, "To capture emotions."

"Did something inspire you to draw these misty skulls?" I needed to know if he'd actually seen the black mist, too, or if it lived only in my delusions.

"Plug's passionate about the occult," Kyla said.

"The what?" I leaned closer, invading Kyla's space, and she started to explain.

"The occult—"

"The practice of evil." Nick waved his hands next to his ears and raised his eyebrows. "Scary stuff, man." He snorted, and Plug—the name was growing on me—shoved him.

"It's difficult to give a factual definition for the occult," Kyla said. "It's something technically undetectable, but some people argue it's the foundation of all world governments."

"Some people say it's esoteric and arcane," Plug said. "Some people will try to convince you the sign language symbol for 'I love you' is an occult symbol. Some people are trying to scare you into being a follower and not a finder. The occult simply explores the paranormal and the unknown. There's nothing evil about it."

"Not according to right-wing extremists," Nick said.

"Stop seeing a conspiracy everywhere," Plug said.

The bell rang.

I was surprised the period had ended already. We had only discussed two pictures. Everyone closed their portfolios and moved out, but Rose stopped me and asked me to stay.

"I understand the counselor gave you special permission to be here because of what happened over the weekend, but I need to know you will work extra hard and take this class seriously. The students in here are exceptional artists and have studied a great deal about the craft and the history. Respect their work—"

"Their work is amazing!"

"You will have to meet the same standards as everyone else in this class, or your grade will reflect it. You will have to work to earn an A in here. Do you understand my terms?"

"Yes. Is there something I should study to try to catch up a little?" Rose handed me a fifty-pound book on art history.

"Start here. And take care of this book. I expect it returned when you're done with it."

I used both arms to carry the massive load to my next class. Two seats remained open in AP Statistics: one next to Mark and one next to Plug. I realized the name fit him perfectly, but I wasn't sure what to call him outside the inner realm of art class. I plunked the massive art book onto the desk next to him, and he raised an eyebrow.

"Steal that?" he asked.

"No!"

"Rose doesn't loan that book."

"How would I possibly steal it anyhow? Sneak it under my shirt?"

He grinned, and my cheeks heated up.

The teacher called out the attendance roll.

"Eugene Polaski?" she said.

"Here," Plug answered.

I coughed twice and smirked. "Eugene or Plug?" I whispered.

"Stop," he whispered back. "Eugene is a hard name to live with."

"It's never bothered me," I whispered and bit back my laughter. "But what am I supposed to call you outside of art? Eugene or Plug?"

He shrugged. "Friends call me Plug."

After class, he carried the huge book for me to my locker, but the sucker was an inch too wide. The door wouldn't close.

"Great," I said. "I guess I have to lug this brick around for two more periods."

"Let's put it in your—" he stopped midsentence. A few seconds passed before I followed his train of thought.

"Right. My car is totaled." I hoisted the book back out of my locker.

"Put it in mine," he said.

"Your locker?"

"My car."

"We only have five minutes," I said. "We'll be late for our next class."

"So?" Plug hauled the book from my arms and headed toward the student parking lot.

When he stopped to unlock the door of an unusual old vehicle, I asked, "What is this thing?"

"Have you never seen a vintage El Camino before?" he asked.

"Apparently not. Its father must have been a truck and its mother a sedan." I grinned at my quick-witted humor.

Plug scowled. He tossed the art book onto the seat and slammed the door. Clearly I'd offended him. Stupid. Cars to boys were like clothes to girls. We all wanted to look nice in the outfit we were riding in, and I couldn't afford to lose my one remaining friend.

"I've just never seen anything like it before," I said.

"It's a classic," Plug said. "The kind of ride my dad had back when he had a mullet." He ran his fingers along the smooth lines of the vehicle.

"Nice." I couldn't think of anything else to say. My blue Mazda had been a "sensible small car" according to Mom. "Should I get the book from you after school?"

"Sure," Plug said. "You want a ride home?" He'd already forgiven me.

"Yeah." I smiled. "That'd be great."

We walked back inside, tardy. At the end of the hall, Plug and I separated, and a weight settled on my shoulders. Something about him had lifted my spirits, and I wanted to drag him with me to all my classes. But that wasn't an option. I had to finish the day alone.

In Spanish class there was a review to figure out what we'd forgotten over the summer. My mind kept drifting to the group of people in art. And then it occurred to me, I hadn't thought of Manny or Lily in a couple of hours. Guilt washed over me. I hoped they were doing better.

The bell rang. One more class to endure. I'd almost made it through the day, but before I entered the creative writing classroom, Chelsea's hee-haw bellowed out. Dread bubbled up inside me. Chelsea, Lily, and I had signed up for Introduction to Creative Writing because we figured it'd be easy, since the teacher was Jordan's aunt. I halted at the doorway. Chelsea ceased her chatter when she spotted me. She and several of our other friends filled in the back row, and together, they gawked at me. I sank into a seat in the front row farthest away from them, but that put me right in front of the teacher's desk. Maybe she was gone today since Jordan's funeral was scheduled for Wednesday. She could be out all week. I hoped for a substitute, but the bell rang, and Mrs. Hilaman stepped into the classroom.

"Okay, class. Welcome," Mrs. Hilaman said. "Get out a piece of paper. I will put a prompt up on the board, and you will spend the entire period writing. Turn in your papers at the end of class. You will be graded for content as well as quality."

She wrote on the board: What I regret most about my summer vacation is . . .

Chelsea spoke up from the back of the classroom. "Mrs. Hilaman, on behalf of all of us, I want to express our sincere sympathies for the loss"—she dabbed the tears from her eyes—"the loss of Jordan. We all loved him so much. He was your nephew, but he was family to us, also."

Mrs. Hilaman hugged Chelsea. "Thank you," she said and wiped her own eyes. "For those of you who are interested, his funeral is Wednesday morning. If you need the details, let me know, but for now, back to your papers." She returned to her desk and frowned when her eyes settled on me.

I lowered my gaze and straightened the ruffles on my blouse. Mrs. Hilaman stepped out of the classroom, and I released the breath I'd been holding.

The day was almost over. I just needed to survive a while longer. Then I could settle into the safety of my bed and forget the world. My eyes burned, but I refused to cry here.

I opened my backpack and pulled out my spiral notebook; the letter I'd written last night was still stuck inside. I considered the prompt on the board and decided to give the letter to Mrs. Hilaman to pass on to Jordan's parents. I opened the notebook and read over the letter I'd written:

Dear Mr. & Mrs. Hilaman,
  It's not my fault that Jordan didn't wear his seat belt. He was a jerk.

Sincerely,
Hannah O'Leary

It was the wrong letter. My vision blurred, and my hands trembled. I dug in my backpack for the correct one. Bits of paper cluttered the bottom of the bag. I pinched a couple of pieces. They were real, but the letter on my desk was real, too, and the handwriting was mine. I glanced around the class, and Chelsea sneered at me. I began to wad up the letter, but I worried someone would still find it and read it. So I tore the paper and shoved the cruel words into my mouth. I chewed and swallowed. I crumpled the rest of the paper into a tiny ball and dropped it into my bag. The edges of my vision pulsed with my increasing heart rate. I covered my eyes and tried to picture Manny. It had worked earlier for me in the counselor's office, but I couldn't imagine his face. I only saw the beady eyes and the mist of darkness from the car accident. I put my head down on my desk and longed for peace.

Mrs. Hilaman came back into the room and tapped the board. "Okay. Finish up and turn in your papers when you leave."

The numbers on the clock showed we had less than five minutes before the bell. Where had the time gone? I yanked out a clean piece of paper and started over.

Dear Hilaman family,
  I regret the accident so very much. No words can ever convey my sorrow. I will understand if you never forgive me.

Sincerely,
Hannah O'Leary

I waited until the rest of the class left, and then I stood. Before I turned in my paper, I read it again to make sure it was the right one and said the right things. It was still the same. I set my paper on top of the pile in Mrs. Hilaman's hands, and she read it.

"Thank you, Hannah," she said. Neither of us moved at first, but then she set the papers on her desk and reached out and embraced me.

"I never intended for any of it to happen. Please tell Jordan's parents how sorry I am."

"I will," she said. "But please don't attend the funeral. They are still angry, and it will make things worse if they see you there. I don't blame you, Hannah, but they are grieving, and it will take them a while to come to terms with the accident."

"Okay." I took a deep breath and settled my nerves.

⇥ • ⇤

I hustled to the parking lot with renewed energy and found Plug perched on the hood of his El Camino joking with Nick and Kyla. Nick wrapped his arm around her.

"Hello, Hannah," Kyla said.

"Hi." I still marveled at the novelty of her crimson hair. Was Nick right? Would she come tomorrow with cerulean hair?

"You survived the day!" Plug held his knuckles out to me. I bumped his with mine and laughed when he pretended his fist exploded, sound effects and all. It had been quite a while since I'd seen anyone do that.

"Weren't sure you were coming," Plug said.

"Why wouldn't I?"

He hopped down from the hood. "You have plans? Or you want to hang out?"

My first choice would be to spend time with Manny, but he hadn't texted me back. My choices were to sit at home alone or do something with these three.

"Let's do it," I said. I texted my mom and let her know I had a ride home, and I was spending some time with . . . friends. Is that what they were? They were speaking to me, and that was nice.

I rode with Plug; Nick and Kyla followed in a black Mini Cooper.

"Where are we going?" I asked.

"Kyla's favorite hangout."

"Which is?" I motioned with my hand for more information.

He smiled and said nothing more. After a few turns he pulled into an old gas station. Large black-and-white signs plastered to the pumps read: OUT OF SERVICE.

Plug parked near several other cars, and Nick pulled in next to us.

"Welcome to Clandestine Coffee," Plug said and hopped out of the vehicle.

I sat there and examined the entrance to the building. There was no business sign. No open or closed sign. No sign of life behind the darkly tinted windows. Plug opened my door.

Kyla smiled and waved us forward.

I followed them inside, surprised by the bustling crowd. Music from a live band played in the distant garage space, and dishes clanked behind the counter. The aroma of freshly ground coffee beans and newly baked pastries filled the air. Against the far wall two baristas worked filling orders and in the main area, tables, couches, and chairs filled the space.

"What do you think of the artwork?" Kyla asked.

I scanned the walls, but she pointed down at the chairs. I was confused. She stepped over to the nearest table and pulled a chair away from it. The wood had been painted multiple shades of blue; stars and glitter and moons covered the entire thing.

"One of mine," Plug said and pulled out another chair. On top of a base of turquoise, branches spanned out with scattered butter-colored blossoms.

"We supply the art here," Nick said and pointed at the posters, framed art, mobiles, and sculptures that filled the entire place.

"Wow," I said, amazed.

Kyla led us through swinging doors to the space behind the bar. We squeezed past the baristas, who were too busy to comment on our presence, and we made our way to the far corner. Where the bar ended, Plexiglas fenced in the space. A wooden easel stood in front of a large window facing out to the sidewalk. A workbench with a sink spanned the back wall. And a canvas tarp covered the floor. In the middle of the tarp sat a wooden chair, already painted white.

"Here." Plug offered me a tattered and stained smock. I followed his lead as he donned an apron to cover his clothes.

Plug opened the lid of a pint of red paint and passed it to me with a long-bristled brush. Kyla grabbed yellow paint. Nick green. And Plug blue. Then they dipped their brushes into the bright colors and flung it at the chair. I questioned their sanity as the paint randomly flew everywhere: on the tarp, on the Plexiglas, and on their smocks.

They laughed at themselves.

"Try it," Kyla said.

I dabbed my brush into the apple-red paint and flicked it at the chair. A smile crept across my face, and I surrendered to the odd pleasure of flinging paint. I dunked my brush, loaded it with color, and pitched it at the chair. A glob landed on Plug's face. He froze.

"Misfire," Nick said.

Plug bit down on his lip ring, and I waited for his reaction. He slowly dipped his brush. Then he yanked it out, and with a quick flick of his wrist, he landed a bombshell of blue smack-dab in the middle of my chest. The smock took the brunt of the hit. Plug flung more paint and hit Nick in the shoulder. His LAST CLEAN T-SHIRT was now dirty. I laughed so hard I doubled over and had to set my container of paint on the floor.

The energy was electric. I hadn't felt this happy since the fair. And then I remembered Manny. And Lily. And Jordan.

I stopped laughing. I picked up the paint and the brush and set them on the workbench. I peeled off the smock and walked out past the baristas. It was insulting to Manny and Lily for me to have fun when they were still in the hospital.

"It's all right," Kyla said as she came up behind me. "Let's order some Italian sodas and sit for a while." I agreed.

She got the drinks, and I found a table in the far corner. From my vantage point, I watched Plug and Nick in the art corner. They cleaned the brushes at the workbench and put away the supplies. When they finished, they helped Kyla carry drinks and pastries to the table.

"Sorry," I said to them.

Plug waved off the apology. "Not necessary."

"I'm glad you had fun, even if it was brief," Kyla said.

I took a sip of the Italian soda. "This is good."

"Have you never had one before?" Kyla asked.

"No, I usually drink Dr. Pepper," I said.

Plug picked at his apple fritter. Then he reached across the table and snatched one of Kyla's chocolate chip cookies.

"Hey!" Kyla protested and yanked the remaining cookie from his grasp. He'd already filched a large bite.

"Do you always just take what you want?" I asked Plug.

"Unjustified sense of entitlement," Nick said.

We laughed at Plug, and he licked his fingers one by one.

"How did you guys find this place?" I asked. "I've lived here for years, and I've never even heard of it."

"My aunt got us the art job here after Plug's mom passed away some years ago," Kyla said. "It's been therapeutic—"

Chelsea and Mark bounded through the main entrance. Her cackle cut straight through the atmosphere and right to my nerves. She spotted us and sauntered over.

"Slumming it, Hannah?" she asked.

"Now you're talking to me?" I asked. "Why are you here?"

"We wanted to see how the lower class lives," Mark said.

"Let's go," Plug said and shoved his chair away from the table. We all stood and moved toward the door.

"What would Manny say if he knew you were on a date with Eugene Polaski?" Chelsea shouted after us.

I whipped toward her. "It's not—"

"Ignore her," Kyla said.

My base instincts urged me to defend myself against Chelsea's accusations, but Kyla was right. It wouldn't do any good. Not here. Not now. The four of us left while Chelsea and Mark lurked inside.

I let out a huge sigh once we were in the sunlight. "Thanks for showing me this place," I said. "Too bad Chelsea showed up."

"Which is weird," Kyla said, "because I've never seen her here before."

"Huh." The tinted windows of Clandestine Coffee concealed what she was doing inside, and I was too tired to pursue it.

"Let's call it a day," I said.

"One more thing to show you," Plug said.

I checked the time on my phone. Mom would be at work for hours still.

"You'll like it," Plug said.

I relented. "Okay."

Nick opened the door of the Mini Cooper.

"We'll see you guys later," Kyla said.

"Wait," I said, and Kyla spun around. "You're not coming with us?"

"No." Nick winked. "We have our own plans." Kyla whacked him in the gut.

"Don't give her the wrong idea," she said.

"Homework," Nick said. "We're doing homework."

"Better." She kissed his cheek, and they headed off.

Plug opened the car door for me, and I tried to relax as I sank into the seat. He drove us to downtown Boise and parallel parked—nailed it first try—on the street in front of a chic restaurant. It didn't seem like an area Plug would hang out. He opened my door, and we stood aimlessly on the sidewalk. I shrugged.

"So, where are we going?" I pointed at the jewelry store across the road, the fine chocolate shop to my right, and the bank to my left. Plug grabbed my extended fingers and drew me down the sidewalk, but I pulled away.

"What?" Plug lifted his hands, confused.

I glanced at his car. I'd had enough adventure for one day. I wanted him to take me home.

"Come on, you'll love it," he said. The sunlight glinted off the rings in his eyebrows, and his gray eyes sparkled. I tucked my hands into my pockets and walked with him.

Up ahead, a vibrant awning popped out from the other monotonous charcoal ones. As we approached it, I studied the colorful collage of Native American images adorning the canopy. The storefront window read: ECLECTIC TATTOO GALLERY. Plug swung the door open and motioned for me to enter first. I stepped apprehensively. I had never been in a tattoo parlor before, and I was surprised when it smelled like a fresh mountain river. Soft instrumental music played in the background, and the large windows in front let in natural light. On the left side of the narrow studio, spotlights brightened framed artwork on the white walls. I turned and reread the name on the window: ECLECTIC TATTOO GALLERY.

On the right side, three partitioned booths—like you'd find at a salon, but stocked with tattoo paraphernalia—spanned the length of the wall. The floor was unadorned concrete, and the high ceiling gave way to exposed beams, ventilation ducts, and shadows.

"What is this place?" I asked. Before Plug answered, a man in dark slim-cut jeans and a clean white tank answered.

"It's a tattoo art gallery," the man said and swung his arms wide, revealing masses of black pit hair beneath his bulky arms. Multicolored tattoos covered most of his exposed skin. The patterns disappeared under his white tank, and tendrils of the designs snaked up his neck. He had a patch of black whiskers on his chin, but the rest of his head was clipped short. Spikes pierced his eyebrows, and his gauge piercings were the size of fifty-cent coins. He was the scariest looking man I'd ever seen.

"Hi, Dad," Plug said and threw his arms around him.

"Dad?" I asked.

"Hannah, this is my dad, Necro."

"As in necrophilia and morbid obsessions with death?" My words slipped out before I had time to filter. "Sorry," I muttered and pinched my lips closed.

"She's smart," Plug said to his dad. "Like AP Statistics smart."

"Yes, Hannah, as in morbid obsessions with death, but I also like to delve into the optimistic folklore of Native Americans." Necro smiled, revealing bleached white teeth. "My friends call me Necro, because most of my tattoo art features death in some regard. If you're interested, I have a portfolio of my work. My next client isn't due for another fifteen minutes."

"Later, Dad," Plug said. "I want to show her the new stuff."

"No problem." He gestured toward the back.

Plug led the way, but a seven-foot canvas with bright red-and-black splashes of paint caught my eye.

"Let's look at these first." I pointed to the contemporary art on the wall.

"I want you to see what inspired the chalk drawing you liked in class," Plug said.

"Oh."

Plug had drawn a picture of the damned, inspired by something in the backroom, and his dad was a necromancer. What was I even doing here?

We moved past the stations with chairs and tattoo accoutrements. Then we went through the back exit of the studio. On the right was a small office with two desks, each stacked high with paperwork, and on the left was a kitchen with counters cluttered with dirty dishes. We passed two closed rooms and moved through another set of doors into a cold and dark space. There were no windows to let sunlight in. My hands began to sweat. Plug flipped a switch and overhead lights lit up the entire warehouse, about twice the size of a home garage.

Plug reached into a box and pulled out white gloves. He offered me a pair. "If you want to touch anything." I slipped them on.

Wooden crates of various sizes lined the walls, and several individual canvases leaned against each other.

"Why does your dad have so much artwork?" I asked.

"He sells a lot in the studio. New stuff arrives daily from around the country." Plug guided me to the back of the building near the freight door. He popped the top off a large crate and set the lid to the side. He slipped on his white gloves and reached inside.

"Ready?" he asked, but he didn't wait for an answer. He lifted out a large canvas and propped it against a crate in front of me.

The air rushed out of my lungs, as if a monster from the depths of Hades had kicked me in the gut. The black-and-white painting took me back in time to the moments after the crash. The smoke. The stench. The shock.

"You okay?" Plug asked.

The room whirled. My lungs burned. I dropped to my knees in front of the canvas. The painting towered over me.

"What's wrong?" he whispered.

I rubbed my hands on my jeans. I took a small breath and then a deeper one. My head began to clear. The brushstrokes of the painting created the illusion of misty smoke around the edges. I traced the swirls to make sure they were inanimate. The middle of the canvas featured a dark vertical cloud, but with closer study, I realized the image had a hooded robe. Featherless wings extended from the backside, and bare-bone arms with claws reached outward. Tentatively, I touched the extended claws and felt a prick. I jerked back, and a red dot spread along the tip of the white glove. I yanked it off and held it against my finger to stop the bleeding.

Plug raised an eyebrow.

"The painting," I said. "It cut me."

Without hesitation, he stroked his glove-covered palm across the surface of the canvas.

"Smooth," he said. He pulled off his gloves and coaxed my fist open. Not a single drop of blood. He flattened out my glove. It was completely white. His touch made my skin tingle as he drew his fingers across my hand and double-checked for any wounds. I pulled away from him, tore off the other white glove, and threw it to the ground.

"This is ridiculous. I need to go home." I took two steps before Plug gripped my elbow.

"Just because I didn't see blood doesn't mean you didn't," he said.

His confidence in me caught me by surprise, and I worried that my friendship with Plug was another one of my peculiar delusions. I choked back my fear and threw my hands in the air.

"Crap like this keeps happening to me!"

"Like what?" Plug asked.

"Ever since the accident . . . no . . . ever since the stupid hypnotist show, I've been seeing strange things."

"Were you seeing things when you bought the fry bread from me at the fair?"

"Ants. They were everywhere, but not just at your food trailer. They also crawled across my hands before I lost control of the car." I pointed at the painting. "I saw this after the crash. It swirled in and out of the windows. But there were no bones, only mist and smoke."

Plug tugged at his ear. I thought I'd said too much, but then Plug gently took my hand. His skin was warm against mine, and I didn't pull away this time.

"It's the Angel of Death," he whispered.

He tightened his grasp, and his rings pressed into my knuckles. He had a quieting effect on me, which I'd yearned for since the accident.

"I don't think the hypnotist did anything to you," he said. "It was Jordan's time to go. You saw the Angel of Death stalking Jordan."

"But I've seen other things since the accident, and that painting pricked my finger."

"I've read a lot about the occult, and there are things in this world beyond our comprehension," Plug said.

"How did this painting inspire your chalk drawing of the skulls?"

"If this is what the Angel of Death looks like"—he let go of my hand and stroked the edge of the painting—"I wonder what his victims look like."

"Is everyone a victim when they die?" Was my dad? Was Jordan?

"I hope not," Plug said, "but you could go crazy thinking about it too much."

"A psychiatrist at the hospital said the hypnotist may have brought an underlying psychosis of mine to the surface."

"Psychiatrists are full of crap." Plug hoisted the canvas back into the crate. "They discount the occult and the Angel of Death."

"You believe that I'm actually seeing things?"

"You and I exist in bodies, but there are also other spirits on this earth. Disembodied spirits. Evil spirits. Sad spirits. Spirits who seek our help, and spirits who wish us harm."

"And you think—"

"They could have attached to you during the accident." He picked up my discarded gloves from the concrete floor.

"How do we get them to detach—"

The room went pitch black, and I shrieked.

"Plug!"

"Right here."

I fumbled in the darkness for him.

"Stay with me, and I'll guide you out." I wrapped my hands around his and pressed into his side. The air around us went frigid, and Plug halted. A high-pitched buzz, barely audible, moved past my ears, as if a horsefly circled my head. I dug my fingernails into Plug's skin.

"You have no power here!" Plug yelled. "Be gone!" The volume of the buzzing increased. Plug stomped his foot and yelled. "Be. Gone."

The lights popped back on, and a bulb above us burst, pelting us with bits of glass. I let go of Plug and shook the shards from my hair and clothes. He did the same. The temperature returned to normal, and even though the room had been cold a second ago, Plug wiped perspiration from his forehead. He scratched at his short black hair and blew out a breath.

"Tell me I did not hallucinate that," I said.

He rubbed his face and said, "Let's ask my dad if he flipped a breaker or if the electricity went out." Plug motioned me toward the doors. We crossed into the studio, and Plug stopped in his tracks. He pointed at his dad. Necro leaned over a customer and continued applying a fresh tattoo. The humming of the tattoo machine contrasted with the soft classical music in the background.

"He's in the middle of a tat," Plug said. "The lights in here must have stayed on the whole time. He couldn't have flipped the breaker and gotten back here so fast, because the box is on the outside of the building."

"One of his employees—"

"No one else is here today," Plug said.

"Tell me you experienced the same thing I did in the warehouse."

He counted on his fingers and spoke. "First, the lights went out. Second, it got really cold. Third, bugs buzzed in my ears. Then the lights came back on, and the bulb popped over our heads."

"Yes."

"But, Hannah, a power surge or a blown breaker—"

"What about the buzzing?" I asked.

"The light bulb above us could have made the sound and then burst."

"And the temperature change?"

"Man. I don't know. I've only read about this stuff. But if a spirit is present, the temperature can, in theory, drop drastically. If something has attached itself to you, we need to get rid of it."

"How?"

"We can start by smudging you with burned sage—"

"Excuse me?"

"The smoke of sage eliminates negative energies," he said. "We can smudge, basically spread smoke around, your room and all your clothes. A tiger-eye will help protect you, too."

I imagined a dead animal's eyeball threaded with a cord and strung around my neck.

"It's a stone called tiger-eye," Plug said, as if he'd read my mind. "Its metaphysical properties will help protect you from uninvited spirits." He pulled several smooth rocks out of his pocket. He selected a brown-and-gold-striped one from the bunch and held it up. It glimmered in the light, like a tiger's eye. He returned the other stones to his pocket, but kept out the tiger-eye and rubbed it with the pad of this thumb. Then he cupped it, closed his eyes, and huffed on it. He mumbled a few words, but I missed what he said. He repeated the process three times. Then he lifted my hand, set the stone in my palm, and folded my fingers over it.

"This is yours," I said.

"Maybe I only carried it because one day you would need it from me."

I was uncertain if I felt flattered or frightened.

"Thanks," I said. "How do you know all this?"

"It's the occult, baby. I love this stuff. Well, I should say, I love researching this stuff. You've brought the first paranormal activity into my life."

"Nice. You're not hanging out with me because of my great hair and fashionable clothes but because I have evil spirits stalking me."

"Fringe benefits." Plug beamed. "My idea of a perfect world includes mystery, art, and friends." He had managed to lift my melancholy and introduce me to a new realm of possibilities. "Come on," he said and motioned me toward the warehouse side of the building.

"No." My mood changed instantly, and my heart beat faster. "I refuse to go back in there."

"Trust me." He tugged at my shirtsleeve.

"No. I can't do it." I swatted his hand away and ran for the front door. Out on the sidewalk, I bent forward and clutched my knees, gasping for air. Plug followed and squatted in front of me.

"Sorry," he said. "I didn't mean to panic you. Let's go get Thai food or something."

Before I could answer, Chelsea's hee-haw chortle rang out behind me. I spun around, but no one was there. I ran to the side of the building and searched the alleyway. A bottle broke somewhere in the unseen distance.

"What?" Plug asked.

"I heard Chelsea laugh."

Plug rushed past me and down the alley. The sun went behind a cloud and cast the alley in a dusky gloom. My muscles went rigid, and I stood frozen. About fifteen feet down the alleyway, Plug closed a metal box mounted on the brick wall of the building. He removed something from the side of the box and came back to me, extending his hand to show me a broken padlock.

"Our breaker box," he said. "Someone broke the lock and messed with the breakers."

"Why is the breaker box on the outside of the building?"

"Old building. Old wiring. Someone popped the breaker for the warehouse lights and then put it back."

"What about the cold air and the buzzing?"

"Could've been paranormal, but someone broke this lock. That's not paranormal." Plug went back inside the tattoo parlor and gave the lock to Necro. Afterward, we headed to a nearby Thai restaurant and debated the occult versus psychiatry while we ate.

⇥ • ⇤

On the way to my house, Plug parked in the deserted lot of a strip mall. He hopped out of the El Camino and ran around to open my door.

"You know," I said, "I am capable of getting my own door."

"Right." He waved me forward, and I followed him to a store called Nirvana. He tugged on the door, but it was locked. He peered inside the window, and I tapped the glass where the store hours were posted. He checked the time on his cell.

"Man. We talked at the restaurant a long time." He rapped his knuckles on the door.

"Plug, they closed at five. It's after seven now. Let's go."

"We need sage." He fidgeted with his lip ring and worried me. "Do you trust me?"

"People ask that question right before they do something stupid," I said.

"Keep an eye out."

"No," I said. "Besides, if you want some sage, we can get it from my neighbor's yard. Sagebrush grows all over the foothills."

"Mmm. Not the same thing," Plug said. "A common misnomer. Sage is from the mint family, and sagebrush is a woody shrub. Not to mention, if you accidentally pick the wrong kind of sagebrush and burn it, people will think you've been smoking marijuana—"

I started laughing. "Okay, I wouldn't want anyone to think we're smoking marijuana."

He plucked a leather case out of his back pocket. "Let me know if anyone comes."

"Plug! We don't need the sage."

"Don't worry," he said. "I know the owners." He slipped two small tweezer-like tools from the leather case. Then he held the leather between his lips and picked the lock of the door.

I plucked at his gray T-shirt. "Stop! Someone will catch us!" But the parking lot was still deserted. Apparently, all the stores in the strip mall had closed for the day. Plug snatched my hand and yanked me inside. Bells jingled against the door as it swung shut. I remained by the window and kept watch.

"A car turned into the lot!" I twirled around to see where Plug was, but in the darkened store, I barely made out his silhouette as he slapped something on the counter. Then he joined me at the front window.

Headlights illuminated the store. Plug yanked some weird bundled weeds off the shelf and tugged me toward the back of the store. The bells on the front door jingled.

"Hello?" a woman's voice called out, and the lights in the store came on. "Eugene?"

Plug trudged out of the backroom, and he dragged me with him.

"Hi, Grandma," Plug said.

I whacked his shoulder.

"Eugene," his grandma said. "Stop picking my locks."

"Sorry, Grandma."

"Who's with you?" she asked and stepped closer.

"My friend, Hannah," he said.

New wrinkles formed as she narrowed her eyes at me. She wore a denim shirt-dress with cowboy boots and a leather vest trimmed with silver buttons. Her thick gray hair hung in two long braids, as it had at the fair.

Plug grinned at me. "This is my grandma, my mother's mother. And this is her store."

I whacked his shoulder again. "You could have told me that before you broke in."

He rubbed his shoulder.

"You knew my daughter?" his grandma asked me.

"No, ma'am."

"A good woman," she said. "You have the same vibrant eyes."

I glanced at Plug, and he grinned.

"You do," he said. "It was the first thing I noticed about you. Legends say pure green eyes belong to strong, courageous women."

Plug's grandma spoke again. "Cherish your loved ones, Hannah. Time on this earth is limited. My daughter's been gone too long now. Seven years."

"My dad died six years ago," I said, surprised at my own frankness.

Plug's grandma clutched my hand and lifted it to her chest. "So you know this hole in the heart. You lost your father. Eugene, his mother. Me, my daughter." My breath caught, and I nodded. She embraced me for a moment, and then she hugged Plug.

"Love you, Grandma," he said.

"Then stop picking my locks." She pulled his ear.

"Okay. We've got to go," he said.

Plug and I walked side-by-side out to the parking lot.

"I can't believe you let me think you were robbing a store!"

"More of an adventure."

"Would you have told me the truth if your grandma hadn't shown up?"

"Probably."

"Plug!"

"I would have," he said, "eventually. There was no harm—"

"You broke into the store and took something that belonged to someone else. That's illegal. And it was unnecessary."

"I left money on the counter," he explained. "More than the sage is even worth, and besides, the store belongs to my grandma. Now we can smudge your room, and you'll sleep better tonight."

"Where did you learn to do that anyhow?"

"Summer job with a locksmith. It's a fine art to pick a lock without breaking it. You have to solve a mystery and overcome obstacles to release the lock."

I studied his round face, his elongated earlobes, and his gray eyes. He barely knew me, but he had picked the lock to get the sage so he could do something nice for me. It baffled me.

⊣ • ⊢

Plug parked in my driveway. Mom's car was gone, probably still at work. He hauled the heavy art book, and I lugged my backpack to the front door. I huffed and dropped my bag on the porch.

"Waiting for me to open the door?" Plug grinned.

"No," I said. "I lost everything when my car exploded, including my house keys." I stepped into the flower bed.

"I can unlock it," Plug said.

I narrowed my eyes at him. "No, thank you." I found the fake rock behind one of the bushes, slid open the base, and plucked out a key. I opened the door and returned the key to its hiding place.

"So," I asked, "do we smudge the whole house or just my room?"

"Let's start with your room, but we will need to do the whole house."

I led the way upstairs, and he set the art book on my bed.

"Matches?" he asked. "And maybe a metal pan?"

"Have you done this before?" I asked.

"I've watched YouTube." He waggled his eyebrows.

I dropped my backpack to the floor.

"Hey," he said, "I'm a researcher of the occult. Not a practitioner."

"Right." I jogged back downstairs to the kitchen and collected the matches and an old pan. When I returned to my room, Plug still stood in the exact same position. "Did you even move?"

"Didn't want you to think I was snooping." He smirked and took the matches. He lit one and held it to the bundled leaves.

"Don't burn the house down," I said.

Plug dropped the match into the pan and coaxed the sage into burning by gently blowing on it. A flame formed, and then Plug blew it out.

"Smokes better this way," he said. "Flame is gone, but it still smolders." He waved it in a figure eight, and the end of the bundled leaves glowed red, creating more smoke. He continued the motion and walked around the room. I followed right behind him with the pan, worried the sage would burst into a raging fire at any second.

"What if we set off the smoke detectors?" I asked.

"Not enough smoke." Plug swept the sage around the clothes in my closet. "Oh, yeah," he said. "Open the window to let the negative energies and spirits leave."

When I did, Mom pulled her red Toyota Prius into the driveway.

"We have to go downstairs," I said. "Now."

He tossed the sage into the pan on my bed.

"What am I supposed to do with it?"

"Leave it. Let it keep smoking while we're gone."

"No way. It could catch my bed on fire." I set the pan on my desk and grabbed a water bottle from my backpack.

"It will only smolder," Plug said. But I suspected he was a rookie at this, and so I poured water over the burning weeds. It smoked more, and I coughed. I dumped the water into the pan and used the butt of the bottle to smash the embers down into the pool.

"Let's go." I motioned him toward the door, and I closed it behind us. We reached the bottom of the stairs right when Mom entered.

Plug stuck out his hand. "Eugene Polaski."

Mom shook his hand. "Beth O'Leary."

"I should go," Plug said, but then he paused at the door. "Need a ride tomorrow?"

"That'd be great."

"See you at seven." He closed the door behind him.

"New friend?" Mom asked and gave me a small plain brown sack.

"Only friend." I opened up the sack and found a new set of keys. "Thanks, Mom."

"Hungry?" she asked.

"No, we ate."

She scrunched up her nose. "Were you two smoking?"

I sniffed my blouse. "Not the way you think." How could I explain it without freaking her out? "We tried smudging my room with sage to get rid of the negative energies."

She cleared her throat. "Let me get this straight, your new pal, Eugene, thought it was a good idea to go in your room while I was at work and light herbs on fire. To expel the negative energies?"

"Right."

Mom's neck reddened like a glowing ember. "Instead of trying Native American rituals, which you know nothing about, you should wait to discuss these ideas with Dr. James."

"I'm not crazy," I said.

"Of course not." She clutched my shoulder. "You hit your head in the accident, but whatever the cause, it's abnormal to hallucinate."

"What if the things I'm seeing are real?"

"Then other people would see them, too." The reddening crept from her neck to her cheeks to her ears.

I stopped myself from telling her what had happened in the art warehouse. It would've added fuel to her fire.

⊰ • ⊱

I lingered at the kitchen table with my laptop and checked e-mails and social media. There was nothing from Manny or Lily. I closed my laptop and carried it upstairs. The stench of burned sage filled every inch of my room. Hopefully, it had worked.

I flopped down on my bed and dialed Manny's home number.

"Hello," Manny said.

I sat upright. "You're home!"

"About an hour ago." The sound of his voice flooded me with relief.

"I texted you earlier," I said.

"Still no cell phone."

"Oh," I said. "Have you heard how Lily's doing? Is there any change?"

"No change," he said. "How was your first day?"

"Pretty bad." I filled him in on everything that had happened at school and started to cry.

"People are probably just in shock over the accident," he said. "I'll be back soon, and it'll get better."

"When?"

"Doctors said if I'm up to it, I can go back on Thursday."

"I miss you so much."

"I've missed you, too," he said. "So, tell me what you did after school."

I told him about Eugene, Nick, and Kyla.

"You hung out with anarchists all afternoon?" Manny asked. The irritation in his voice surprised me.

"I wanted to be with you," I said, "but you were still in the hospital. And they're not anarchists."

Manny cleared his throat. "I guess Eugene is a good enough guy. I had a couple of classes with him last year. He's smart for someone like him."

"What does that mean?" I asked.

"You know," Manny said. "Someone who is more concerned with rebelling than—"

"That's unfair," I said, but what did I really know about him?

"I'd feel better if you didn't hang out with them so much."

"It was one afternoon," I said.

"Do you want to come over here after school tomorrow?"

"Of course I do." Even if he was being condescending, I wanted to see him as soon as possible. I needed Manny to get better and for things to improve. After we said our goodnights, I plugged the phone in to charge and set it on my nightstand. Then I shut the window and yanked the drapes closed.

In the stillness of the room, I undressed and tossed my jeans and blouse into the far corner. I tugged an extra-large baby-blue T-shirt over my head, and a shiver ran up my spine. I remained still and listened for a few seconds. Silence. But the hair on my arms stood. I scanned the room, and my gaze settled on the chair behind my closed door. The pink elephant, singed with its stuffing falling out, sat on the chair. I sank to the carpet. Plug had told me that the tiger-eye would help protect me, but I'd left it in the pocket of my jeans—on the other side of the room.

"Be gone," I whispered. Nothing happened. Those words had worked earlier in the warehouse for Plug. I crawled over to the corner and dug into the pocket of my jeans. I clutched the stone and rubbed it like a magic wishing lamp. I closed my eyes and yelled, "Be gone!"

When I opened my eyes, Mom stood in the open doorway, staring down at me.

"What are you doing?" she asked.

"Behind the door." I pointed.

She closed the door, and the stuffed animal was still there.

"Tell me you can see it," I said.

"See what?" The color drained from her face. I pointed at the elephant.

She picked it up and ran her fingers along the scorched trunk.

"You can see it." I slouched with relief. I didn't want her to worry about me the way she had about Dad. All those times he embarrassed her. His behavior made more sense to me now that I knew he had schizophrenia, but I hated that he'd been so tortured he'd committed suicide. Most likely, no one had believed him when he said he saw things. At least Mom saw the pink elephant. She had to know I was telling truth. The elephant was real.

"Of course I can see it," she said. "Where did it come from?"

"Manny won it at the fair. It was burned in the accident."

"How did it get in your room?" Mom rotated the elephant in her hands and inspected it.

"I thought it was destroyed when the car exploded," I said.

Mom's eyes widened, and then she stormed out of the room, with the elephant still in her clutches. "I'm calling the police," she said.

"Wait!" I hopped up after her. "You can't!"

She whipped around, her neck and face red with anger.

"It will be more proof that I'm nuts."

"Just the opposite, Hannah. Someone is tormenting you. They've been in our house and left what can only be classified as a taunting reminder of the horrific accident. You're not delusional!"

I snatched the elephant from her grasp, rushed downstairs to the kitchen, shoved the pink atrocity into a trash bag, and ran outside. After I threw the bag into the trash bin, I darted back inside and slammed the front door behind me. I glanced down at myself. I wore only my T-shirt and underwear.

"Hannah!" Mom waited at the base of the stairs.

"I don't want the police here," I said. "I want it to be over. Let the elephant go to the junkyard."

Mom wrung her hands. "We need to report it."

"No, Mom." I used my T-shirt to wipe my tears and smeared black mascara across the baby-blue fabric. "The neighbors will see a cop car at our house. People will talk about it at school tomorrow. I can't handle it."

Mom tried to give me a hug, but it was awkward. We both wanted everything to be normal, but we both knew it wasn't.

"All right, Hannah." She tucked my hair behind my ears.

"I just need a good night's sleep," I said.

"I love you. Do you know that?" she asked. I nodded and stepped away.

I climbed the stairs and turned toward Mom. "I love you, too."

I closed my bedroom door, picked up the massive art book Rose had loaned me, and climbed into bed. I flipped pages, skimming the pictures, until I came to a section of artwork depicting death. I scrutinized each painting. The victims of death expressed terror: their mouths opened wide, screaming for help; their hands held high, trying to shield themselves from pain. The reapers of death expressed joy: their eyes bright and lips wet.

I closed the book and set it on the floor next to my bed. I reached for the lamp to switch it off, but my cell phone rang with an unknown number. I clicked End Call and turned out the light. I fell asleep clutching the tiger-eye.

TUESDAY
AUGUST 27

I slapped my alarm silent and rubbed the sleep from my eyes. Morning sunlight peeked around the edges of my bedroom drapes. I stretched and threw off my bedcovers, surprised by the bright orange-and-black Princeton T-shirt I had on. I glanced around the room for the blue shirt I'd worn to bed, and my gaze settled on the chair behind the door.

The pink elephant had returned.

I let out a skull-scraping scream until the tips of my fingers tingled.

Mom threw open my door and ran to my side. I gasped for air and pointed at the evil creature and the trash bag wedged beneath it.

"Hannah," Mom said. "You brought it back inside." Her eyebrows creased.

"No!"

"Yes. I got up to check on you last night when I heard the front door open. You'd gone out and returned with the trash bag. I asked you if you decided to keep the elephant. You ignored me. I thought maybe you were sleepwalking. I made sure you got back to your room, and I let it go."

"I've never sleepwalked before. I wouldn't suddenly start last night." I threw my pillow and knocked the rotten beast from its roost. I patted around on the bed for the tiger-eye. It was supposed to protect me last night, but apparently it had slipped from my grasp. I swept my hands through the sheets.

"Hannah?"

"Someone sneaked into our house and put the elephant back," I said.

She perched on the edge of my bed. "Sweetheart, I saw you with the trash bag. Plus, I made sure the doors and windows were locked. No one got in."

I remembered how Plug had picked the store's lock with ease.

"It's a good thing we didn't call the cops last night," Mom said. My heart sank.

Her mouth dropped open, and she tried to retract her words. "I just meant—"

"You figured I brought the elephant into the house the first time, too."

Mom clutched my fingers. "We will get you in sooner to see Dr. James."

I yanked away.

"Hannah, neither one of us likes this, but the way you acted last night was abnormal. This fascination with that thing is abnormal. We need his help."

In my mind, I retraced my steps from last night. I threw out the elephant. I went to bed. I flipped through the art book.

The art book.

I leaned over the edge of the bed. It was gone.

"What?" Mom asked.

"The book my teacher loaned me is gone. I set it there." I pointed at the floor. Mom got down on her knees and searched under the bed.

"This?" She tugged out the book and set it on my lap. "Are you okay?"

"Ask me a different question."

Mom groaned as she stood. "We'll figure this out, Hannah, but we need Dr. James's help." She reached out to touch me, but I shrugged away.

"Get ready for school," she said and left the room.

I traced the spine of the book. Something wedged inside made the pages bulge. I opened it and found the tiger-eye stone crammed into the gutter of the book's binding. I removed the rock and set it on my nightstand. It had marked a page I'd not seen last night.

A sculpture by Rodin: *Iris, Messenger of the Gods*.

She was headless and naked. I traced the detailed muscles of her legs up to her neck—where a head should have rested. Heat rose from the pit of my stomach, and I flipped to the next page.

Another sculpture by Rodin: *Head of Iris*.

My hand trembled. Dirt was caked in my cuticles. I flicked some off, and it landed in the book. I brushed it away and read the caption beneath Rodin's sculpture. "He wanted to achieve more than a mere similitude of his subject; he wanted his art to possess the inner conflicts and emotions." I studied the *Head of Iris* more closely. What could her inner struggles have been? Maybe the fact that her head was disconnected was trouble enough.

I slammed the book closed.

The elephant peered out from under my pillow on the floor. Today was trash day. I hopped up and plucked the plastic bag off the floor. I stuffed the elephant in, and then I grabbed my rhinestone jeans and ruffled blouse and threw them in also. I had bought them to coordinate with Lily and Chelsea, and that was an utter failure. I wanted it all hauled to the city dump with thousands of other people's discarded junk.

I dropped the bag in the hallway and contemplated changing clothes. Earlier in the month, I had planned out my entire wardrobe for this first week of classes. I wanted to make a great impression with my teachers, leaders, and friends, but now as I lifted my sleeveless navy dress from the closet, I just wanted to stay in my pajamas. That wouldn't go over well at school though. I was already getting enough stares and whispers. So I changed into the dress. The wide flowing skirt hung beneath my knees, and the fabric was soft against my skin. I slipped my feet into some white wedge sandals. Then I reached for the coordinating necklace with large white beads, but when I hooked the closure, I felt as if I was choking to death. I removed it and tossed it back into my drawer. The dress alone was enough to keep up appearances. I'd skip the accessories today.

In the bathroom I used my pearl-handled brush to smooth my hair back into a ponytail. I avoided making eye contact with myself in the mirror. I didn't want to study myself or examine my inner conflicts and emotions. It was easier to analyze art. I swiped a new coat of mascara over yesterday's, wiped the black flakes from under my eyes, and spritzed on a generous amount of jasmine body spray.

The doorbell rang.

I remembered the dirt around my fingernails and darted to the sink. I halfheartedly washed and tried to recall how the grime got under my cuticles. Maybe it was from the sage yesterday. I ran back to my room, snatched the tiger-eye, and slipped it into my skirt pocket. Then I grabbed my backpack and the trash bag, hollered goodbye to Mom, and rushed out the front door. I nearly crashed into Plug.

"Need help?" he asked.

"Nope."

But he helped anyhow. He lifted my backpack from my shoulder and carried it over to his car. I threw the trash bag into the bin and rolled it to the curb.

Plug held open the door, and I plopped into the passenger seat.

"You smell great," he said and closed my door.

I hoped he was serious, since I skipped taking a shower today. My mom would be mortified by the idea, but she'd be even more bothered by the fact that I neglected to make my bed. I'd left a mess.

Plug sank into his seat. He wore the same gray waffle-knit shirt and worn-out jeans from yesterday. He started the vehicle and drove down the street. "Seriously," he said, "you smell like sage and jasmine—"

"Sage?"

Plug nodded.

I lifted the fabric of my dress and sniffed it. "People will think I smell weird."

"So?" Plug said. "Did the smudging work?"

"No."

Plug frowned. "We need to do the whole house for it to work right."

"Why does it even matter to you?" I blurted out. "You hardly know me." He'd been in my house yesterday; he knew the layout. He could've been watching when I took the elephant out to the trash the first time. He could've sneaked in and put it in my room. And he gave me the tiger-eye, which was wedged next to the picture of the naked sculpture.

Plug thumped the steering wheel and pulled to the side of the road. He twisted in his seat and faced me. "Hannah, I do know you, and you know me. Maybe we haven't been best friends, but we've been in broadcasting together for the last two years, and before that we had biology together, and before that . . . well, we went to middle school together. I know you—"

"Like an obsessed stalker? That would explain why you're going out of your way to be nice to me." Maybe Manny was right about Plug, and I should've stayed away from him.

He glared at me. "You want me to stop helping you?"

I held his gaze. He didn't fidget at all. Not with his lip ring. Not with his ears. He was upset with me. I covered my face with my hands. I was an idiot to accuse Plug. I needed him on my side.

"Sorry," I muttered.

"Why are you so angry, Hannah? What happened?"

I swept away my tears and gasped for air. "I'm losing everything, including myself."

He reached over and clutched my hand. I flinched and started to pull away, but he tightened his grasp.

"Tell me," he said.

I prattled on and on about the elephant appearing, reappearing, my mom's version, my version, and the tiger-eye marking the nasty page in the book.

"I must have botched the programming of the stone," he said. "I know I messed up the smudging, because I researched it more last night. After school today, we need to put salt in every corner and olive oil above your doors. And we're supposed—"

"I can't today. I have plans with Manny."

Plug loosened his grip, and I pulled away.

"You know Manny is my boyfriend," I said.

"And why is that exactly?"

I stared at Plug, astonished by his boldness. My relationship with Manny was none of Plug's business.

"Why are you with Manny?" Plug asked calmly. "It shouldn't be hard to answer."

"It's personal." I loved Manny because we were best friends. I loved him because he watched out for me. I loved him because he was sweet to me. I loved him because he had thick, messy chestnut hair and dark, piercing eyes. Manny reminded me of my father. Plug spoke again and interrupted my thoughts.

"He's an arrogant—"

"He's my boyfriend," I said defensively.

Plug started the car.

"And he's good to me. That's all that should matter to you."

"Okay," Plug said.

I'd already lost so many friends this week. I refused to lose Plug, too. "Look," I said, "can we be friends without discussing Manny?"

"Sure," he said.

"Maybe you and I could work on smudging my home later tonight," I said, but I was unsure how long I'd be at Manny's house.

"Maybe." Plug cranked up the volume on the radio.

⊰ • ⊱

Plug and I walked together to first period, and Mr. Arnold stopped me at the studio door. "How are you today? Are you up to this?"

Just beyond Mr. Arnold, Chelsea sat in my chair at the anchor desk. She winked at me, and my gut wrenched.

"Up to what exactly?" I gritted my teeth.

"Hannah, I know you've been through a lot, but we need this morning's broadcast to go smoothly." Mr. Arnold set his hand on my shoulder, and I jerked away, surprised by my own reaction. Mr. Arnold had always been one of my favorite teachers, but he'd let Chelsea sit in my chair again. The chair that I had earned.

"She can work the booth equipment with me," Plug said.

I reached into my skirt pocket and gripped the tiger-eye. Even if it hadn't protected me last night, the simple motion of stroking it calmed me now. I kept my mouth shut and my hands to myself.

"That's a great idea," Mr. Arnold said to Plug. It was going to be another long day.

Most people gave me a wide berth in the halls, but some still whispered as they passed. And Chelsea continued to lead my former friends in ignoring me.

The bell for third period rang, and instead of running to the Commons to join the student council gang, I trudged off to my new psychology class. The room was quiet when I arrived, and I spotted Kyla and Nick. Maybe it wouldn't be awful after all. I gave the teacher my revised schedule and then took the seat behind my surrogate friends.

"Love the cerulean hair," I said, marveling at her nonconformity.

Kyla twisted in her seat and faced me. "Thank you."

"She's beautiful in any color," Nick, in his knit-cap-cameraman disguise, said.

"I love your shirt, too," I said to Kyla. The bright, bedazzled tangerine blouse made her eyes seem even bluer.

"What about mine?" Nick asked with a wink. He motioned toward his brown T-shirt, which featured the heads of Chuck Norris and Waldo with the caption: CHUCK NORRIS IS THE REASON WALDO IS HIDING.

I smirked. "Right."

He cocked an eyebrow, leaned toward me, and whispered, "Your mind would be blown if you knew some of the conspiracies Chuck—"

The teacher cleared his throat and started class.

Nick and Kyla turned in their seats and faced forward. I'd never given conspiracies a thought before meeting Nick. He seemed like the right guy to help uncover the reason behind Chelsea's recent scheming.

⊨ • ⊩

The bell rang at the end of class. I picked up my backpack and headed for the hall.

"Plans for lunch?" Nick asked.

"Nope," I said.

"Well, come on then." He wrapped one arm around my shoulders and his other arm around Kyla, and we headed toward the parking lot.

Plug heaved a cooler into the back of his El Camino, and then he climbed in. Nick and Kyla followed him and hoisted themselves up and over the side of the truck bed. I set my backpack on the asphalt and considered whether or not this was better than eating alone. I straightened my dress and wiggled my toes in my wedge sandals. I was clueless how to climb over the side.

Plug motioned me to the back end, and he released the tailgate. He reached down for my hand and helped me up. I stepped into the bed, and a breeze blew my skirt. I dropped Plug's hand and held my dress in place.

We perched on the walls of the truck bed, and the cooler served as a table between us. I reached down and stroked the AstroTurf.

"What's with the grass?" I asked.

"Makes it more like the classic vehicle it truly is," Plug said.

Nick lifted the cooler's lid and opened a plastic container full of pepperoni pizza.

"Leftovers from a cooler in the back of an El Camino with green AstroTurf."

Everyone's eyes lifted to meet mine.

"Did I just say that out loud?" I asked.

"You don't have to eat with us," Nick said.

"Cut her some slack. She had a bad night." Plug passed me a cold Dr. Pepper. I turned it over in my fingers and wondered if he'd brought it because it was my favorite or if it was a coincidence.

Nick closed the cooler and set the pizza on top. "To apologize, you can bring lunch tomorrow."

"We take turns," Kyla said. "And if you'll give it a chance, you will discover it's quite fun to eat out here away from everyone else. It's like our own little oasis in a sea of chaos."

"I am really sorry. Sometimes I speak without thinking." I popped the top on the Dr. Pepper and took a swig.

"There's enough for everyone," Plug said and pointed at the pizza.

"What happened last night that upset you?" Kyla asked.

I told them about the pink elephant, but before I finished, Kyla interrupted.

"Before second period, I heard Chelsea bragging about a pink elephant."

We all stared at Kyla.

"And?" Nick prodded her.

"What did she say?" I asked. "Did she use my name?" I leaned forward and spilled soda on the AstroTurf.

Plug pressed a napkin against the fake grass and mopped up the puddle.

"Chelsea's voice is so piercing," Kyla said, "it was hard to avoid. She said she found just the right kind of pink elephant. I walked past her in the hall so I missed a lot of what she said, but I never heard her use your name. If I'd known it mattered, I would've listened better."

"Hannah, you heard Chelsea's laugh at the tat shop," Plug said. "Any chance she's causing these weird things?"

"She's been acting differently toward me since the accident, but I don't know why. She has nothing to gain from taunting me," I said.

"Trust me," Nick said, "she'd do anything to connive her way into the rich bit—"

"Nick!" Kyla cut him short.

"No offense," Nick said to me, "but I'm sure she's conspired for a while to fit in with your group."

"She doesn't have to fit in," I said. "She's already in."

Nick raised his eyebrows. "She pretends to have money. She's dirt poor."

"How do you—"

"She lives in the same low-income apartment building I do. I see her every day," Nick said.

"But you drive a brand-new Mini Cooper," I said.

He jerked his thumb toward Kyla. "Her Mini."

Kyla nodded.

"The way I see it," Nick said, "if Tall-Tree-Chelsea got revenge for Jordan's death, that would earn her points with his group. Or even if she turns them against you, then she gets your spot, your friends, and your anchor chair in broadcasting. She wins."

My mind lingered on the idea of Chelsea being poor. We usually hung out at the mall, and when we weren't there, we were either at my house or Lily's house, never Chelsea's. I flashed back to the day Lily, Chelsea, and I went shopping and bought the coordinating outfits, the rhinestone jeans and cute tops—she had forgotten her wallet that day. Lily paid for her things. And Chelsea constantly borrowed my clothes, shoes, and accessories. Some things she still had. But it was easier to believe Plug broke into my house than Chelsea.

I took another sip of the Dr. Pepper, and a small burp escaped. "Sorry," I said. "Pop does that—"

Nick released a monster belch and stared at me. "You got nothing on us. I am the champion wind breaker in this group."

"Yes," Kyla said and patted his back. "Certainly something to be proud of."

I laughed at Nick, and he let out another burp, smaller than the first one. Lily would have been appalled. I missed her terribly. I wanted to call, but I knew the nurses wouldn't give me any information, and after the incident in the waiting room, Mrs. Sloane probably never wanted to talk to me again.

"What other unusual things have happened?" Kyla folded her slice of pizza in half and bit into it.

I wiggled my toes and studied the AstroTurf. Then I told them everything from the shadows and black mist to the spider and the Angel of Death pricking my finger.

"Wait," Kyla said.

I scrunched my toes and glanced up.

"When did these creepy things start happening to you?"

"After the hypnotist show."

"You're certain?" Kyla asked.

"Maybe during."

"Do you remember the hypnotist's name?" she asked.

"Geero. Gyro. Something like that."

"I'll research him," Kyla said.

"If anyone can find the truth, it's Kyla," Plug said.

"Have you documented any of this?" Nick asked. "Pictures, video, journaling?"

"No, I've been too freaked to stop and snap a picture."

"Do you have a computer in your room?" he asked.

"I have a laptop."

"Turn on the webcam before you go to bed."

"I don't want people watching me."

"That's not what I meant." Nick tore his remaining crust into bite-sized pieces and tossed them into his mouth, one at a time. "I'll e-mail you a program that you can download onto your computer. When you turn on the camera, it will record everything that happens in your room and save it on your hard drive. It doesn't even have to be only at night. We'll set it up to record twenty-four-seven, and if someone like Tall-Tree sneaks into your room, we'll catch her, and have evidence."

"What if it's not Chelsea? What if it's not even a real person? Or worse, what if it's me?"

"Then we'll catch it on video. Knowing is better. Do you want me to come over and set it up for you?"

"No. E-mail it. I can figure it out."

"Be pretty sweet to catch demons on video," Plug said.

"Sweet for who?" I asked. "I would hate to see a recording of evil spirits haunting me while I'm asleep."

"Hannah, you need to reclaim your life," Kyla said.

"I never gave it up." I gnawed off a tough piece of cold pizza and imagined my student council friends eating fresh hot pizza, made to order, at Flying Pie Pizzeria. I hungered to have my old life back. I never chose to give it up in the first place.

"I'm not referring to your social status," Kyla said. "I mean you need to take back control of your own choices."

"I am in control." Another breeze blew my skirt. I caught the fabric in time and tucked it between my thighs.

"You sure?" Nick asked.

⊰ • ⊱

We stepped into the art room, and Rose told us to select our preferred medium and sit without talking. I had no idea what "preferred medium" meant, so I followed Plug. He selected two long, slender pieces of charcoal from a side counter. He motioned for me to pick from the array of supplies: colored pencils, paints, brushes, markers, chalks, crayons, and even sand. I picked a bottle of red paint, and we joined Nick and Kyla at a table. Nick had three different shades of blue pencils in front of him. Kyla had two vials of tinted sand and a can of spray adhesive.

"What are we doing?" I whispered.

Kyla brought a finger to her lips.

I bounced my knee and peered around the room. A small string of smoke drifted upward from an engraved silver dish on Rose's desk, and I recognized the aroma of burning sage. Soft harp music played in the background.

Rose finished giving instructions at the door. Then, when everyone had taken their supplies and their seats, she moved to the front of the room.

"Thank you," she whispered. "There will be no talking today while I introduce you to a different way of creating art. Get out your sketchbooks." Everyone at my table pulled out thick spiral-bound books and opened to a blank page. I was about to raise my hand when Rose set a brand-new sketchbook in front of me and smiled. I mouthed the words "thank you" and she nodded.

"Consider the medium you selected. I'm going to take you on a journey, and as I do, you can follow along with me, or you can walk your own path. Visualize and experience the journey in your mind. Use your chosen medium and create art while your eyes remain closed."

Before Kyla closed her eyes, she sprayed adhesive on two opposing pages in her sketchbook. I opened the lid to my bottle of paint, but I had no brushes. I still knew nothing about art. And this felt a lot like hypnotism. I peeked at Plug. He opened his eyes and looked right back at me. He reached over and squeezed my hand. I valued Plug's friendship, and so I squeezed back. I also wanted to be loyal to Manny, and so I eased my hand away.

"Get comfortable in your chair," Rose said. "Uncross your legs and plant your feet on the floor. On your thighs, set your palms up."

Plug and I followed Rose's instructions. He closed his eyes again and so did I. He was right next to me. I recalled how calm he'd remained in the warehouse when the lights went out, and I knew everything would be fine.

"Focus on the sound of my voice. Inhale deeply and hold it for five seconds. One. Two. Three. Four. Five. Release it through your mouth. Take in another breath and feel your lungs expand. Relax. Let the breath out through your mouth. Keep your breathing steady. When you decide the time is right for you, create your art, but remember to keep your eyes closed and trust your instincts.

"Now, imagine you are in a chaotic hotel lobby. People are rushing with their luggage and talking loudly, but you are peaceful. You slowly inhale, and you refuse to let their chaos influence you. You move through the crowd with a purpose. You find the elevators and press the down button. The crowded lobby is behind you and has no influence over you. The elevator opens, and you step inside. Alone. Press the button for the basement level, because you want to descend deeper—"

"Into the depths of the underworld," a man interrupted.

I opened my eyes wide, but there was no man in the room, and Rose continued speaking. Everyone else created their art with their eyes closed. No one else reacted to the deep, husky voice. Only I had heard it.

Kyla began to sprinkle sand over the page in her book. Plug lightly sketched a large oval that extended off the top of the page. Nick sat still, with his pencils untouched.

I pulled in a long breath and focused on Rose's voice. I'd be fine. I squirted a blob of paint onto my right index finger and then swiped some of it onto my left one. I rested my forearms against the edge of the table and closed my eyes.

"The walls of the elevator are mirrors," Rose said. "Study your reflection. You're tired, and your shoulders sag. A soft bell dings, and the doors open. The elevator has brought you to a safe level. You step into the comfort of this place and relax even more. The sense of happiness floods over you. The lush grass beneath your feet comforts you.

"Under a large shade tree you see an ornate box. Touch it, and trace the intricate design. When you lift the lid, you find a paper and a pencil. Write your concerns and your worries. Only you will see the list. Once you have finished, set the list back inside the box and close it. Your troubles are secure inside. They will be there when you return, but you do not need to carry them with you now. When you move away, you feel lighter than ever before. Float if you want. Fly if you want. Enjoy the sensation of being free.

"Beyond the rise of grass is your ideal place. Possibly a bed next to a river, or a couch near a rose garden, or a cloud in the sky, whatever it is, create tranquility and joy in your safe place. Once you've created it, you can revisit it whenever you want and build upon it, add details, and smooth the edges. Today is the basic creation. We're staying a short time today, but you can come back whenever you please. Commit your details to memory. The colors. The textures. Travel toward the tree where you left the box. Continue to breathe deeply. Kneel in front of the box, but before you open the lid, know that you have the power within you to overcome the items on your list. No problem is too great for you to handle.

"Return to the elevator and step inside. Face yourself in the mirror. You stand taller. Your eyes shine brighter. Your smile is larger. You are confident, strong, and sure. The elevator rises, and you inhale deliberately. The bell dings, and the doors open. The lobby isn't as chaotic as it was before. People move slower, talk softer, and carry lighter loads. You greet people with kindness, and they are happy to see you. As you move toward the hotel exit, you feel refreshed and energized. Ready to conquer the day. When I count to five you will open your eyes and be fully alert. One. Two. Three. Four. Five. Open your eyes."

All my fingertips were covered in paint now, and in my sketchbook I had drawn a sloppy outline of a small square cabin that I'd pictured in my safe place. It sat near the rise of a hill. My clumsy artwork was worse than the stick drawings of a five-year-old, the roof disjointed from the body of the cabin. Smoke swirls extended and flourished across the remainder of the page and carried over onto the opposing page. In the lower corner was a crude box—my representation of the ornate one Rose had described. Red pooled beneath it. I laughed at my ridiculous effort.

Plug passed me a wet paper towel. "Let's wash up," he whispered. Other students returned supplies and washed their hands in the side basin. Before I stood, I gazed at the sketchbooks on the table. Nick had used his three colored pencils to create an abstract drawing. Kyla had created a windstorm of sand on her pages, and she now sprayed adhesive on a thin plastic sheet and pressed it over her art. Plug had drawn a portrait of a girl, who looked a lot like me, using shadows and illuminations to play with the features. I leaned closer for a better view, but Plug closed the sketchbook and slipped it into his bag. He motioned me toward the side basin.

After the students had returned to their seats, Rose said, "This method of creating art allows you to explore your innermost being. Sometimes the art you create will match what you envisioned in your mind. Other times, it will have no resemblance to anything you saw. Perhaps it more closely resembles your emotions. Research has shown that colors influence and reflect our deepest feelings. For example, cool colors like blues and greens can have a relaxing and nurturing effect. That's why decorators use these colors in spas. It's also why people in positions of authority will wear these colors—to have a comforting influence over the individuals they manage. Warm colors like yellow, orange, and red convey more fervent emotions, not only rage and anger but also happiness, passion, and courage. And interestingly enough these warm colors can trigger hunger, and that's why you'll see red tones in a lot of fast-food company logos."

Several students snickered and named the companies with red in their logos.

Rose lifted a hand to quiet them. "Remember, art is not necessarily about finding hidden meaning, but if you explore it closely, your art can be a mirror reflecting your soul."

The bell rang.

"Thank you, everyone, for participating," Rose said. "If your sketchbooks are wet, set them on the counter to dry." I carried mine to the back of the room and set it among the others.

Plug and I walked together to our next class. "What'd you think of that?" he asked.

"I've never done anything like it," I said.

"Neither have I."

"Really? Everyone's art seemed as if they'd done this a million times before. Did you see Nick's drawing?"

Plug nodded.

"Did you have your eyes closed the whole time?" I asked.

"Pretty much."

"Your charcoal drawing was amazing," I said. "You must've had your eyes open."

He quickened his pace toward statistics, but I grabbed the back of his shirt and pulled him to a stop in the hallway.

"Why did you draw a picture of me?"

Plug bit down on his lip ring.

The bell rang, and he motioned me into the classroom. We didn't have a chance to talk during class. So afterward, I asked him again.

"It was only a sketch," he said.

"It was beyond incredible."

"Rose said to create our art and trust our instincts. You were in my thoughts. I drew a picture of you."

"Which means you stared at me when my eyes were closed." That troubled me, even though I had stolen a glance at him during the exercise, too.

"It's a drawing, Hannah. Let it go. Especially if you still want me to drive you to your boyfriend's house after school." Plug turned away, and we headed in separate directions.

⧓ • ⧓

After my last class, I met up with Plug in the parking lot. It seemed wrong to bum a ride to Manny's house from him, but Plug claimed to be my friend. So it shouldn't matter. "Do you want to meet Manny when we get there?"

"I already know who he is." Plug got into the El Camino without opening my door for me.

"You're mad at me," I said after we belted in.

"I've been thinking about the conversation at lunch. Kyla told you to take back your life, and it made me curious. If you could choose who to eat lunch with tomorrow, would you still hang with us, the outcasts, or would you return to the uptight rich clique?"

"They're not uptight," I said.

Plug glared at me.

"And I never called you an outcast," I said.

"That doesn't mean you want to be with us either." Plug started the engine, but then he draped his forearm over the steering wheel. "Why do you care so much about what other people think of you?"

"Why do you care so much about your artwork?" I asked.

"What do you want from our group? From me?" Plug asked.

"I don't know," I said.

"Right." Plug shifted into reverse. "Where are we going?"

I explained how to get to Manny's house.

"You two live in the same neighborhood?" Plug asked. I nodded. We listened to a rock station on the radio and drove into the foothills. Neither of us said a word until he pulled to the curb in front of Manny's house.

"Please don't be mad at me," I said. "You're my only friend. I'm sorry for the stupid things I said and did today."

"I know." He tapped his rings against the steering wheel. Then he killed the engine, hopped out, and ran around to open my door.

Before I stepped out of the car, I said, "Thanks, Plug."

I glanced across the street to Lily's house. I didn't even know if she had regained consciousness yet. I missed her.

Plug walked with me across Manny's lawn.

"What are you doing?" I asked.

"Walking you to the door."

"Why?"

"Why not?"

My heart beat faster at the thought of Manny opening the door and seeing me with Plug. He reached out and rang the doorbell.

Zeus—the Santos family's small half-breed beagle—howled inside. Mrs. Santos opened the door with Zeus cradled in her arm. She wore a cranberry blouse and a KISS THE COOK apron. She hugged me with her other arm, and Zeus sniffed my ear with his wet nose.

"How are you feeling, child?" she asked.

I shrugged.

She tilted her head to the side and said to Plug, "Hello."

"Mrs. Santos, this is . . ." I hesitated, because now that I'd gotten used to calling him Plug, the name Eugene felt strange on my lips.

"Eugene," Plug finished for me. Then he reached out and shook her hand.

"Well, come on in you two." She motioned us in, but Plug hesitated.

"Actually, I can't stay." He stepped away but then turned back to me and said, "I'll see you at seven tomorrow morning."

I nodded and followed Mrs. Santos inside.

She closed the door, and Zeus squirmed. When she set him down, his tail wagged and he ran toward me. I squatted to scratch him behind the ears, but he tucked his tail between his legs, and he began to whimper.

"What's bothering you?" Mrs. Santos asked Zeus and picked him up.

I set my backpack by the door and followed Mrs. Santos down the hall to the family room off the kitchen. To my right, fresh homemade bread lined the counter on cooling racks. To my left, Manny lay sprawled out on the couch. He pushed up to a sitting position when he saw me and carefully moved his feet from the couch to the floor. Joy flowed through me, and I relaxed. Mrs. Santos set Zeus down, and he ran out of the room. She went back to baking in the kitchen.

I stooped in front of Manny. "How are you?"

"I'm better now." He twined his fingers with mine. I peeked toward the kitchen to see if his mom was watching. She mixed something in a lime-green ceramic bowl. Manny lowered the volume on the television with the remote.

"Was someone at the door with you?" Manny asked.

"Eugene dropped me off."

Manny's jaw clenched. "I thought you weren't hanging out with him anymore."

"I don't have a car, and he offered me a ride. We're friends—"

"I don't care," Manny said. "I don't trust him."

"There's nothing to worry about with him." I sidled up to Manny on the couch. "Do you still hurt?"

"Yes, but at least I've been able to cut back on the pain pills. Soon I won't need them at all." He touched his torso. "It hurts to breathe because of the cracked ribs, but the doctors say it will take time to heal."

"Have you heard any news about Lily?" I asked.

"Didn't her mom call you?"

"No. What's happened?" My chest tightened with fear.

Manny grabbed my hand. "She woke up this afternoon."

Tears of relief flooded down my face. "Can she talk? Can I call her?"

"No, she's still in ICU, but Mrs. Sloane told us they plan to move her to a regular room tomorrow. So you should be able to talk to her then."

I gazed downward.

Manny lifted my chin. "She'll get better. The accident was not your fault."

"Of course it was. And I can't fix it. Our friends on the student council hate me. Chelsea's convinced them I'm to blame. And I'm being stalked by evil spirits or something."

"Chelsea told me some weird stuff has happened at school, but she—"

"When did you talk to Chelsea?"

"She's called to check on me."

"Chelsea is up to something. And I'm serious about the evil spirits. I know it's hard to believe, but remember that pink elephant you won at the fair? It burned in the fire. I know it did. But now it keeps reappearing in my room. I threw it out with the garbage this morning."

Manny's face paled. "That sounds really crazy," he said. "Have you been home to see if the trash men took it away?"

"No. I came here right after school. I don't want to go home and see it again. But Manny, I'm telling you the truth. I've seen the Angel of Death or some sort of evil spirit."

Mrs. Santos dropped a pan in the sink. We jerked our heads in her direction. She closed her eyes and whispered a prayer.

"Mom?" Manny perched on the edge of the couch to get up, but he clutched his ribs.

"Mrs. Santos?" I approached the counter.

"Amen," she whispered and opened her eyes. She wiped her hands on her apron and moved around the edge of the counter.

"Do not play with evil spirits, child. When you spoke of them just now, I felt a darkness lurking."

"You believe in evil spirits?" I asked.

"Of course I do. Not only is God real, but Satan too. Angels and demons battle each other."

"Does saying a prayer protect you?"

"It helps if you have faith. We've also blessed our home. No malevolent spirits can enter here unless they are invited inside. The prayer I said reinforced that blessing. You are protected in our home. But, please"—she clutched my hands—"never tempt these spirits. Once you invite them into your life, your house, your mind, they are hard to get rid of."

"I haven't invited them in," I said.

"You took part in a hypnotist's show," Mrs. Santos said.

"Yes, but I wasn't actually hypnotized."

"How can you be certain?" A bead of perspiration rolled down Mrs. Santos's forehead. She pulled a tissue from her sleeve and wiped the sweat away.

"I guess I can't."

She led me back over to the couch where Manny waited.

"If you gave up your free will during hypnosis," Mrs. Santos said, "evil spirits may have connected with you and then with your house. If you want, we can have your house blessed, but only if your mother agrees to it."

"Why does my mom need to know?"

"Because you're her daughter, and it's her house. If you have faith, God will bring good things to you, but you have to invite him in, because God will not violate your will."

"But evil spirits can? Are they more powerful than God?" I asked.

"No, that's not what I said. Satan can cause havoc, but he cannot extinguish true faith. He has no real power here. You can tell him to depart, but you must decide to either act or be acted upon." She rubbed my shoulder before returning to the kitchen.

Sometimes Mrs. Santos's words spun like riddles in my mind, and the meanings escaped me. Was her faith strong enough to overcome my doubts?

I slipped off my sandals and scooted next to Manny. I wanted to enjoy my time with him and forget about seeing strange things. I wrapped my hands around his, and we watched television. I wished I could move in here with Manny and be with him forever.

Mrs. Santos walked down the hall, and I snuggled into Manny.

"My mom will be back any second," he said.

I groaned. I needed to cuddle closer. That was all. But I scooted away. Manny's mom returned a few seconds later with her purse dangling from the crook of her arm.

"I need to run errands," she said. "Your dad will be home from work in a few minutes, and your brothers will be home from soccer soon. Is there anything you need before I leave?"

"Nope." Manny changed the channel.

The front door clicked when Mrs. Santos left, and I grinned at Manny. I reached across him, grabbed the remote, and clicked off the television.

"What are you doing?" he asked and fidgeted with the collar of his shirt.

"Why are you nervous?" I pushed his hair away from his face. Then I traced his features, starting with his eyebrows and working down the bridge of his nose to his lips. I leaned in to kiss him, and he lifted a hand between us.

"Wait," he whispered.

"You don't want to kiss me?" I asked.

"Of course I do." He rubbed his face. "But someone could barge in on us at any second."

"It's only kissing. Besides, we'll hear the front door long before anyone gets back here." I kissed his palm and then his wrist. He sighed. I leaned in and pressed my lips against his.

I drew back and studied his dark eyes. Then I carefully maneuvered onto his lap and kissed his neck. He gave in to me this time. Soft as a feather, I traced the tip of my tongue along his full lips. They parted, and our tongues touched tentatively at first, but then we sank into a deep, long kiss. Manny moaned. His hand found the hem of my dress. He stroked the bare skin of my knees, and then he pushed me away.

"What has gotten into you?" Manny asked, breathless. He wiped his mouth with the back of his hand.

"It was only a kiss," I said. "Manny, we almost died." I moved away from him and stroked the plush carpet with my toes. "Everything we have could be gone in a blink. Just gone." Student Council. Lily. Jordan.

"Are you going to the funeral?" I asked.

"Yes. Are you?"

I locked eyes with him. "His family doesn't want me to." I told him how Jordan's mom slapped me at the hospital and what his aunt said after creative writing class.

Manny pulled me closer.

"I don't want to lose you, too," I said.

"You won't."

I nestled my head against his neck, and he wrapped his arms around me.

"Where did you learn to kiss like that anyway?" he whispered.

I pulled back from him to see his face. He was serious. "You are the only guy I have ever kissed. The Ferris wheel was my first time. Ever. I waited years for you to be interested in me."

"But now you're hanging out with Eugene, seeing evil spirits, and climbing all over me."

There was a click at the front door.

"Hello? Anyone home?" Manny's dad bellowed. He walked into the kitchen area. "Oh, hello, Hannah. How are you?"

"I was just leaving." I slipped on my sandals and stared at Manny for a moment. I wanted to scream at the top of my lungs for one short, little second . . . just to see what would happen. Would it freak Manny out? Would it scare Mr. Santos? Was it possible to behave erratically for one lousy minute and still be normal? Acceptable? Lovable?

I turned away and hustled down the hall before either of them said anything else. And before I said or did something I'd regret. I loved Manny, but I'd never seen this critical side of him before, and I was unsure what to do about it. I wanted to be one with him so badly my stomach ached, but he'd asked, *What has gotten into you?* I'd been propelled by instinct and desire, but it wasn't as if I'd stripped him naked. I'd only kissed him. He almost died in the accident. I nearly killed him. My best friend. My true love. Would Manny and I survive this? Would he still want to be with me when he returned to Peregrine?

I checked the time on my cell and slipped it into my dress pocket. Then I grabbed my backpack and stepped outside. The sunlight blinded me momentarily, and as I walked across the grass, an uncomfortable heaviness settled on me. I stopped on the sidewalk and faced Manny's house. Mrs. Santos had said no evil spirits could enter their home without invitation, but I was outside now. I pulled the tiger-eye stone out of my pocket and stroked it with my thumb. I felt alone and unprotected.

My legs began to itch.

I glanced down and shrieked.

The sidewalk swelled; legions of ants swarmed over the concrete in waves. They blanketed my sandals, my toes, and my ankles. Several scampered past my knees and beneath my dress. I stomped and screamed and swatted at the evil pests. They bit into my flesh. I darted out into the road to get away from the mega-colony, and I shook my skirt, lifting it up and down. I needed to get the insects off me. Red welts spotted my legs.

A minivan pulled into Manny's driveway, and I continued flipping my skirt and brushing my legs. Manny's younger brothers, Miguel and Michael, hopped out of the van.

"What's going on?" Miguel asked.

My cheeks heated up with embarrassment. "Ants." I pointed at the sidewalk.

The minivan backed out and drove away. Manny's brothers moved over to where I'd pointed.

"What ants?" Miguel asked.

I inched over to them. No bugs. Not a single one remained on the sidewalk, but welts covered my legs. I pointed at the red bumps. "They bit me."

"Ants don't bite," Miguel said.

"Carpenter ones do," I said.

Miguel scrunched up his face in disbelief.

"Never mind." I walked away. I brushed off my dress to make sure no more bugs remained. The welts on my legs were evidence bugs had bitten me. It was not a delusion. I was not crazy.

When I arrived home, the driveway was empty. Mom was probably working late tonight. As the general manager of the largest hotel in town, she often got called in at strange hours of the night. The hotel had more than 500 rooms, two restaurants, and three lounges, and that kept her busy.

I headed upstairs to my room and found it in the same condition I'd left it that morning, with the bedcovers on the floor and dirty clothes in the corner. I kicked off my sandals and sat at my desk to check e-mails. Nick had sent the information to configure my computer for capturing videos. I downloaded the program and modified my computer settings to get it to work. I had just finished when I heard a bang come from downstairs. It echoed through the house.

"Mom?" I called.

Silence.

I skipped testing Nick's program and clicked the start button. Then I moved to the top of the stairs and listened for noises. The house was so quiet I heard the refrigerator kick on in the kitchen.

I tiptoed downstairs. No one. Nothing unusual.

In the kitchen, Mom had left a note on the counter:

Working late. You can reheat the pizza in the fridge for dinner.

Great. More leftover pizza. Mrs. Santos undoubtedly had prepared a delicious five-course meal for her family. Most likely, they had circled the dinner table and eaten together. I wanted what Manny had. I opened the fridge and lifted out the box, but before I saw what toppings Mom had ordered, another loud noise reverberated through the house. I set the pizza box on the counter and went to investigate the sound.

The front door hung wide open. I could've sworn I'd shut it already. I closed the door and flipped the deadbolt. I scanned the living room. Nothing. I hesitated at the base of the stairs. Did I really need to search the whole house? But I knew I'd enjoy my pizza more if I checked things out first. I darted up the stairs and inspected Mom's bedroom. Nothing. I swung open the door to my room.

The pink elephant sat on my neatly made bed.

"No."

I snatched the elephant and screamed until my lungs burned. I wrenched my fingers into an open seam and ripped him apart. I yanked out his stuffing and tore off his limbs. I threw the pieces across the room, as far away from me as possible. How did this charred monster get back in my room? The smell of smoke became stronger and stronger. I coughed. I chucked the last piece of elephant to the far corner and ran to the top of the stairs. A dark vapor swirled around the base and climbed one step at a time.

Moving backward, I crept to my room and slammed the door. I leaned against it and kept my gaze on the torn bits of elephant. The smoke detectors beeped, and a thick gray haze seeped under the door. What if this wasn't my mind playing cruel tricks or even demons taunting me? What if the house was really on fire? I didn't want to burn to death. I threw open my door and ran back downstairs. A black cloud clung to the ceiling. I stayed low with the breathable air. I unbolted the front door and swung it open. Then I crawled to the back door and opened it to let fresh air inside.

The smoke seemed thickest in the kitchen. I covered my nose and searched for the source. There were no flames anywhere, but red indicator lights glowed on the stove, and gray haze streamed upward from the rear vent. I opened the oven door, and black smoke billowed out. I gagged and closed the door with a thud. I shut off the oven and flipped on the water in the sink. I found the barbecue tongs, held my breath, and opened the oven. I reached in with the tongs and tugged out the blackened pizza box, dumped it into the sink of water, and turned off the faucet. I dropped the tongs on the counter and ran out to the backyard. I collapsed on my knees in the middle of the lawn and gasped for air.

Black clouds continued to stream out of the house, and the smoke detectors continued to beep at a ridiculous volume. Would the neighbors notice? I should have opened more windows for better circulation, but I couldn't bear to go back inside. I needed fresh air. I lay back on the cool grass and tried to clear my lungs. I recalled the aroma of freshly baked bread at Manny's house. His mom probably never burned anything in the oven. I wheezed with each breath I took. I couldn't remember putting the pizza box in the oven or turning it on.

I jolted upright. I was certain I had set the pizza on the counter. Then I went upstairs. Found the awful elephant. But I never put the pizza in the oven. Someone must have been in the house playing a cruel joke on me. I needed to see if Nick's program recorded anything on my computer, but there was still too much smoke in the house.

The welts on my shin itched, and I scratched them. They bled, but I scratched anyway. Maybe Chelsea got inside my house and burned the pizza. My fingers slipped, covered in blood. I rubbed my hand in the grass, but the sticky red mess smeared across my skin, and my leg continued to bleed. I needed a towel.

I took a deep breath of clean air and ran back inside. I opened the windows downstairs. Then I grabbed a towel from a kitchen drawer and darted outside. I wrapped the dishcloth around my leg and tucked the corner underneath to secure it in place. Good enough for now.

Mom would freak when she saw the mess I'd caused. Everything reeked of smoke, and stains darkened the wall behind the stove. I sank down to the grass, and after about five more minutes, the detectors stopped blaring. I moved over to one of the patio lounge chairs and curled up on it.

What if the demons tried to kill Manny the way they'd almost killed me tonight? If I had stayed in my room, the pizza box would have eventually burst into flames, and the whole house would have caught fire. I needed to warn Manny. Make sure he was all right. I pulled my phone from my pocket, but before I texted him, the phone rang.

❧ • ☙

Mom startled me awake. The sun had long since set, and the moon dominated the sky.

"What are you doing out here?" Mom asked. "And why on earth is the house wide open?"

"I burned the pizza in the oven. I had to open up the house to let out the smoke."

She glanced back at the house. "I didn't smell any smoke."

"What time is it?" I asked.

"After ten. Let's go inside."

She was right. The house smelled normal. We walked into the kitchen together, and Mom opened the refrigerator.

"You said you burned it?" She lifted an unblemished pizza box from the fridge. I peered at the sink where the damaged box should have been. Nothing. But the barbecue tongs remained on the counter where I'd left them.

Tears streamed down my face. I didn't know how much more of this I could take. It had happened. The smoke in the house. The smoke in my lungs. It was real. I reached down to my shin, but I was wearing jeans . . . and a sweatshirt. I yanked up my pant leg to see the welts. My skin was clean and smooth. No welts. No blood smears. No bites. I examined my fingernails. My manicure looked better than ever.

"Mom, can I sleep with you tonight?" I asked.

Mom set the pizza back in the fridge. Then she leaned her hip against the countertop.

"Hannah—"

"Tomorrow's Jordan's funeral," I said. "I don't want to be alone tonight." Because I am freaked out, I wanted to add. I'm afraid to go into my room and see the elephant has reassembled itself. I don't trust myself anymore.

Mom clutched my hand. "Yes, you can sleep in my room. You will recover from this. You need to hang in there until our appointment with Dr. James. I called and moved it to Thursday afternoon. That was their earliest appointment." Mom hugged me and stroked my back. "It's been a long day for both of us," she said. "Let's get changed and—"

"Did something happen at the hotel?" I asked.

"Nothing out of the ordinary. We've had a lot of extra work finishing the remodel of the fourth-floor lounge, and today we started auditioning new lounge acts," she said. "So I'm tired, but it's all fine. Get your pajamas on and meet me in my room." I nodded, and she left the kitchen.

I picked up the barbecue tongs and sniffed the ends. No residual smoke.

I trudged up the stairs dreading what I'd find in my room. I considered staying out, but Mom had told me to change.

I opened the door to my room, steeling myself for what I would find. But it had reverted to the way I'd found it after school. The bedcovers were on the floor. The dirty clothes rested in the corner. And there was no pink elephant. No stuffing. No charred fur. Maybe I had dreamed the whole incident. If it had been a dream, I didn't want to go back to sleep.

My laptop was closed. Had I even installed Nick's program? I sat at my desk unable to make myself open the laptop and discover that I'd never even checked e-mails. I opened the art book from Rose instead. The tiger-eye was lodged in the gutter, marking the same nasty picture it had that morning. I studied the picture on the page, and a chill ran up my spine. I pinched the stone out of the book and tossed it across the room. Then I grabbed a clean T-shirt and a pair of pajama bottoms from my dresser. My whole body ached as I changed clothes.

In a moment of determination, I opened the laptop and typed in my password. I clicked on Nick's e-mail and installed the program. After I made sure the settings were correct in my computer, I clicked the start icon, angled the laptop toward my bed, and left for Mom's room.

Nothing would happen to me while I was with Mom, because she didn't think anything was happening anyhow. We settled into her king-sized bed; she took the left and I took the right. She reached for her lamp and switched it off, but the lamp on my side still illuminated the room.

"Good night, Hannah," she said.

"Mom?"

"What?" she rolled onto her side and faced me.

"Could we have the house blessed?"

She scrunched up the pillow under her head.

"Manny's family is religious," I said, "and his mom thinks it might help to have our house blessed."

Mom sat up and massaged her scalp.

"What if evil spirits are haunting me?" I asked.

"There are no such things as evil spirits." She reached across the bed and held my hand. "You feel guilty for the car accident. You feel guilty for disliking Jordan, and now he's dead. Your mind is trying to work through these emotions. You will be okay. This doctor will help you get better. I will help you. But you have to take responsibility for your own emotions and not blame what's happening on evil spirits."

"So my mind will keep playing these tricks on me while it works through the emotions? Honestly, Mom, what am I supposed to do?"

"If you're interested I can show you how to meditate. That may help you cope with the trauma of the accident."

"How?"

"You can strengthen your mind and strengthen your will through meditation."

We sat crossed-legged facing each other and joined hands. "Close your eyes," she said. "Fill your lungs with—"

I opened my eyes. "How is this different than hypnotism?"

"I won't tell you what to do, think, or feel. I'll show you how to relax and find the place within your mind where you can deal with these emotions from a place of safety."

"Okay." I closed my eyes and followed her instructions. Her meditation routine resembled Rose's exercise in art class, which made it easier for me to follow. I had already built the foundation within my mind. I found the cabin and added new details around it: colorful flowers, rolling hills, and a grassy patch beneath large cottonwood trees. A wisp of black smoke curled up from the top of the cabin, but before I had time to investigate it, Mom brought the meditation to an end.

"As you practice this on your own," Mom said, "you can face your emotions from within your protected space. Nothing can hurt you there. Things will improve with time."

"But it's getting worse with time."

"It's only been a few days." She patted my hands. "Now get some sleep." She scooted back down under the covers and rolled in the other direction. Maybe she was right. Maybe the hallucinations were just my mind's way of working through the tough emotions. I flipped off the light and settled into the bed.

WEDNESDAY
AUGUST 28

Mom jiggled my arm. "You need to get up and get ready," she said.

I squinted at the clock on my nightstand: 6:45 A.M.

I jerked upright.

"I slept in your bed last night," I said.

"No," Mom said. "You haven't slept in my bed since you were a child. And I wonder how you slept in yours." She pointed at the mattress. It was bare.

"Not again," I whispered and drew my knees up to my chest. Exasperation pumped through my veins. I wanted to tell Mom my version of last night, but even a hint of disappointment in her eyes would crush me. I ignored the sense of dread and focused on steadying each breath, in and out.

"Come on, Hannah," Mom said. "If you're late, I can't drive you. I have too much going on at the hotel."

"Please let me stay home," I said. "Today is Jordan's funeral, and I can't imagine being at school while it's happening. People will ask why I'm not at the service."

Mom perched on the bed next to me and remained quiet for several seconds.

"Please, Mom."

She wrapped an arm around me and said, "You can stay home, if you promise to go back tomorrow."

"I promise," I said.

"And you need to call me if anything unusual happens."

"I will." Maybe. Probably not.

She stood and stroked my hair. "You can spend the day picking up your room and catching up on your laundry." She smoothed her blazer and stepped over the various land mines in my room. "Don't wait up for me tonight. I'll be late."

I sat and listened to her leave; the front door opened and closed.

Blankets and sheets snaked across the carpet. My mattress had been stripped bare. Clothes were strewn about the room. Dresser drawers dangled open. Papers speckled the remaining spaces. And at my desk, shredded pages from Rose's art book stuck up from the gutter of the binding.

"No, no, no!" I jumped off the bed and ran over to the desk. I drew my finger along the feathered edges of the pages. Every single one had been ripped out.

"Who would do this?" I whispered.

Someone must have been in my room last night. I moved over to my window. Not only was it unlocked, but it also hung wide open, the screen gone. I leaned out and spotted it two stories below in the grass. Mom backed out of the driveway and talked on her cell at the same time. She didn't see me leaning out the window or the screen lying below on the grass. I lifted my gaze to the ancient oak tree, and my jaw dropped open.

Branches pierced my ruffled emerald blouse and my rhinestone jeans like fish speared in the ocean. I closed the window and yanked the drapes across it.

I sidestepped obstacles to make my way to the closet. Inside, scattered across the carpet, were my family snapshots. And splayed open in the middle of the mess was my family album. I fell to my knees and picked up the pictures: Dad holding me on his hip when I was a baby; Mom, Dad, and me on the boardwalk in Atlantic City when I was four; me burying Dad in the sand at the beach. I scooped all the photos back into the brown box and set the album on top of them. I cradled the box in my lap and rocked back and forth. What was happening to me? Was I schizophrenic like my dad? I snatched the lid off the floor, covered the box, and then stashed it on the shelf behind a pair of tennis shoes.

Wiping tears from my face, I returned to my desk and plopped down in the chair. The drawers of the desk had been emptied onto the carpet, but the caricature from Disney World hung on the wall again. I traced the edges of the closed laptop.

"Leave it," a voice whispered. "Like it never happened."

I clenched my teeth, unplugged my laptop, and picked up my cell. After another quick glance around the room, I left and slammed the door behind me. Downstairs, I set my laptop on an end table, and then I opened the blinds and curtains in the kitchen and adjoining family room. I flipped on all the lights. I needed brightness. No lurking darkness.

My heart beat faster as I stared at my laptop across the room. I scratched at my cheeks and debated whether or not to open it. There had to be a recording on it, but I would come entirely unhinged if I watched a video showing me tearing apart my own room. Proof positive that I'd become a complete nutcase.

My cell buzzed with a text from Plug: I'm heading to your house. See you soon.

I replied: Don't need a ride.

He messaged back: Remember to bring lunch today.

I texted: I'm not coming.

I tossed my phone on the couch and reached for the computer, but my hands trembled. I tightened them into fists and paced the room, too chicken to do it alone. Resigned, I foraged through the kitchen cupboards. Sugar and caffeine would help keep me awake.

With two cans of Dr. Pepper and a bag of chocolate chips, I curled up on the couch. I emptied the first can of soda and half the bag of chips while Manny and I texted back and forth. But then he left for the funeral. Everyone I knew was going. Would they notice my absence? Would they talk about me? I let out three enormous burps in succession. Then I popped the top on the second can of Dr. Pepper. At least Manny felt well enough to go, which suggested his ribs were healing. And that meant he'd be back at school soon.

Last night Manny had said Lily regained consciousness. I snatched my phone and dialed the hospital.

"Hello?" Lily said.

"Lily!" I sat up straight. "Is it really you?"

"Hannah? Are you calling from the funeral?"

"No, I'm at home."

"Oh"—Lily cleared her throat—"because Jordan's mom slapped you? Did you really brag to her about going to the mall?"

"I didn't brag. I wasn't thinking straight. I said stupid things."

"I still can't believe he's dead." Lily's voice diminished.

"I never meant for any of it—"

"I know," Lily said, "but Hannah, are you okay?"

"I only have bruises."

"No, I mean—"

"What?"

"Chelsea told me you punched her in broadcasting—"

"She stole my anchor chair."

"She said Mr. Arnold asked her to fill in—"

"Don't believe Chelsea's lies."

"Are you saying you didn't punch her?"

"I swung at her, but I never actually touched her." I suddenly realized how petty I sounded when Lily was stuck in the hospital. "I'm sorry. I shouldn't be ranting about Chelsea when I called to find out how you're doing. Are you in pain? What do the doctors say?"

"Yeah, I'm in pain. The doctors say I'll be here a while. Something about internal damage and a traumatic head injury. They shaved off my hair."

"It'll grow back," I said.

"I wish Jordan could come back as easily," Lily sobbed into the phone.

I cried along with her. "Is there anything I can do for you?"

"No. A grief counselor is supposed to visit me sometime today. My mom's worried that I'm depressed. What else would I be? I just woke up and found out that my boyfriend is dead!"

"I'm so sorry."

"I know, Hannah," Lily said. "I should go, but can you visit soon?"

"Absolutely." We hung up. I rested my head on the arm of the couch, and at some point, I fell asleep.

⚜ • ⚜

My phone chimed with a new message from Manny: I'm home. Want to come over?

I texted him back: I'll be right there.

I darted upstairs to change, but halted when I touched my bedroom door. What would I find inside? I pressed my forehead against the closed door. Everything had been perfect before the accident. I wanted a chance for my life to go back to normal, but if I was spending the afternoon at Manny's, I had to get out of my pajamas first. I flung the door open. The room was still a mess.

Nothing had changed.

I yanked on a T-shirt and shorts and then shoved my feet into some flip-flops. I snatched my purse from the floor and ran outside, but before I hit the driveway, I hesitated. Did I lock the doors? I walked back and made sure the front door was locked.

But what about the back door? And my bedroom window?

I pulled my keys from my purse and let myself inside. I latched the back door and double-checked the windows, upstairs and down. Then I grabbed the broom from the hall closet and lugged it out to the front yard.

The bright sun pounded down on me, but beneath the shade of the old tree I planted my feet, and with great satisfaction I fished my clothes from its branches. I threw them into the trash bin and propped the broom next to it.

Anticipation filled every ounce of me as I walked to Manny's house. He was my anchor, my remaining piece of normal. I rang the doorbell and thumped my fingers against my bare legs. He swung the door open, looked me up and down, and smiled. He still wore his suit from the funeral. Black slacks, black jacket, crisp white shirt, and skinny black tie. His hair was smoothed back, and his face was cleanly shaven.

I wanted the pleasure of touching him, but I waited for him to invite me inside. He backed up and motioned me in, but Zeus growled and bared his teeth.

"Zeus, stop it! It's Hannah!" Manny shooed him down the hall. "Apparently he's a guard dog today, but I can't imagine why he thinks I need protection from you."

I remained on the porch.

"What are you waiting for? Come in!" He snatched my hand, and the hairs on my arms stood when I crossed the threshold of his home.

"Is your mom here?" I asked.

"Nope." He led me back to the family room. Sunlight streamed in through the sliding glass doors, and muddy paw prints streaked the lower half of the glass. Before we reached the couch, I lifted Manny's hand and drew my thumb across his smooth knuckles.

"Are you still sore today?" I asked.

"Yeah." His wristwatch ticked, and the seconds passed.

I slid my hands around his waist. His muscles tightened. "Does this hurt?" I asked.

"No," he whispered.

I drew him closer until our hips touched. "Does this?"

He shook his head.

I lifted up on my toes and kissed his lips. "This?" I ran the tip of my nose along his jaw and breathed in the lingering fragrance of shaving cream.

He raised one hand to my waist and the other to my cheek. He leaned in for another kiss and tugged me closer to him. He kissed me greedily. I craved him just as badly. Our mouths stayed locked on each other, and we staggered over to the couch. Manny pulled back. We both breathed hard.

I slid his jacket off his shoulders, and he grimaced.

"My ribs hurt when I move a certain—"

"So sit still," I said.

His eyebrows rose, but he lowered to the couch. I propped a throw pillow behind him and I knelt at his feet. I loosened his tie, unbuttoned his shirt, and tugged it out from his pants. The sight of his skin made me tremble. Last week I would never have been this brash, but today I needed to be touched, to be loved, to feel wanted. I opened his shirt wider and explored the lines of his muscles with my fingers. I traced the hair that ran from his belly to his belt buckle. I slipped off his shirt and freed his arms. I gently caressed his tan chest. He raised my chin and pressed his full lips to mine. Warmth flowed through me.

He leaned back and stretched out on the couch. I straddled his lap and balanced my weight to avoid touching his ribs. I leaned forward and pressed my mouth to his. Manny's hands slipped under my shirt.

The front door clicked. Opened. Closed.

I pressed against his hips and kissed his nose, his cheek, his lips. Manny muttered incoherently and pushed my shoulders.

"Hannah!" Mrs. Santos said.

I jerked up and twisted to face her.

Her eyes narrowed, and her cheeks reddened.

I cleared my throat and climbed off Manny. "I have to use the bathroom." I sounded lame, but I grabbed my purse and ran down the hall to the guest bathroom.

My mouth dropped open when I assessed myself in the mirror. I wore my missing baby blue T-shirt from the other night. Dirt and grass stains covered it. Panic welled. I tried to take a breath, but I stifled a scream instead. I ran my hands along my shorts. At least they were clean, but I had on two different flip-flops: a bright pink one and a brown suede one. I scrutinized my reflection. Yesterday's mascara was smeared beneath my eyes, my hair knotted and disheveled. I was mortified. Why didn't Manny flinch when he first saw me? Mrs. Santos probably assumed I was a mess because Manny and I had been fooling around. But we had only gotten started. I ran my fingers through the mop of hair on my head, but that made it worse. I rifled through my purse and found a ponytail holder. I fixed my hair the best I could as fast as I could. I spit on the hem of my shirt and used it to wipe under my eyes.

"Hannah?" Manny called from the back of the house. I dreaded facing his mom, but I returned to the family room where they waited. Manny had put his shirt back on and tucked it into his slacks. His wavy chestnut hair fell across his forehead.

Mrs. Santos pursed her lips when I made brief eye contact with her, and that was a knife through my heart.

"Hannah," she said and clacked her tongue against the roof of her mouth. "I have loved you like a daughter, but you are no longer allowed to be in the house with Manny alone. I know you care for each other, and you both have gone through a traumatic experience. It's normal to want to be together. But you're young. And if you got pregnant—"

I gazed at Manny, and his eyes widened with shock. I did not want to have this conversation with Mrs. Santos.

"Mom!" he said.

Mrs. Santos held up a finger. "Let me finish." She turned and glared at me. "If you got pregnant, Hannah, your plans for Princeton would be over. You would have to change your priorities to take care of a baby, and remember, Manny has goals, too." She took a deep breath and wrung her hands together. "Hannah, what happened, or almost happened, here is unacceptable in my house. Do you understand?"

I nodded.

Mrs. Santos left the room without another word.

Manny and I stared at each other for a few seconds without moving.

"I'm going home," I said.

"That's probably a good idea." He held his side, took several gasps, and moved to the kitchen. He swiped the prescription bottle from the counter and twisted off the lid.

"I'm so sorry," I said and got him a glass of water. "I don't know what got into me. You're injured. I should never have—"

He put his soft fingers on my lips. "It wasn't just you." My heart beat faster. He traced a line from my lips to my jaw, and then to my neck. His gaze fixed on my lips.

"I love you," I whispered.

"I've loved you longer." His eyes darted toward the hallway before he leaned in and kissed me. He lingered there for a moment, and his breath on my skin made me believe we'd be okay. He drew back, took the glass of water from me, and downed a couple of pain pills.

"Why didn't you tell me I looked so awful when you first saw me?" I asked.

He swallowed more water before setting the glass on the counter. He took my hand in his and said, "You never look awful to me."

"Liar," I said. "You must've noticed."

"I noticed you're using a different perfume," he said.

I lifted the collar of my T-shirt to my nose. It smelled musty and a bit like sage.

He leaned in and kissed me again. I wanted to stay, but I doubted my ability to keep my paws off him, and I dreaded hanging around under Mrs. Santos's condemning eye.

"Will you walk me home?" I asked.

"I can't." He pointed to his ribs. "I hurt too bad to even think about walking."

"Sorry."

"It's not your fault," he said, "but Hannah, something's changed."

"You mean, I've changed, and you hate change."

"No, I mean we can't do this."

"Do what?"

"Hannah, we crossed a line today, and we can't do it again. I can't disappoint my mom like that."

My chin quivered, and I turned away before he saw me cry. I dreaded going home by myself to an empty house with malicious surprises waiting inside, but it would be better than feigning restraint and status quo in front of Manny and his family.

Manny led me to the front door and opened it for me. "When do you see that doctor?"

"I'm not crazy," I said.

Manny bit his lips together.

"Your mom believes I've seen spirits—"

"Hannah, I doubt spirits have the ability to do everything you've described."

"You think I made it up?"

"You're confused," Manny said and reached for my hand, but I yanked it away. "Hopefully that doctor can sort things out."

"I'm not crazy."

"I know. That's what you keep saying. Hannah, I love you, but you need to get help so you can go back to your old normal self."

"And what if I never go back to my old normal self? Will you still love me?" The uncertainty in his eyes made my stomach twist. "Forget it," I said. I walked across the lawn and headed toward home.

"Of course I'll love you," Manny called out from behind me, but I didn't believe him.

⊱ • ⊰

From a distance, I spotted Plug's El Camino parked at the curb in front of my house. I jogged the remainder of the way home but found his car empty. I moved toward the house, and Plug came through the side gate.

"What are doing here?" I asked.

"Worried about you," he said. "You haven't answered your phone this afternoon." He pushed his sleeves up past his elbows.

I dug my cell out of my purse. It was silenced. I toggled the volume back on and checked for messages. Plug had sent several, but I didn't take the time to read them right then.

"Why were you in my backyard?" I asked.

"You said you were staying home, but you didn't answer the door." He lifted my hand and entwined his long, callused fingers with mine. My stomach tightened. I wanted to pull away, but my fingers had a mind of their own and intermingled with his.

"Weird stuff has happened," Plug said, "and I wanted to make sure you were okay."

I needed to let go of him. I loved Manny. A bead of sweat rolled down my back. I peeked up at Plug, and I had an overwhelming urge to kiss him. I desperately wanted to know if his thin lips would feel different from Manny's fuller ones. I wanted the pleasure of toying with Plug's lip ring. My heart rate increased, and I stepped closer to him.

But then Plug dropped my hand and walked away.

I snapped out of the trance I'd fallen into and shook my wrists. Why was I even considering the idea of kissing Plug? I rubbed my lips.

Plug moved to the driver's side of his car.

"You're leaving?" I asked.

"Just came by to make sure you were okay." He opened his door, but before he got inside, he asked, "Want me to stay?"

Yes, I don't want to go into the house by myself.

No, I don't want to be tempted to kiss you.

"Doesn't matter," I said. Please stay.

"We could go get something to eat," he said, "but you should shower first. You're kind of a mess." He grinned and pointed at my shirt and shoes.

I plucked at one of the larger stains on my shirt and groaned. How could I have gone out in public like this?

"Come on," I said. "I think we have your favorite in the fridge."

"Cold pizza?" he asked.

I laughed and fished the keys out of my purse.

"Nice to see you have your own set," Plug said.

My heart stopped. He knew where the spare house key was hidden. I stepped off into the flowerbed to retrieve it, but it was gone.

"Did you take the fake rock?" I asked.

"Why would I?"

"You said you came to check on me. Maybe you went inside."

"I wouldn't need a key."

"It's missing." I rifled through one bush and then another. Plug stepped next to me and helped. I smashed a daisy in my frantic search for the fake rock. "Where is it?" I yelled.

"It's gone," Plug said.

"It has to be here!" Because I didn't know what to think if it was gone. I kicked a geranium. I scoured the dirt with my fingers. Manny knew we kept it here. I yanked a tulip like a weed. Maybe it was underneath. Lily knew the key was here. I flung dirt against the house.

"Chelsea knew it was here," I said.

Plug gripped my shoulders and pulled me away from the flower bed. We sank to the ground, and he embraced me.

"Things will get better," he whispered.

I buried my face in his chest and cried. He held me and rocked side to side.

My sobs slowed, and I whispered, "I'm such an idiot." I started to pull back, but he held on tighter.

"No. You're not." He rubbed my back, then loosened his hold.

I sat and rested my hand on his knee. Plug wiped my tears with his fingers, his skin rough against mine. He held my face and caressed my ears.

Heat lit from my head to my toes, and I imagined reaching up and stroking his short clipped hair. I imagined him lowering me back onto the soft bed of grass and kissing me. I wanted to tease his lip ring with the tip of my tongue, tug at the slick, hard metal. I ached for him to kiss me deeply—

"Hannah?" he said.

I gasped and glanced toward the blue sky. "I have a boyfriend," I whispered. And I just betrayed him by fantasizing about Plug.

"Your boyfriend is not my concern." Plug moved his fingers from my face to my hand.

I studied Plug, hoping to figure out his intentions.

"You are my concern, Hannah," he said. "I need to make sure you're okay, as a friend or more than that. Whatever you want." He let go of my hand and swept the loose hairs from my face. "I care about you." His fingers lingered on my skin.

I yearned for someone to be on my side, to fight for me, to fight with me. I wanted to stop worrying about losing control and disappointing everyone around me. Plug had never criticized me or blamed me for the crazy things happening around me. He'd been kind and helpful. He'd been here for me when nobody else had.

Plug stood and extended his hand to help me up. I took it.

We ate pizza at the kitchen counter, straight out of the box, and I told him about the recent demonic chaos in my life.

"Did you set up your laptop to record?" Plug asked.

I pointed across the kitchen toward the adjoining family room.

"Why's it down here instead of in your room?" He walked over and picked it up.

"I wanted to see if it recorded anything, but I was too scared to watch it alone."

Plug pushed the pizza box out of the way and set the computer on the counter.

"We'll do it together," he said.

"Wait!" I set my hand on his before he opened the laptop. "What if none of it happened? What if it was all a delusion?"

"One way to find out." He opened the computer. "Password?"

"Let's go upstairs first and see if my room is the same. Maybe nothing really happened." I wanted to ignore the idea of the videos, because if I found out for certain that evil spirits were messing with me or that I was crazy out of my mind, I'd fall completely apart.

I darted upstairs and threw the door open to my room. Still a disaster. I sank to the floor.

Plug stepped over to the desk and fingered Rose's art book. He closed the cover and traced the edges. Then he picked up the tiger-eye stone from the desktop, which I hadn't even noticed earlier. He immediately dropped it, as if it had burned him. He grabbed the half-empty glass of water from my nightstand. Then he used a piece of paper to scoop up the rock and let it plunk into the water.

"What are you doing?" I asked.

"The stone needs to be cleansed and reprogrammed."

"And the water will help with that?"

"It should. Leave it in there for now." He set the glass on the desk next to the art book. "You know, Chelsea could still be the one terrorizing you. You said she knew where the key was hidden. But whoever or whatever it is, you can fight it."

He reached up and lifted the caricature off the wall, leaving a blank spot next to the family photo and homecoming snapshot.

"Is this new?" Plug asked. "I don't remember seeing it when we were up here Monday."

I walked over to him, took the picture from his grasp, and dropped it into the bottom desk drawer.

"When was it drawn?" Plug asked.

"What does it matter?"

He retrieved the caricature and examined the sketch of me with my distorted head and exaggerated eyes. "Because I'm interested. When did you go to Disney World?"

Ants still dotted the edges of the red-and-white-checkered blanket and moved in a uniformed line into the picnic basket. I rubbed my eyes.

"I was eight," I said.

"Special occasion?" Plug asked

"We were celebrating my dad getting into Princeton for his master's program."

With the caricature still in one hand, he pointed at the family portrait on the wall. "This is you with your mom and dad?"

I gritted my teeth.

"How did he die?" Plug asked.

"He had schizophrenia. He committed suicide when I was eleven."

Plug was unflustered by the revelation. He stared at the portrait and said quietly, "My mom died from pancreatic cancer. She was in a lot of pain at the end. Your dad must have been, too, for him to commit suicide."

A tear ran down my cheek.

"Where was the picture of your family taken?" Plug asked.

I wiped my cheeks. "On the East Coast. We lived in New Jersey back then, but less than a year after my dad died my mom was so upset she changed our last names, dyed her hair brown, and moved us out here—clear across the country."

"A bit extreme," Plug said.

"She wanted to forget everything about my dad. She wanted to sever all ties with our lives back there."

"I can still remember when you joined our class halfway through the school year. You were the most beautiful girl I'd ever seen." Plug hung the caricature back up on the wall. "Keep this on the wall as a statement of defiance against what's happening around you."

"Defiance?" I asked.

"Caricatures are a ridiculously inappropriate exaggeration of reality," he said. "You need to laugh in the face of all this."

"Plug, whoever is doing this is getting inside my house. Inside my head. Making me nuts. What if it is a demon?" Zeus came to mind. He had growled and bared his teeth at me, and I had felt compelled to wait on the porch until Manny actually asked me inside.

"What if an evil spirit has possessed me?" I asked Plug.

"Be defiant. Laugh in its face. And to be on the safe side, we'll finish smudging your whole house tonight. The supplies are in my car. And we'll fix the tiger-eye, too."

"What if it's schizophrenia?"

"It's not. Western medicine wants you to think it is. So you'll buy their pills and stay within the boundaries of their system—"

"My mom hated my dad. What if she ends up hating me, too?"

"You're not crazy."

"Maybe you're the one who's crazy," I said.

"Maybe that's why I like you so much." He surprised me with a quick kiss on the forehead. "Go take a shower and change your clothes. It'll make you feel better. While you're doing that I'll check your laptop and pick up your room."

"You're offering to clean?"

"We'll see how far I get." He slipped his hands into mine and pulled me closer. Fire burned within me. He leaned toward me, but stopped a fraction of an inch away from my lips.

He hovered there.

And my breath trembled.

My head seemed disconnected from my body, as if my inner conflicts and emotions were buried in stone like Rodin's sculptures. Unexplainable urges filled my mind.

"The dirty clothes hamper is in the hall closet," I whispered, trying to restrain myself. "And the password to my laptop is Princeton." I studied his lips. "According to Nick, you have an unjustified sense of entitlement."

A smile spread across Plug's face. "That's a matter of opinion. The real question is: how long can you ignore your overwhelming desire for me?" Plug winked at me. He was teasing, but he had no idea of the truth he spoke.

"Take a shower," he said. "I'll pick things up."

We lingered for a moment longer. My head still floated in a fog. And then Plug stepped away from me and toward the hall closet.

I plucked a pair of gray yoga pants, a pink shirt, and clean underwear from the disaster on the bedroom floor.

Once in the bathroom, I studied myself in the mirror. My eyes were darker. I leaned in toward my reflection and poked at my cheeks. My vision blurred for a second and when I refocused my irises were brown instead of green. I blinked. Green. I set my palms against the mirror.

"Are you still in there, Hannah?" I whispered to myself. My breath fogged the mirror, and a dark silhouette appeared behind me. In a split second the image took shape and lunged at me. I spun around to defend myself against the decaying flesh and rotting talons, but nothing struck me. I was alone.

I faced the mirror, and everything seemed normal. I reached for the doorknob and considered asking Plug to come inspect behind the shower curtain for me, but that was silly. I was capable of showering by myself, but my mind drifted toward the idea. Images of the rings on his long fingers touching my skin came to mind. His body pressed to mine.

I steadied myself against the counter. My muscles trembled. I touched my chest to slow my breathing, but then my hand moved, as if it had a will of its own. My fingers traced the line of muscles from my shoulders to my waist—like I had multiple times with Rodin's sculpture in the art book. Heat spread throughout my body. I bit my lip and closed my eyes. Both of my hands caressed my body. A moan escaped my lips.

"You okay?" Plug tapped on the door.

I opened my eyes, and the reflection in the mirror showed a man behind me. His image shimmered. His face was darkened by shadows. I gripped the counter, and he stroked my body.

162

I screamed.

His bulky, hairy hands groped me and yanked me against him. His laughter reverberated off the walls of the small bathroom. I clawed at his grasp and dug my nails into his flesh.

"Stop!" I yelled. "Stop!" I wedged my fingers beneath his. "Let go!" I shrieked.

Plug pounded on the door. "I'm coming in!" he yelled, but I had locked the door.

My hands slipped with sweat, but I continued to fight the man. He shoved me against the counter, and I threw my weight backward against him. He hit the wall, but his grip on me tightened.

Plug threw the door open.

"Help me!" Tears ran down my face. "Get him off!"

Plug's eyes widened, and he stepped back.

I screamed. "Help me!"

"Be gone! You have no power here!" Plug wrenched his arm back and smacked the wall next to me with his open palm. I flinched. "Be gone!" he yelled.

Plug stepped past me, yanked open the shower curtain, and turned on the water. He held his fingers under the flow for a few seconds. Then without looking at me, he said, "Get in the shower."

I stepped toward him and caught my reflection in the mirror, completely naked. I gasped. I could not remember removing my clothes.

"Get in," Plug said again.

"I can't." I was sinking into hysteria, and I couldn't depend upon myself anymore. "I can't trust my own hands. This isn't who I'm supposed to be."

"Stand under the water. Remember how Rose taught us to visualize a safe place? Go there. Make your mind do what you want it to do," he said.

I stepped into the shower, and he started to slide the curtain closed.

"No!" I said. "Leave it open."

"All right." He lowered the lid of the toilet and sat with his back to me. "I'm staying right here."

My hands trembled, then my arms, and then my entire body shook. I steadied myself against the wall of the shower and doubted my strength.

"Picture your safe place, and I'll talk to you," Plug said.

There was no way I could close my eyes. I took a breath and reached for my jasmine shampoo. I lathered up and pretended the water was a soft rainfall. But as I scrubbed my head, I worried that his hands were doing the work. I extended my hands in front of me. I squinted at my fingernails and scraped out the flesh from beneath them. His flesh. My breathing sped up. I gasped for air, as if I was drowning.

"No!" I screamed and slapped the tile of the shower wall. Pain shot from my wrist to my elbow.

"I'm right here," Plug said. "Control your thoughts."

I leaned against the tile and focused on Plug's voice.

"Everything will be okay." He told me stories in a quiet and steady voice. He explained what it was like to grow up with a tattoo artist for a dad, and the fact that he never wanted a tattoo. He described how he earned his black belt in karate two years ago. He talked the entire time, and the constant chatter helped soothe me.

I rinsed my hair. Then I plucked my loofah from the wire basket and squirted shower gel into it. A single ant crawled out from the loofah and scampered up my thumb. It wasn't alone. Behind it more ants swarmed out, as if I'd kicked their nest. They ran up my arms in waves. I dropped the loofah and screamed. Ants covered my entire body like a blanket. I backed into the corner of the shower, swatting the ants from my skin.

Plug clutched my shoulder. "Hannah!"

I continued to scream and bat the ants away.

Plug shook me. "Stop! Whatever you're seeing isn't there. Picture the chaotic hotel lobby and run to the elevator. Push the down button. Get to your safe place. You can do it."

I scrunched my eyes shut and created the images in my mind. I ran to the small log cabin. Smoke rose from its chimney. I spotted a straw broom propped on the steps. I grabbed it and swept the porch of the cabin clean. No ants. No dirt. Nothing but wooden planks. My breathing slowed, and I calmed down.

"You are okay," Plug whispered. After he switched off the shower, he draped a towel over me. He turned away and leaned against the frame of the door.

I stepped out of the shower, dried off my hair, and then I wrapped the towel around me, insulating myself from my own hands. My fingers trembled when I reached for my underwear. I skipped the underwear and tugged the yoga pants up and over my hips as fast as possible. I fiddled with the fabric of the bra. It would be impossible to fasten it and pull the straps over my shoulders without grazing my skin. I let the bra fall next to my underwear. I grabbed my clean shirt and pulled it over my head. The soft fabric brushed my chest, and the tingles began all over.

"No!" I screamed. Plug spun around. He reached out to touch me, but he stopped himself when I jerked backward.

I didn't want anyone touching me. Ever. Again.

He moved out of my way, and I went to my bedroom. He had picked up my room and even made my bed. I yanked a sweatshirt from a hanger in the closet and slipped it over my head. Too loose. I tugged it off and grabbed a new bra from my drawer. I fastened it over my shirt. Problem solved. I avoided touching my skin with the bra on top. I pulled my sweatshirt back over my head. No one would ever know.

I snatched my robe from the hook on the closet door and pulled it on, over all my layers. I wrapped it tightly around my waist and knotted the tie around my rib cage. Better. I tugged on a pair of athletic socks and tucked the hems of my yoga pants into the socks. No ants could crawl inside. I relaxed long enough to notice the fresh odor of burned sage.

"How long was I in the bathroom before you pounded on the door?" I asked.

He waited in the doorway, his gray shirt soaking wet. "Long enough for me to clean your room and smudge the entire house."

I grabbed a clean T-shirt from my closet and held it out to him. He tugged his shirt up and over his head, revealing his long, lean muscles. His arms were tan, but his chest was white, with black hair circling each of his nipples. He took the oversized black Princeton T-shirt from me and pulled it on. It fit him fine.

I perched on the edge of my bed and took a deep breath. "Why do you always wear gray shirts?"

"Because life is gray."

"That's depressing," I said.

"No. It represents the fact that there is truly no black and white in the world, only—"

"But you're an artist. You should want more color in your life."

He smiled and plucked the black T-shirt with bright orange lettering. "With you in my life, I definitely have more color. You've changed me forever."

Plug dropped his wet gray shirt into the trashcan by my desk. He lifted my pearl-handled brush and asked, "May I?" I was unsure what he meant until he pointed at my hair.

I began to bawl.

He sat next to me without touching me. "We'll figure this out. I'll do more research about demons and possession, but I think you had a breakthrough tonight."

"A breakdown, you mean." I wiped my eyes and huffed.

"You survived. You controlled your thoughts."

"Only with your help." I used to love the solitude of a long shower. Now the idea made my gut wrench. At least Plug had been there.

"It's a start," Plug said, "and I think the smudging will work this time." He waggled the brush.

"Only my hair. Do not touch anything else. Not my shoulder. Not my hand. Not my face." I couldn't believe he wanted to brush my hair. Plug: the guy with multiple piercings, a tattooist for a father, and a passion for the occult. He tenderly brushed the knots from my hair, and I tried to imagine Plug without the piercings. An image came to mind of when we were in the sixth grade. During PE, a boy had stolen my jump rope, and Plug, Eugene back then, kicked him in the shin and returned the rope to me.

"Back in sixth grade," I said, "do you remember the jump rope? When you kicked that boy?"

"Yes." Plug continued pulling the bristles in a rhythmic motion. "I was suspended for three days."

I stared at Plug.

"Really," he said. "The PE teacher told my dad I attacked that kid. So my dad enrolled me in martial arts to teach me self-restraint." Plug continued with the brush.

"What else should I know about you?" I asked.

He shrugged and continued brushing my hair. Hopefully, Plug was right. If I practiced my own self-restraint, by changing my thoughts, tonight could be a turning point. Surely things would get better from here.

"All done." He rose and set my brush on my desk next to the laptop.

I pointed at the computer. "Did you see if it recorded anything?"

Plug twisted a ring on his finger. "After everything that's happened tonight, let's forget about the computer for now.

We'll check it tomorrow." He walked toward the door. "Let's go downstairs and watch television until your mom gets home."

I was too exhausted to argue. I followed him out of my room.

Once in the family room, he picked up the remote and plopped into a side chair. The guy who was so eager to touch me before kept his distance now.

"Thanks," I said and curled up on the far end of the couch, but then I reconsidered. If I wanted things to improve, I had to do something about it. Make my own choices rather than react to everything and everyone around me. I moved to the end of the couch closest to Plug and extended my hand to him. He raised his eyebrows.

"I'm sure," I said.

He reached out and held my hand. No tingles. No hallucinations. No panic. Just comfort.

Plug flipped through channels on the television. He settled on *Ultimate Cage Fighting*.

"Seriously?" I asked.

"Hey, we're fighting the unknown here. We need all the inspiration we can get."

"Right." A grin crept across my face, and Plug smiled back at me. I focused on the skills of the fighters and limited my thoughts. It was tiring, and I fell asleep.

Thursday

August 29

I sat on the front steps and waited for Plug to pick me up for school. The brilliant sunshine and fresh morning air reinforced my sensation that things were about to improve. Plug parked at the curb and hopped out to open my door for me.

He wore a V-neck T-shirt as blue as the sky. And I smiled. I brushed past him to take my seat. He smelled like fabric softener, clean and crisp.

"Better today?" he asked.

"Much," I said. "Last night's smudging must have worked, because I feel better than ever." He ran around to the driver's side and slid into his seat.

"You cold?" He motioned toward my outfit.

"No." I plucked at the sweatshirt. "Do I look stupid?"

"If that's what you want to wear, don't worry—"

"I care what you think," I said.

"I'm used to seeing you in fewer clothes."

Images of last night popped into my head, and my chest lit on fire.

He held up his hands. "Wait! I meant you normally wear flip-flops, shorts, and a shirt. Today, you're wearing boots, big jeans, and a sweatshirt." He fidgeted with his lip ring.

What he didn't know: Beneath my jeans, I still had my yoga pants tucked into my athletic socks, and under the bulky sweatshirt, I still wore my bra on the outside of my pink shirt.

I was lying to myself about being better than ever.

He leaned forward and rested his forehead on the steering wheel. "I'm sorry."

"We had some success last night," I said, "and that makes me think things can return to normal, but I'm not there yet. I still need a barrier. I don't want anyone to touch me, and more layers equal more protection."

"What about me?" Plug peeked in my direction. "Should I keep my hands off you?"

"Probably," I said, but even now, as Plug sat back and licked his lips, desire for him churned in my stomach. I longed for his lips to press against mine. A tinge of guilt pricked my heart, and I recalled the tenderness in Manny's eyes, his fingers at the back of my neck, and the shivers along my spine when he first kissed me on the Ferris wheel. I had feelings for them both.

"Hannah?" Plug said.

I halfheartedly smiled. "Just keep your hands where I can see them."

"Promise." He waggled his fingers in the air and then slipped them beneath mine. "Are you ready to talk about what happened in the bathroom last night?"

If I told him, maybe it would minimize the fear lurking in the back of my mind. I squeezed his hand. "My eyes changed color in the mirror. Then something like a demon appeared behind me, but it disappeared when I turned to face it."

"You tried to face it," Plug said. "That's huge." His reassurance comforted me.

"But I lost time. I don't remember undressing. Then when you knocked, I opened my eyes, and there was a guy behind me." My breathing sped up, and my armpits grew wet with sweat. "He groped me with his big, hairy hands."

"He can't hurt you here," Plug said. "You're okay now."

"His facial features were in shadows. I only saw his hands and felt his body against mine." I glanced at Plug's long fingers. "Did you see him when you came into the bathroom? Or was it another one of my delusions?"

"I only saw you, but a demon could've manifested as a man and been only visible to you," Plug said. "Did anything else happen after I left?"

"I have no idea when you left. I slept hard on the couch until my mom woke me this morning when she left for work."

"Your mom got home around midnight. She was surprised to see me, but I told her we'd fallen asleep watching a movie. I doubt she bought it. I apologized and left. But when I was there, nothing else weird happened."

"Maybe the evil spirit used up his energy reserves attacking me physically."

"You researched that?" Plug asked.

"No." I laughed. "The extent of my knowledge comes from horror movies, which, by the way, I will never watch again."

Plug smiled and rubbed his callused thumb across the back of my hand. "So everything was fine in the bathroom this morning?"

"Well, I couldn't bring myself to open the door."

"That's okay," Plug said. "Policing your thoughts and practicing the guided imagery will help you overcome all of this."

I pointed at the time on the dashboard clock. "We're late," I said. Peregrine was a five-minute drive away, and the first bell was about to ring.

Plug twisted the key in the ignition, and we rode in comfortable silence.

We turned into the parking lot, and my phone chimed. Plug pulled into the spot next to Kyla's Mini Cooper, where Nick and Kyla still sat inside. I checked my phone before I got out of the El Camino.

A text from Manny read: Where RU?

I messaged back: At school. Why?

I slipped the phone into my pocket and stepped out to join the other three at the front of the vehicle. Plug held out a huge, wrapped present to me.

"Happy birthday!" they chimed.

"It's not my birthday," I said.

"Today, it is," Kyla said. In the bright sunlight, her violet hair complemented her marigold blouse.

"Can't believe you found one," Plug said to Kyla.

"It was a challenge with such short notice." She patted the gift. "Open it, Hannah. It's from all of us."

I set my backpack on the ground, and my phone chimed in my pocket. I ignored it and focused on the surprise. I tore off the wrapping paper, and my breath caught. I drew my fingertips across the pristine cover of the art history book, still wrapped in cellophane, untarnished by anyone's hands.

"We're a team," Plug said. "We'll help you through this." He pulled me into a hug. I tensed at the full contact, but I closed my eyes and reminded myself I was all right. I relaxed, and then Kyla joined our embrace. I no longer felt as if I was drowning. Plug was my life preserver, and I could conquer anything as long as I held on.

"Okay. Let the girl breathe," Nick said. Plug and Kyla drew back from me. The air was crisp, the sun was bright, and today was a new beginning.

I lifted the heavy book. "Let's take this to Rose now, so there's no possible chance it can get damaged."

"Sounds good," Plug said and nudged the book from my clutch into his own.

The tardy bell rang.

"Who will work the equipment for the broadcast if we're late?" I asked.

"They'll survive without us," Nick said. His white T-shirt with simple black letters read: IF LIFE GIVES YOU MELONS, YOU MAY BE DYSLEXIC. "Mr. Arnold will replace us with other students without even thinking twice."

Plug linked his free arm through mine and said, "As far as I'm concerned, you are irreplaceable."

"Thanks, Plug."

"Rose has a work period first hour," Kyla said. "Let's use the outer door." She pointed toward the end of the building.

"How do you know?" I asked.

"We've been her students for the last three years," Kyla said. "She's like a mother to us, and she'll give us a pass to get into first period late."

Kyla knocked on the locked door, and few seconds later, Rose opened it. The fragrance of freshly brewed herbal tea and crisply toasted bagels washed over me. I could always count on Rose's room having a delicious new aroma.

"Good morning," Rose said.

Plug set the book on the desk next to her cream-cheese-covered bagel.

"What's this?" Rose asked.

"I tore a page in the book you loaned me," I said. "My friends were generous enough to help me find a replacement for you."

Rose reached out and squeezed my hand. I remained calm.

"Thank you," she said, "but you are all tardy. You need to get to class." She stepped away from me and tore four passes off of a tablet.

Plug stole a bite from Rose's bagel, and she smacked his hand.

"That does not belong to you," she said. He laughed through a mouthful of food. She plucked the half-eaten bread from his clutch, and then she gave us the passes.

Nick said goodbye to Kyla, and she headed down a different hall. The rest of us jogged toward broadcasting.

We skidded to a stop at the studio entrance. Nick blocked my view, but I knew the broadcast was already in progress, because Chelsea's bone-grating voice carried a mile away.

Plug wrapped his arm around my waist, and I relaxed into him. I caught his gaze, and electricity lit through me. Plug leaned in and paused. I knew he wanted to kiss me, but his eyes waited for my consent. The ache and hunger I felt for him eroded my fidelity to Manny. We were at school, and anyone could see us. Someone would tell Manny, but I almost didn't care anymore, because with Plug I felt invincible. All my problems and the world around us faded away. I closed the distance between us and kissed Plug. He tasted like cream cheese.

Nick cleared his throat, but Plug and I continued kissing. Plug pulled me against him, and I stroked the silver ring in his lip with my tongue.

"Dude!" Nick said and whacked Plug's shoulder.

Plug drew back from me, and Manny tackled him to the floor. Rage flushed Manny's face, and carpet burns covered his elbows.

Chelsea screamed from the other room, and the lens of the abandoned pedestal camera drifted toward the floor. Students rushed around Manny and Plug to watch them fight. My cheeks heated up. Why didn't Manny tell me he was coming back today?

"Go to a public service announcement!" Mr. Arnold yelled at the broadcast crew.

Manny pounded Plug over and over with his fist. His class ring bit into Plug's flesh. The class ring I'd talked Manny into getting so we would remember our senior year together. Plug did nothing to fight back. He just lay there and watched each blow come at him.

I clutched Manny's shirt and tried to pull him off, but I was too scrawny. Nick grabbed Manny's fist and prevented another swing from connecting.

"Don't hurt him!" I yelled. Nick glared at me. His biceps bulged as he restrained Manny.

Mr. Arnold gripped Manny's shoulders. Together, he and Nick hauled Manny off Plug. Manny got in a swift kick to Plug's side before Nick shoved Manny in the chest. Manny bent forward, held his ribs, and howled in pain.

"Stop!" I yelled.

"Take Manny to the nurse," Mr. Arnold said to Mark.

Mark slipped his arm under Manny's shoulder to support him. I grabbed Manny's hand, but he yanked it away.

Mr. Arnold clutched my elbow.

"Let go!" I wrenched away from him.

I reached out for Manny, but he staggered backward. "Manny—"

"I don't even recognize you," he said. His eyes welled, but he lifted his chin toward the ceiling so no tears would fall. Mark urged him through the door.

"Go help with the camera," Mr. Arnold said to Nick. But Nick ignored Mr. Arnold and helped his friend stand. Blood dripped from Plug's lip, his cheeks were cut, and one eye had already begun to swell.

The group of gawking students parted to let Chelsea through from the studio to the center of the action. Her eyes widened at me, and she broke into her donkey laugh.

"What are you wearing?" Chelsea flipped her long blond hair over her shoulder.

"What are *you* wearing?" I mocked her and stepped toward her. "My tennis shoes you borrowed. The jeans Lily paid for. And that's my blouse." I reached out, clutched the collar, and ripped. Buttons popped off. But Mr. Arnold seized my wrist before I finished tearing the fabric off her.

Chelsea's tan face paled, and she covered her chest.

Mr. Arnold steered me away with his sweaty hand, but I yelled at Chelsea. "You can't even afford to buy your own clothes. You're an imposter. A fake. A no one."

"At least I showered today," she said. The onlookers laughed, and Chelsea turned her back to me.

Mr. Arnold escorted me to the hallway. "Hannah, I've been patient with you this week, but this behavior is unacceptable. You could be expelled."

"You don't have the authority to expel me," I said.

Mr. Arnold glared at me, but before he said anything more, Plug staggered between us.

"We'll go," Plug said.

Mr. Arnold pulled a handkerchief from his pocket and wiped the perspiration from his face. He repositioned his glasses, and then he shook his head slowly as he said to me, "Hannah, you've changed from the girl I knew last year. I don't know what's possessed you, but you've become violent and mean. You are unwelcome in my classroom."

"Come on," Plug said and pressed my back.

"It wasn't my fault." But it was. I'd kissed Plug, even though I loved Manny. It was senseless. If I had been faithful to Manny none of this would have ever happened.

Nick followed us into the hall. "Plug, are you okay?"

"Go help Mr. Arnold," Plug said, "before he kicks you out of class, too."

"Is she worth this?" Nick whispered.

"I can hear you," I said.

Nick glared at me for a second and then went back to broadcasting.

When Plug and I rounded the corner of the hall, he pulled me into the boys' bathroom.

"I can't be in here," I said. "Someone will see us."

"Stop worrying about what other people think." Plug dampened some paper towels in the sink and held them against his bloodied lip. He grimaced in pain. He lifted the paper towels and examined the damage in the mirror. His silver ring had been ripped out, and the flesh was torn.

"You need to see the nurse," I said.

"Manny's there." Plug tried to speak without moving his lips.

"Why didn't you fight back?" Tears ran down my face.

"He saw us kissing."

"But you didn't fight back."

"If I hurt him, I'd hurt you."

I rested my hand on his back. Plug had been so loyal to me when I'd done nothing to deserve it.

"Go check on him," Plug said through his clenched jaw.

"And leave you?"

"You don't belong to me." In one swift motion, Plug spun around and kicked the stall door. It banged against the wall and then swung back and forth until it finally slowed and stilled.

"You belong to him," Plug whispered. "I should have respected that sooner, especially with everything going on around you right now. I'm sorry for hurting you, Hannah."

I studied his gray eyes. "You didn't hurt me. You've helped me."

"I'm going home." He dabbed the paper towel against his bloodied lip.

"You need stitches. Let me go with you." I squeezed his hand.

"The office probably called your mom," Plug said. "You need to be here."

"What about you, and when your dad gets here?"

Plug shook his head. "He left for Vegas today."

I reached up and traced Plug's jaw, but he pulled my fingers away.

"Hannah, you're going to be all right."

"Not without you," I said.

"Yes, even without me," Plug said. "Go check on Manny. It will ease your mind."

I wrapped my arms around his waist and pulled him into me.

"Call me when you get home," Plug said.

"I have an appointment this afternoon with the psychiatrist."

"Call me after," he said and pressed his forehead against mine.

We left the bathroom together, but separated at the end of the hall.

"Go home," a man's voice said behind me. I spun around to see if Plug was still in the hallway, but I was alone. I rubbed my face, and then I covered my ears.

"Control your thoughts," I whispered to myself. To help focus, I counted each step to the nurse's office.

Mark huffed when he saw me. "Haven't you caused enough trouble?"

My throat tightened, and I feared if I spoke, I'd start sobbing. So I kept quiet. The room smelled of antiseptic. Manny sat on top of the nurse's desk, and she wrapped his ribs. Bruises peeked out from the edges of the white tape.

"Only leave this on for a few hours," she said, "to help you get past this immediate pain."

Manny nodded, but his face contorted.

The nurse noticed me and said, "Hannah, you can wait in the front office. They've already phoned your mother. She'll be here soon."

"Can I have a minute with Manny?" I asked.

"One minute," she said and prodded Mark to leave with her.

He bumped into me as he left. "Slut," he said, loudly enough for the whole world to hear.

Manny huffed, as though he agreed. And in that moment I knew things had changed between us forever. I flashed back to the fair when Jordan had said obnoxious things about me stuffing his shorts with money and Manny had come to my defense and told him never to talk to me that way. But now, when Mark called me a slut, Manny did nothing to defend me. The difference was at the fair I'd done nothing wrong, and today I had.

Manny fumbled with his shirt. He started to lift it, but he stopped and groaned with the pain. The desk squeaked under his shifting weight.

"Let me help you." I reached for his shirt, but he held up a finger.

"No," he said.

I moved closer and touched his wrist. "Manny, let me—"

"No!" He jerked away, and for a split second I feared he would hit me, just like my father had, just like Jordan's mother had. But instead, he stopped himself and clenched his fingers into a tight fist. Through gritted teeth, he said to me, "You kissed Eugene Polaski in front of everyone. He was all over you. Is that who you are now? Do you let anyone put their hands all over you?"

Images from last night in my bathroom flooded my mind. Those large, hairy hands touching me. Panic bubbled inside of me. I peered at Manny's hands. His were smaller, smoother, and hairless, but his knuckles were covered with blood from Plug's face. I gasped for air, and the edges of my vision blurred. I stumbled over to the desk chair and sank down. Manny kept yelling at me.

"We had something special. Something forever. But now, how am I supposed to get the image of you kissing Eugene out of my head? I used to think we were alike—we wanted the same things—but ever since the accident, you've changed."

"I have not."

"Can't you see how Eugene is making you different? You used to care about your appearance, but now you're dressed like a bum in winter."

I covered my face and leaned forward. Nausea overtook me, and the bitter taste of bile filled my mouth. I hung my head between my knees and tried to breathe.

A deep voice said, "You're just like your dad."

I jerked up and glared at Manny.

"What'd you say?" I asked.

"I said he's changing you. He's manipulating you. Convincing you to do things you never would have done a week ago." Manny rubbed his knuckles against his pants. "Has he convinced you to spread your legs for him, too, or just your lips?"

My mouth dropped open. And my heart sank. His words hurt worse than any slap across my face could have.

"Never mind," Manny whispered. "I don't want to know."

"You have no right to judge me," I said and stood up.

"You kissed Eugene!" Manny moved closer to me. "We were supposed to go to Princeton together. Be together forever. And instead you kissed Eugene." Manny set a hand on his taped ribs. "I never want to see you again."

"Manny, we've been friends for years." I clutched his bare shoulder, and he jerked away.

"And I can't erase the image of Eugene's lips all over yours. I can't even look at you without seeing him touching you."

"Manny—"

"No."

We reached an impasse. There was no way he could excuse what I'd done. And there was no way to erase the awful things he'd said. We would never return to the way we were before the accident.

I ran out the front doors of the school, sank to the curb, and bawled. I replayed the incidents in my mind. Less than thirty minutes ago, I had believed things could return to normal, but Manny made it sound as if I wasn't even myself anymore.

A shadow moved across the asphalt, and I glanced skyward. Storm clouds formed and drifted in front of the sun. A breeze kicked up the dirt next to the curb where I waited, and the temperature dropped. Hopefully, Mom would get here before the clouds burst open. Ants scurried over the leaves and debris, searching for shelter. Several darted up the side of my boot. I let them explore. They could bite me, but even if they did, it wouldn't be real. I set my fingers in their path and let them crawl across my skin.

Mom drove up to the curb. I stood and dusted myself off.

I opened the door of the Prius and slid into the passenger seat. "Glad you got here before the rain dumped on me," I said and buckled in.

Mom leaned forward and scrutinized the sky through the windshield. Then she reached over and clutched my hand.

"I need to go into the office and sign you out," she said.

"Can we please just leave?" I asked.

"The school said there'd been a fight. Are you hurt?" She eyed me up and down.

"Manny attacked Plug," I said.

Her eyebrows lifted. "Plug?"

"I mean Eugene."

Mom shifted into drive. "The boy who was at the house last night?" Mom asked and drove away.

"Yes."

"What provoked the fight?"

"Manny saw Eugene kiss me."

"I thought you and Manny were together."

"I thought we were, too." More tears spilled down my cheeks. "But Manny just broke up with me." I wiped my face with the sleeve of my sweatshirt.

"Are you sleeping with Eugene?" Mom asked.

"No! How could you even ask that?"

"Because Eugene was at the house late last night, and Manny's a nice boy. I can't imagine him punching a guy unless he deserved it."

"You're taking Manny's side?"

"No, I'm on your side." She parked in the driveway of our house. "Run inside and change your clothes."

"Why?"

"I refuse to take you to the hotel like that. Brush your hair, too."

"Let me stay home." I said.

"We've got the doctor's appointment in a few hours, and I'm missing auditions as we—"

"What auditions?" I asked.

"For the hotel's new lounge. I told you about it the other night. Don't you remember?" Mom tilted her head toward me, but she didn't wait for me to answer. "You're coming with me where I can keep an eye on you. Then we'll go see Dr. James." She pointed to the house. "Go. I'll wait here and make some phone calls." She lifted her phone from her purse.

I walked to the front door and let myself in. The fragrance of sage filled the house, and I pulled in a lungful. I felt peaceful, as if I'd left my problems outside. I ran up the stairs and paused in front of the bathroom door.

I didn't remember Plug smudging the bathroom—he said he'd done the rest of the house while I was in the bathroom. I moved away from the door and went to my bedroom. I stood in front of my full-length mirror and pulled my sweatshirt over my head. My white bra looked absurd on the outside of my pink shirt, but I couldn't bring myself to touch it. I kicked off my boots and stepped out of my jeans.

My cell phone fell to the floor, and I snatched it up. I had missed a message from Manny. I clicked on it. He had replied to this morning's message. I'd ignored it when I opened the wrapped art book.

He'd written: I'm in broadcasting. Where RU? I can't wait to spend the day with you.

If I had checked my phone before we ran to broadcasting, things would have turned out differently today, but there was no going back now. Manny had been my anchor, and the weight of losing him tugged me down. I was drowning. I needed Plug to keep me afloat. I sent a text to Plug and asked if he got stitches.

My phone vibrated with a new message. It was from Lily: What in the world happened at school today? Call me ASAP!

How could I answer when I was still uncertain myself about what had happened?

I set my phone on my bed and wiped my face. Then I examined my reflection in the mirror. Athletic socks, yoga pants, and my bra on the outside of my shirt. No makeup. My hair looked as if I'd been through a hurricane. I brushed it and braided it down the back. In my closet, I found my thin white hoodie—better than a sweatshirt in August—and pulled it on. I zipped it high enough to conceal my bra. I removed my socks and slipped my feet into a pair of matching flip-flops. I re-evaluated myself in the mirror. Almost good enough. I leaned into the mirror and swiped on some mascara. Green eyes. I blinked. Brown eyes. I closed my eyes and willed them to change back. I peered into the mirror. Brown eyes still. I dropped the mascara to the floor.

Plug smudged the house, but he didn't smudge me. An evil spirit could be inside of me. My heart raced, and my hands began to itch.

I grabbed my phone off the bed and bolted out of the house.

Mom was still talking on her cell when I plopped into the seat next to her. She ended her call and turned to me.

"Are those the only clothes you could find?" she asked.

"What color are my eyes?" I leaned toward her and opened wide.

"Green," she said. I flipped down the visor and opened the embedded mirror. Mom was right. Green, again.

"My clothes are fine." I wished I was too. "My shirt is Nike, my hoodie is Aéropostale, my yoga pants are New Balance, and my flip-flops . . . well, they might be from Walmart. Want me to change?" I wiggled my toes.

Mom started the car and pulled out of the driveway.

"Could we visit Lily before we go to the hotel?"

"I'm missing auditions, Hannah."

"I'll be quick," I said. "I just need to see her in person, to know for myself that she's okay."

Mom glanced at me and then to the road. "Okay, but it has to be a fast visit today."

"I promise."

"And I spoke with your principal," Mom said. "He's agreed to let you come back to school tomorrow and try again, but you'll spend first period in the library from now on. Do not try to speak to Mr. Arnold, or Chelsea, or Manny. Those are the conditions. Can you do that?"

"What choice do I have?"

⇥ • ⇤

Lily's new room was dreary. Slatted vertical blinds covered the window, and shadows shifted in the corners. I hurried to the window and yanked open the blinds, flooding the room with sunlight.

"No, too bright." Lily shaded her swollen eyes.

I tugged the blinds back across the window until Lily's face was cast into the darkness. Then I stopped and allowed a bit of light into the remainder of the room.

"Where's your mother?" my mom asked Lily.

"Cafeteria." Lily's lips were engorged and covered with an ointment. A gloomy pallor still masked her formerly tan and vibrant face.

Mom moved to Lily's bedside and set her hand on the railing. "We can't stay long today, but we're so glad to see that you're doing better."

I clutched Lily's fingers, and she jerked away. She covered her nose and mouth with both hands.

"What?" I asked.

She slowly removed her hands from her face. An oxygen tube dangled beneath her nose and snaked back to an outlet in the wall.

"What is that awful smell?" Lily asked.

I sniffed the cuff of my hoodie. "Burned sage."

Out of habit, Lily lifted a finger to twist a strand of her hair, but it was all gone. She plucked at the gauze wrapped around her head instead.

"Hannah, what's happened to you?" Lily asked.

Nothing. Everything. I didn't really know for sure.

Mom answered for me. "She's had some bumps and bruises of her own, but we're working through it."

"I'm still the same person I was last week," I said.

"I know," Mom said.

"Chelsea called me," Lily said.

"Don't believe her lies."

"She said you ripped the blouse right off of her."

Mom pursed her lips.

"She's been horrible to me," I said. "And technically it was my freaking shirt."

"At least ten other people have texted me about it," Lily said.

"And?" I asked.

Lily tilted her head toward my mom, signaling that she couldn't say in front of her.

"Go ahead and say it," I said. "The principal already told her his version of the events."

"Did you . . ." Lily gripped my fingers, lowered her voice, and spoke quickly. "Did you really make out with Eugene Polaski in front of everyone?"

"It wasn't like that."

"Hannah, I'm worried about you."

"So am I," my mom whispered.

I scratched at my neck. "Come on, let's not waste our time talking about the idiots at school. Let's talk about you," I said to Lily. "Are you feeling any better?"

Lily shook her head. "I hurt worse today, but the doctors keep saying I'll make a full recovery." Tears streamed out of the corners of her swollen eyes. "They're changing my medication to see if it'll make a difference, but I'd give anything for this pain to go away. I'd give anything to be with Jordan again."

I wiped a tear from my own face. "I wish I could fix it for you." Lily's busted and bruised face made me realize just how broken her spirit was too, and knowing I'd caused that was more than I could handle on top of everything else that had happened today.

A nurse came in to check on Lily.

"We should be going," Mom said and checked her wristwatch.

"Hang in there," I said to Lily and squeezed her hand.

"You, too," she whispered back.

⇥ • ⇤

Mom drove to the far corner of the hotel's underground garage and parked. We rode the freight elevator to the fourth floor, walked through the back halls, and entered the new lounge through an employee entrance. A locker room led to a small kitchen, which opened to the main part of the lounge. On the stage, a pianist played a jazz piece.

We wandered over to a table where two men sat. I recognized Mom's assistant manager, Mr. Holloday, but not the other guy. Mom joined them, and I took a seat at the table right behind them. When the audition ended and the pianist left the lounge, Mom apologized.

"How many did I miss?" she asked.

"Five auditions, but trust me, you didn't miss any talent," the guy said. He reviewed some of the various details with her. When he finished, Mom waved me over to them.

"Hannah, you remember Mr. Holloday," she said.

He rose and extended his hand to me. I shook it. Mr. Holloday wore a business suit similar to Mom's and was somewhere near her age.

"Nice to see you, Hannah," he said.

"And this is Kevin, the new lounge manager," Mom said.

He also shook my hand, but he was younger, and he dressed in slacks and a pinstriped oxford shirt.

"Nice to meet you," I said, as if it was just another take-your-daughter-to-work day.

"Who do we have up next?" Mom asked.

"Several more singers, a comedienne, and a hypnotist," Kevin read off a list.

"A hypnotist?" I asked.

"Yes," Kevin said, "his description says he can hypnotize anyone, anywhere, in less than fifteen seconds through a method called rapid induction. Sounds cool, right?" The hairs on the back of my neck stood.

"What's his name?" I asked, but before Kevin answered, Mom rose and touched my arm.

"I need you to wait quietly while we finish these auditions. Do you have a book to read or something?" She guided me to a table farther away from the stage and back in the shadows. I dreaded sitting in the darkness by myself.

"Hannah?" Mom said.

"What?"

"Do you have a book to read?"

"Why would you want a hypnotist in your lounge? Shouldn't you hire a band or something?" I rubbed my neck and tried to relax my nerves. I wanted to stay far away from any hypnotists.

"Just sit." Mom stepped away but turned back to me. "And stay put."

I slid down in the seat and pulled out my cell. I texted Plug: You okay?

I slid the phone onto the table and watched the auditions.

The first guy walked onto the stage and shaded his eyes from the spotlights. "Does it have to be so bright?" he asked. "I can hardly see you three."

"Sorry," Kevin said, "the lights are preset for the auditions. Do the best you can."

I leaned back and closed my eyes while the singers performed. They took forever. I checked my phone to see if Plug had replied yet. Nothing.

The comedienne started out kind of funny, but then her language became vulgar and her jokes nasty.

Mom interrupted her. "No, thank you. Your act isn't right for our lounge."

The lady stared forward with her hands on her hips.

"You can go," Mom said and pointed to the doors. The comedienne capitulated and left.

A few moments later an older man stepped onto the stage. He wore black shiny shoes, a black suit, a white shirt, and a black glittered bowtie. His face, too tan. His hair, too black. He clapped his huge hands together, and his bleached teeth glowed under the glare of the spotlights.

I gasped.

He squinted in my direction. I shrank down in my seat before he shaded his eyes from the bright lights.

"Are there other people in here?" he asked.

"What is your name?" Mom asked him.

The hypnotist smiled at the managers. "Harry Hurricane—Hypnotist in a Hurry and Master of the Rapid Induction."

"It says on your application," Kevin said, "that you can hypnotize anyone, anywhere, in less than fifteen seconds. Is that—"

"Not your stage name," Mom interrupted. "What is your actual name?" My mom, ever impatient, did not wait for him to respond. "Do I know you?"

The hypnotist ignored her. "Yes, fifteen seconds, but I'll need a volunteer for my demonstration."

Mom kicked back her chair and stood. "John Harrison?"

The hypnotist's smile faded.

"More than five years later and you're still a street peddler."

"Hey, don't insult—"

"No, don't insult me. You're a fool if you think you can barge into my life. Get out of my hotel," she said.

He narrowed his eyes at her and raised a hand. "Wait a minute—"

"Not open for discussion. Leave, or I will call security," she said.

Mr. Holloday rose from his chair and blocked my view of the hypnotist. Mr. Holloday stepped toward the stage.

"I'll go," the hypnotist said, "but don't think this is the end, Beth."

Mr. Holloday escorted the man out of the lounge.

Kevin muttered something to Mom that I couldn't hear from where I sat.

"No," Mom said to him. "You need to think about what type of clientele you want coming to the lounge. The act we select will determine the mood. There's a huge difference between a jazz pianist and a—"

"I think—"

"We're done for today," Mom said. "I have to take my daughter to a doctor's appointment. You narrow it down to three options, and we'll revisit this in the morning." She gathered her papers and stepped away from the table.

"Hannah!" She barked at me. I stuck my phone in the pocket of my hoodie and hustled down to meet her. She clutched my elbow and herded me out the rear door of the lounge.

"I think that was the same guy from the fair," I said and marched down the back hallway of the hotel next to Mom.

"What guy?" Mom asked.

"The hypnotist."

She stopped walking and faced me. She opened her mouth, as if she was going to say something, but then she closed it. She frowned and then finally said, "Let me get this straight, you're telling me John Harrison, the man who was just in the lounge, was the hypnotist at the fair?"

"I think so." I shifted my weight from one foot to the other. "The guy at the fair had white hair and wore jeans and sneakers, but they both had these big—"

"Hannah, what was the name of the guy at the fair?"

"Gyro, Jeero, I'm not sure, but he was really tan like this guy—"

"Hannah, they're all tan. It's stage makeup."

"But the voice—"

"A deep voice is necessary for their performance, but . . ." Without finishing, Mom turned and moved down the hall. I hustled to keep up.

"You acted as if you knew this guy," I said.

"We met at Princeton," she said.

"How?"

"A department barbecue for your dad's graduate program."

"And you still hate him?" I asked.

She stopped walking again. "Yes, Hannah, I still hate him. And I'll check into it to see if he was the hypnotist at the fair. But right now we have to hurry up or we'll be late to your appointment."

⇥ • ⇤

Everyone in the reception area sat in pairs: one crazy person for each companion. The patients had nervous twitches and darting eyes. The companions read magazines or novels. At least we were different, but then I glanced at Mom. She read a magazine, and my knee bounced up and down. I held my breath and stilled my knee. I grabbed a magazine from the side table and flipped through the pages, but nothing interested me. I tossed it back onto the pile and rubbed my palms against my yoga pants.

Was crazy contagious?

I needed to remember to wash my hands after we left.

The doctors probably made patients wait out here forever to weaken their resolves, lower their defenses. Sunlight glinted off the windows, and higher up in the panes near the ceiling, scratches in familiar patterns marred the glass. I stepped closer for a better angle and tilted my head to the side to study them. Six sets of five. Like claw marks in the dirt. Or fingernails on a chalkboard. Or like talons from a demon trying to scratch its way out of the

191

room. I stepped up onto a nearby chair and reached up toward the marks. I stretched on my tiptoes to reach them. The streaks were unmarred by my touch. They were etched into the glass.

"Hannah?" Dr. James called my name from the side door.

Mom set her magazine down and noticed me. "Hannah! What are you doing? Get down!"

Dr. James waited at the door. His shoulders lifted as he inhaled through his giant crooked schnoz.

I hopped down and followed Mom across the reception area.

"How are you, Hannah?" He patted my shoulder, and I jerked away. "I apologize. I shouldn't have touched you without asking."

His hand was bulky but not hairy. He stepped away from me and fingered his black-and-white-striped tie. I took a deep breath and reminded myself I was okay. I was with my mom. Everything would be fine.

He motioned for me to move down the hall. "Second door on the left," he said. We entered. Two oversized leather chairs, a two-person couch, and a desk filled the room.

"Have a seat, Hannah," he said.

I sank into an oversized leather chair. Across from me on the wall hung the typical framed diplomas and certificates, but in the middle of them was a mesmerizing piece of art. Framed and matted, the picture was sketched on paper torn from a large tablet. The paper—yellowed with time—had been torn down the middle and pieced back together with discolored Scotch tape. The right half of the paper featured a fine-line drawing of a beautiful girl with flowing hair, a vibrant smile, and a piercing eye. The left half used a heavier hand, with charcoal instead of a pencil. Her hair hung like spider legs tangled together, her lips drooped like a thirsty flower, and her eye was suspended like a specter in the night. Even though the sketch appeared to be two separate pieces taped together, a large brushstroke of red paint carried from the lower left of the paper, over the top of the tape in the middle, across to the right corner, and up the right side of the yellowed paper.

"Have a seat, Hannah," Dr. James said again.

He paused in the doorway, and I stood inches away from the artwork. I couldn't remember moving across the small office from the chair that I'd already sat in.

Focus.

This time, I settled into the leather chair that faced the door.

He took the other chair, and Mom perched on the couch.

"Normally, my appointments are only with the patient, but I figured you both would be more comfortable if we started out together with the three of us."

Mom clutched her purse in her lap.

"I'll begin with some general questions. Then we'll get to specifics. Sound all right, Hannah?"

I nodded.

"First, Mrs. O'Leary, how do think your daughter is doing?"

"Things have changed."

"Why do you say that?" he asked.

"She's become apathetic toward things that used to matter to her." Mom set her purse on the carpet.

"How do you know this?"

"Simple observation. She's less interested in her appearance and less interested in school. She's forgotten things."

The doctor's forehead wrinkled. "Can you tell me more?"

"Appearance"—Mom waved up and down at me. "A week ago, she would have never gone out in public in that outfit. She's wearing exercise clothes. Plus, it's hot outside, and she's bundled up, as if it's cold. Schoolwork"—Mom crossed her legs. "She dropped several of her classes, and today she was nearly suspended. Forgetting things"—Mom wrung her hands together. "Perhaps she's sleepwalking, but she has forgotten where she's been and forgotten things she's done."

The doctor took notes before lifting his head. His eyes went from her to me. "Hannah, what do you think of all this?"

Mom looked at me the way she used to look at Dad, fearing an outburst at any moment. I needed her to be proud of me, but could she still love me if I ended up being like Dad?

"Hannah?" Dr. James said.

"What?" I asked.

"Do you disagree with anything your mother said?"

"No."

He wrote more on his legal pad. Then he relaxed back into his chair and crossed his right ankle over his left knee.

"Hannah, since we spoke in the hospital have you seen things other people haven't? Heard things? Smelled things? Basically, have you sensed things that no one else has?"

I studied the floor and worried about how to answer. If I admitted to the evil spirits, Dr. James would for sure diagnose me as crazy and sentence me to weekly sessions. I'd refuse to come back for regular sessions alone with him. I never wanted to be alone with any man. An ant crawled along the floorboard toward Mom's purse. She'd freak if she found it in there later. Scream and drop her purse in the middle of a restaurant or store. But then she'd understand how I've felt this past week. I wouldn't be alone. So I remained quiet, and the ant crawled up the side of her purse, along the clasp, and vanished inside.

"Hannah?" The doctor's voice brought me back to the moment.

"What?" I asked.

"She sees things all the time," Mom answered for me. "Today, when I picked her up from school, she believed the clouds were going to burst open and dump rain on her—"

"They were," I said.

"The sky has been clear and cloudless all day." She twisted the watch around her wrist. "She thinks evil spirits have attached themselves to her. She sees black smoke where there is none. She thinks someone is stalking her, taunting her with a pink elephant—"

"You saw the elephant. You know that's real," I said.

"The elephant was real," Mom said, "but it's not moving on its own, and no one else is moving it. You are the one moving it from place to place."

That was a lie.

"Okay." The doctor lifted his hand toward Mom and then turned toward me. "Hannah, let's talk about your emotions for a minute. Have you experienced less emotion than normal the past few days, or have you expressed inappropriate emotions in some situations, or is it harder to experience pleasure?"

"Jordan died," I said. "Yes, it's harder to experience any kind of pleasure." And Manny broke up with me. That was not pleasurable.

"What about inappropriate emotions?" Dr. James asked.

Images of me lunging across the desk at Chelsea popped into my head alongside images of me pawing all over Manny in his family room. And Manny said he could never get the image of me kissing Plug out of his mind.

"No," I said.

Mom groaned. "She was kicked out of class today because she was kissing one boy, and her boyfriend punched him. Afterward Hannah ripped the blouse off of a girl in the class."

"Hannah, have you had any more hallucinations?" Dr. James asked.

I glanced at Mom.

"Tell him," she said. I shook my head. She described the incidents she knew about: The pizza burning. The elephant moving. Sleeping in her room. She had no clue about the warehouse, the ants, the letters, or the man in the bathroom.

"Based on the things we've discussed so far and your family history, it's very likely you're suffering from schizophrenia."

Mom's head snapped toward the doctor. "No, she is not."

"What do you think the problem is, then, Mrs. O'Leary?" he asked.

"Post-traumatic stress disorder. That's all. It's fixable."

"Sure. It could be," he said, "but let's be prudent and start Hannah on some antipsychotic medication and begin daily therapy."

"Daily?" I asked.

He tapped his pen against his legal pad. "With the drastic behavior changes in the few days since I saw you in the hospital, daily therapy is necessary if you want to improve."

My mom nodded her consent, but his gaze was glued to me. He leaned forward in his chair and rested his elbows on his knees.

"In order for you to get better," he said, "I need you to promise to do a few things."

I waited for him to continue. I watched him and reminded myself to focus. Don't think about the ants trailing along the floor and into Mom's purse. Focus on what he's saying.

"I need you to promise you'll take the prescribed medication. I need you to promise to keep a journal of everything you experience, especially the things you think are unusual. And I need you to promise to keep your appointments with me. Can you do these three things?"

He held the authority here, and so I conceded.

⇥ • ⇤

I lingered in the downstairs' guest bathroom and read the tiny words on the gargantuan pamphlet that came with the prescription.

Side effects: fever, shaking, confusion, sweating, pain, weakness, twitching, palpitations, diabetes, high cholesterol, weight gain, fainting, dizziness, feeling of inner restlessness, missed menstrual periods, leakage of milk from the breasts, problems with erection.

Warnings: avoid driving a car, avoid doing things that require you to be alert, be careful when exercising, do not drink alcohol.

Except for a few things on the list (like diabetes, milk leakage, and erectile dysfunction) I already had these symptoms.

I removed the child safety cap from bottle and poured several of the pills into my hand. My fingers twitched. My heart palpitated. Would these pills help me or make me worse? I funneled the pills back into the bottle and threw away the warning sheet.

I ran up the stairs to my room. My laptop was just as I had left it, but the tiger-eye stone and pearl-handled hairbrush sat a few inches away from the computer. I reached out and touched each of them. Whether or not Plug had fixed the stone didn't matter anymore. Clearly the freaking rock offered no protection against psychotic delusions. I lifted the brush and then whacked it against the rock, as if I'd hit a fly with a plastic swatter. No result. I was tired of the stone showing up in unexpected places. I smashed the head of the brush against it again. And again, until the handle of the brush cracked and broke free from the head. The tiger-eye remained undamaged. I swept it and the brush to the floor and pulled the laptop closer.

I opened a new window and Googled symptoms of demonic possession: fever, confusion, sweating, twitching, palpitations, dizziness, feeling of inner restlessness, uneasiness around animals.

At least with evil spirits, I could exercise without worrying about my breasts leaking milk. I peered at the Disney World picture hanging on the wall. Plug had said, *Caricatures are a ridiculously inappropriate exaggeration of reality.* My life had become exactly that—an inappropriate exaggeration.

I Googled guided imagery and read for a while. Then I lifted the bottle of pills. The side effects scared me more than the idea of seeing more black smoke, but not more than seeing a man grope me. If a pill would keep the terrors away, I should take them. I began to sweat. I removed my hoodie and laughed at myself when I saw the bra on top of my shirt. I appeared insane. Things were never going to improve at this rate.

I clicked on Nick's recording program. I should have watched the previous recordings, but I couldn't bring myself to do it. I didn't want to see proof that I was schizophrenic. But I clicked the record icon and stepped away from the desk. I climbed onto my bed. I kicked off my flip-flops and scrunched up my pillow under my head. I closed my eyes, and I dreamed of Manny and his family, protected in their blessed home. I sneaked around the perimeter of his house, unable to get inside. Circled it and circled it. Smoke swirled everywhere and made it hard to breathe and hard to see. The smell reminded me of when my car exploded after the accident. Reminded me of that moment when I feared Manny was burning to death.

BOOK THREE

Skepticism

A blind acceptance of absurdities leads
to the undertaking of atrocities.

Friday
August 30

I jolted upright in bed.

Plug shook my shoulder. "Hannah!"

"What are you doing here?" I squinted at the clock: 7:15 A.M.

"We're late."

"Did you sneak into my room?" I asked. "Or did my mom let you in?"

"Haven't seen her."

I glared at him.

"You didn't answer your phone," he said. "I was worried about you."

Had I really slept since yesterday afternoon? I flung myself back onto my pillow.

"Hannah, get up." Plug pulled at my quilt, but I tugged it closer. He let go, and then he climbed over me and lay at my side.

"If you're staying, I'm staying," he said.

I tilted my head toward him, our noses inches apart. His left eyelid had become purple and puffy since yesterday, and black stitches held his lower lip together.

"Does it hurt?" I pointed but then touched my own lower lip.

"It's okay," he said.

"Doesn't look okay."

"Neither do you."

I rolled over and threw off the quilt. I swung my legs over the edge of the bed, surprised that I was fully dressed and wearing shoes. A horrible stench made my stomach knot.

"What is that smell?"

"You." Plug climbed off the bed. He wore a new dark teal T-shirt, which made his gray eyes seem brighter. "Did you sleep like that?" He motioned toward my outfit.

I fingered the grimy, tattered sweatshirt that I'd never seen before. I ran my hand over the unfamiliar baggy jeans. Flakes fell to the floor as I tapped the mud-encrusted shoes together. Gasoline fumes from the sweatshirt made my head spin. I pinched my nose, and I tried to stand. But the room blurred, and my knees gave out. Plug caught my elbow and helped me to the edge of the bed.

"I have such a headache," I said.

"You need a shower."

"No."

"Eventually, you'll have to shower. You stink."

"Rude."

"Truth," he said. "Would you prefer I lie?"

I covered my mouth and nose and attempted to filter the air I breathed. Maybe this was how Lily felt when she smelled my stink yesterday. I stumbled to my closet and tugged off the wretched sweatshirt, which then exposed the bra and pink shirt I'd worn since Wednesday night. My clothes were absurd, and my body odor was ripe, but I refused to change. Not today. I slipped on a clean navy hoodie and zipped it up to my neck. Then I moved to my desk and spritzed myself with jasmine body spray. I squirted more onto my fingers and rubbed the scent beneath my nose. I ran my hands over my day-old braid. Loose strands of hair stuck out, but it was good enough.

Plug picked up the prescription bottle from my desk and read the label. "Did you start taking these?"

I plucked the bottle from his grasp and tossed it to the bed. "No, but I should have."

"You are not schizophrenic," Plug said.

"You do not know that."

"Let's watch the videos on your laptop," he said.

"No, we're late."

"You're avoiding this. The only way to defeat the unknown is to meet it straight on."

I shuddered and turned away from him. "We can check it in the library. Let's go." I spotted my cell phone on the floor by the bed and snatched it up. Plug carried the laptop, and we headed downstairs.

A note taped to the inside of the front door read:

Called into work. Phone if you need me. Mom

I pulled the note off the door and wondered if she had gone into work last night or early this morning. Didn't matter. I swung open the door. The air was murky, and I gagged when I breathed in the smoke.

"Something's burning," I said, but then I regretted saying it aloud. I was probably hallucinating.

"Must be a fire nearby," Plug said.

"You smell it, too?"

"Of course I do, Hannah."

He set his hand on my back. His warmth radiated through my layers of clothes. Plug understood what was happening to me better than anyone else. I studied the cuts and bruises on his face, reminders that he hadn't fought back against Manny.

"Yesterday, in the nurse's office," I said, "Mark called me a slut, and Manny said he never wanted to see me again."

Plug stroked my ear with his callused thumb. My chest tightened, and tears threatened to spill. Plug stepped away and walked to the El Camino. He opened the door for me, but I hesitated on the porch. He had been so patient with me when everyone else had turned away. I needed him to help me get through this day.

I trudged across the grass and sank into the passenger seat. Dried mud flaked off my shoes onto the floor mat.

"No respect for a classic work of art." Plug poked my shoulder and grinned.

"Sorry," I said. "I don't know how they got so dirty."

"No worries," he said. "I'll clean it later." He set the laptop behind my seat, walked around to the driver's side, and got in. He started the engine, and even though I'd changed out of the other sweatshirt, the aroma of gasoline still filled the interior. Plug rolled down his window and set the fan to high. "Things will improve," he said and drove down the street.

Plumes of gray smoke billowed across the pale blue sky, highlighted with swirls of white at the top and tinted with black at the bottom. I asked Plug to turn a different direction than normal through my neighborhood to follow the smoke. We came around the corner, and two fire trucks obscured the front of Manny's house.

"Pull over!"

"Not a good idea," Plug said.

"Pull over or I'll jump out!" I released my seat belt and reached for the door.

Plug swerved to the curb, and I had my door open before he came to a complete stop. I bolted across the lawn toward the house, but a fireman grabbed my arm and stopped me.

"Let me go!"

"You can't go up there." He tugged me back to the curb where the neighbors hovered.

I clutched the fireman's jacket. "Where's Manny? Where's his family?"

He radioed someone, told them to come to the sidewalk, and continued to restrain me.

I beat my fists against his chest. "Answer me!"

"You need to stay back," he said.

Plug ran over to us and pulled away my fists, but the fireman kept his grip on my arm. Plug stood to the side of me and rested his hand on my shoulder.

The flames had already been extinguished, but the house continued to smolder. Firemen picked away at the darkened, charred remains of the house's siding. A gaping hole at least four feet wide marred the second-story face of the house. Windows had been knocked out. Screens lay on the ground. And broken glass sparkled in the puddles glistening in the morning sun.

The fireman tightened his grip on my arm.

"Let go of me," I said and stomped on his boot. I tried to pull away, but he refused to release me.

"You need to stay here," he said.

A guy in a business shirt and slacks marched over to us.

"Hannah O' Leary?" he asked.

"Yes," I said.

"I'm Detective Samuelson." He looked me up and down, and his eyebrows creased. He plucked a handkerchief from his back pocket and covered his nose.

"Is Manny okay?" I struggled to maintain my composure. Someone needed to answer me soon, or I would explode.

The detective turned to the fireman. "You can go. I've got this."

I slipped my fingers through Plug's and squeezed. Out of habit, he started to fiddle with his lip ring, but it was gone, and he winced when his tongue touched the stitches.

"Did you set fire to the Santos's home?" the detective asked.

"No, I would never—"

"Where were you this morning?" he asked. "I went to your house, but there was no answer at the door."

"I was asleep," I said.

"Where were you between ten P.M. and two A.M.?"

"At home asleep."

"Was anyone with you?"

"My mom." But her note said she was called into work, and I had no idea when that was.

"Did you leave the house during the night?" he asked.

"No." But my shoes were caked with dirt, and I smelled like gasoline.

"We have a witness who called nine-one-one," Detective Samuelson said. "She said she saw you, specifically, at the scene."

"What witness?"

Another fireman called out to the detective and waved him over toward the damaged house. The detective locked eyes with me. "Stay put. I have more questions for you." He jogged toward the house, and the waiting fireman held up a red gasoline can.

"I have a bad feeling," I said to Plug.

"Understatement."

"I don't remember anything," I said, "but I would never hurt them."

The people milling about were focused on the smoldering house. No one paid any attention to Plug and me. Without discussion, we moved to the car and slipped inside.

I watched the detective at the edge of the house, and Plug started the engine. With the noise of the fire trucks running, no one noticed Plug drive away from Manny's house.

At the first stoplight, Plug yanked his seat belt across his chest, and I gasped for air. The light changed to green, and Plug sped down the street to the next red light. He pounded the heel of his hand against the wheel.

"We have to figure this out," I said. "I reek of gasoline. My shoes are caked with dirt. That cop smelled my stink. I saw it in his eyes. He thinks I set fire to the Santos's—"

"You didn't," Plug said.

"There's evidence." I clutched my chest. My heart pounded faster.

Plug fished his cell from his pocket and dialed a number. "Nick? Get Kyla. Meet us at the studio. Yes, now. Park in the back." The light switched to green, and Plug wedged his phone next to his thigh.

⧼ • ⧽

Plug swerved into an alley and drove to the back of the tattoo studio. He parked perpendicular to the doors and killed the engine. He hopped out and ran around to open my door. He let out a huge sigh and waited for me. I leaned my head against the dashboard and began to cry.

Plug crouched next to me. "Hang in there, Hannah."

"We just fled the scene of a crime," I said in between sobs. "What does that make us?"

"Determined." He took my hand and pulled me from the car. He reached behind the seat, grabbed the laptop, and then we moved toward the doors.

I stopped midway. My skin crawled. The last time I'd been inside the warehouse, the painting pricked my finger and the lights went out. I could believe Chelsea popped the breaker, making the warehouse go dark, but it was impossible for me to believe she rigged the canvas to draw my blood, or the temperature to suddenly drop, or the bugs to buzz around our heads. I had to figure out what was going on before I completely unraveled.

Plug unlocked the door and reached inside to flick on the lights. I took a deep breath to steady myself and followed him in.

We maneuvered through the crates, and I avoided glancing at any of the uncovered canvases propped against the boxes. I did not want to tempt any evil spirits or hysterical delusions to mess with me today.

We sat at the kitchenette near the office.

"Do you live here?" I wondered if his room was behind one of the closed doors.

"Yes," Plug said.

"Does your grandma live here with you?"

"No, she lives near her store," Plug said. "Did you start the recording program on your laptop before you went to bed yesterday?"

"Yes."

Plug's cell chimed. He thumbed it and read a text.

"They're almost here," he said.

My cell rang, and I checked the caller ID.

"Who is it?" Plug asked.

"No name. Unknown number."

"Ignore it," Plug said.

"But it could be important."

The back door of the warehouse squeaked open, and a spider scampered across the floor, just like the monstrous spider from the hospital bathroom. I shrieked and dropped my phone on the concrete flooring. The case popped off, and it stopped ringing.

"It's only Nick and Kyla," Plug said.

I scanned around for the spider and made sure it was long gone before I reached down and grabbed my phone and its case. I snapped them back together, and Kyla rushed in.

"What's the emergency?" She stopped and scrunched up her face. Her indigo hair swished when she flipped her head, and then she pulled the collar of her orange T-shirt over her nose. "Geez, Hannah, you reek."

"Thanks," I said.

"What's going on?" Nick asked and straddled a chair.

"Someone set Manny's house on fire," I said.

"Were you involved?" Nick asked and pulled the knit cap off his head.

Kyla whacked his arm. "No, she was not," Kyla said and grasped my hand.

"Someone called nine-one-one and said she saw me start the fire," I said.

"Chelsea?" Kyla asked.

"I don't know," I said.

"We'll find answers on here." Plug opened my laptop.

"I have some answers, too," Kyla said. "You'll be stunned by what I found with my research last night." She unclipped her bag.

"What?" I asked.

"Here we go," Plug said. He clicked on the file dated yesterday and expanded it to full screen. We scooted closer for a better view and waited for the video to begin.

"Have you watched any of it yet?" Nick asked.

"Not this one," Plug said.

"You watched a different one?" I asked.

"Only one," Plug said. "We can watch them all right now, but let's start with the one from last night."

The video began, and my face filled the screen; I had been sitting at my desk with my laptop. I remembered. Everyone got a great view of my white bra on top of my pink shirt. My cheeks heated with humiliation as we watched the video.

I climbed onto my bed, kicked off my flip-flops, scrunched up my pillow under my head, and closed my eyes. The drapes had been left open, and shadows danced across the walls and bed as the sun began to set.

Minutes passed. No one moved out of fear of missing something. Nick broke the silence.

"What's with the bra over the shirt? New fashion trend?" He pointed at the laptop. I wished for instant death and double-checked to make sure my hoodie was zipped up high.

Plug kicked Nick. "Shut up."

After ten minutes of watching me sleep, Plug fast-forwarded the image. When my mom walked into the room, he backed the image up and hit play.

Mom stepped next to the bed. "Hannah?" she said. I rolled over but didn't respond. She touched the strap of the exposed bra. She sighed and left the room. A few minutes later, my cell rang. I stirred and switched on the bedside lamp. The phone continued to ring. I got up from the bed, walked over to the desk, and sat while I answered my cell.

"Hello?" I asked. My shoulders sagged, and my chin sank to my chest, and yet I still held the phone to my ear.

"Yes," I said.

I ended the call, rose from the desk, and dropped the phone to the floor. I moved out of the view of the camera, which had a wide shot of my room with the bed centered.

A minute later, I re-entered the room, and a man walked in behind me. I stood next to the bed and faced him. He stepped in front of the laptop, but his head was out of the view of the lens. He turned, and with a bulky, hairy hand, he pointed at me.

"Why are you dressed like that?" he asked.

"To protect myself," I said.

"From what?"

"From you."

My stomach churned. I did not remember any of this. Where was my mom while this was happening? Was this after she'd left for work? Plug pulled at his ear and glanced at me. Kyla touched my shoulder, but I flinched away from her.

"Swallow this." The man handed me something small. I set it on my tongue and swallowed.

"Sit on the bed." His deep voice was familiar.

I perched on the edge of the bed and stared straight ahead. He moved toward me with a large paper sack in one hand. He set it on the floor and knelt in front of me. He spoke, but his words were inaudible.

Plug increased the volume on the laptop and rewound the playback. We leaned closer and strained to hear what the man said, but he faced the other direction and spoke too softly.

The man stroked my shoulder and then my face. I remained still, not responding to him verbally or physically. He sat back on his heels and pulled on leather gloves. Then he opened the sack and lifted out a small red gasoline can, a sweatshirt, a pair of jeans, and a pair of my tennis shoes that I hadn't seen in months.

He asked me a question.

"Yes," I said.

He rose and glided toward the door. Shadows drifted along the wall. He kept his back to the camera, but when he neared the computer his words were clear. "Do not answer the phone if it rings. Do not answer the doorbell. After you return to your bed, remain there until someone physically wakens you. Do you understand?"

"Yes," I said.

"Avoid contact with the police at all costs. Understand?"

"Yes."

"I will count backward to one. When I reach one, you will follow the instructions I've given you without hesitation." He paused at the door. "Three, two, one." He left.

I pulled the jeans over my yoga pants and slipped the sweat-shirt over my head. I walked to my dresser, pulled out socks, and then tugged them onto my feet. I laced up the tennis shoes. Then I picked up the gas can and left.

Plug fast-forwarded the video. According the time marker on the video, I was gone for over an hour, between 11:15 P.M. and 12:30 A.M.

I walked to the bed, lifted the covers, and climbed in, muddy shoes and all. I reached up and switched off the bedside lamp. The room went dark.

Plug fast-forwarded again.

The sunrise brightened the room, but I hadn't moved a millimeter the entire time I'd slept in the bed. The alarm went off, and it didn't faze me. I continued sleeping, dead to the world. The alarm blared for five minutes before falling silent. My cell phone chimed with multiple texts, but I did not move. My cell rang, but it still resulted in no response from me.

Plug entered the room.

"Hannah." He moved to the bed and touched my shoulder with the tips of his fingers. "Hannah?" No response. He grabbed my shoulder and shook me. "Hannah!"

I jolted upright in bed.

Plug clicked stop on the video.

"Why would you wake up to the phone call that came late at night from that guy, but not my phone call this morning?" Plug asked.

"Dude, she was hypnotized," Nick said. "He told her to only wake up when someone woke her physically." Nick tilted his chair forward, propped it on two feet, and waited for us to say something, but when no one did, he continued, "Think about it. He hypnotized you, gave you some sort of drug, and then instructed you to set fire to the Santos house. He wanted you to stay asleep up until your mom or someone else shook you awake. You most likely left the gas can at the scene with your prints all over it."

My breathing increased. My hands trembled. And my gut clenched. I lurched forward and threw up. Most of the puke landed on the concrete floor.

"Oh!" Kyla yelled and covered her mouth.

"So. Not. Cool." Nick popped out of his chair. Vomit had splattered his 6 OUT OF 7 DWARVES ARE NOT HAPPY T-shirt. He pulled it over his head and walked away from the kitchen.

Plug snatched a towel from the counter and handed it to me. Then he went to the sink and dampened a cloth and returned to wipe my face.

"I thought it wasn't possible for you to smell any worse," Plug whispered to me and winked with his good eye. He swiped the excess puke off my shoes and scooted my chair away from the mess.

Nick returned with one of Plug's gray V-neck T-shirts halfway on. He shoved his arms into the sleeves and said, "The CIA has used mind control for decades."

"You're talking fiction," Plug said. "*The Bourne Identity*. I saw the movie like everyone else." Plug mopped the mess off the floor.

Nick tapped Plug's head. "I'm serious. This crap happens. There are documented cases all over the Internet of people who've been inducted against their will. They're called Monarch slaves. They're programmed with triggers, given drugs, and then told to do things that they'd normally consider wrong."

"You're saying some evil government entity has recruited Hannah to set fire to Manny's house." Plug chucked the puke-soaked rag into the trash. Then he washed his hands in the sink.

"No." Nick rubbed his smooth scalp and paced the room. "I'm saying it's possible some jerk-off has manipulated Hannah against her will."

"Not just any jerk-off." Kyla pulled a stack of papers out of her bag. She thumbed through them, singled out one, and pointed at the names. "I researched the hypnotist from the fair. Master Gira is also known as Harry Hurricane, also known as—"

"John Harrison," I whispered.

"And is also known as," Kyla said without missing a beat, "Chelsea Harrison's dad."

"What?" Plug said.

Chills ran along my spine.

"Yes," Kyla said, "and before that, he attended Princeton. The official report said he was expelled from the psychology program for cheating, but the chatter around campus said he was booted for experimenting with demonic rituals in the basement of the psych building." She locked eyes with me. "Isn't Princeton your dream school?"

I nodded.

"Strange coincidence," Kyla said.

"Not a coincidence," I said. "Harrison was in the same graduate program as my dad. Apparently my parents knew him. And he auditioned at the hotel yesterday when I was with my mom."

"And you didn't recognize him then?" Nick asked.

"My instincts have been a bit unreliable lately. Plus, his hair was different. And so much has happened since the fair."

Nick turned to Kyla and asked, "Does your dad know you used his computer for these searches?"

"No."

I needed to tell Mom about Harrison, but before I could do anything, my phone rang.

"Ignore it," Plug said.

I read the caller ID. "It's the same number as before."

Plug snatched the phone from me.

I tried to grab it back from him, but he was faster. He tapped the reject button and then scrolled through my phone log.

"The same number called you last night. It's the only number in your phone log that doesn't have a name attached to it." He scrolled more. "He's been calling you since Sunday."

"I don't know who it is," I said.

"Seems obvious," Kyla said. "It's the hypnotist."

Plug set my phone next to Nick at the laptop. Nick pulled up the Internet and typed the number into a reverse directory. "Nothing."

"It's probably a disposable," Kyla said. "I have an idea." She leaned in closer and typed the same number into her cell.

"What are you going to say?" I asked, but she shushed me.

My heart raced, and the seconds ticked by. Finally, she ended the call.

"No answer. No voice mail," she said.

"Why wouldn't he answer?" I asked.

"Worse yet," Plug said, "now he can do a reverse search on your number."

"Doesn't matter," Kyla said. "The phone is registered to my dad's work. They have gazillions of cell phones. This guy will never know we had anything to do with the call."

"Let's see if these other videos captured anything," Nick said.

"Wait," I said. "I want to know what else Kyla found out. I've known Chelsea for a year. She would've said something if her dad was a freaking hypnotist—"

My cell rang.

Nick held my phone. "Same number."

"Let me answer it." I reached for the phone, but Nick kept it. "I've had enough of this. Let's answer it." I thrust my hand at Nick.

"Put it on speaker," Plug said and began fiddling with my laptop.

Nick set the phone on the table. I sat down and pressed the green button.

⇥ • ⇤

I fumbled with the phone and ended the call.

"It was just a wrong number," I said. My friends stared at me with open mouths.

"Oh no," I said. "What happened?"

Plug and Nick moved over to the laptop.

"Did you get it?" Kyla asked.

"Yes." Plug clicked play on yet another video.

I drummed my hands against the table. The screen showed Plug's kitchen, and my heart raced. Plug clicked the mute button.

"Watch," he said.

The video showed Nick setting the phone on the table.

"Turn up the volume," I said.

"Not yet." Plug let his finger hover over the button.

"What are you hiding from me?" I asked, but they ignored me. The images played out on the computer screen. After I had slumped in the chair, Plug increased the volume.

"Are you alone?" a man's voice asked from the phone's speaker.

"No," I said.

"Where are you?" he asked.

"In the kitchen—"

Plug reached for the phone, but Kyla grabbed his hand.

"Is anyone watching you or listening to you?"

"Yes."

"Repeat these words: You have the wrong number."

"You have the wrong number."

"Okay, when I count to three, you will wake and feel more anxious and fearful than you have in days. You will not remember any of our conversation. You will believe the call was simply a wrong number. Understand?"

"Yes."

"One, two, three." He disconnected the call.

I fumbled with the phone and ended the call.

"It was just a wrong number," I said. "Oh no. What happened?"

"That was the hypnotist's voice." I knew beyond any doubt, and panic welled up from the pit of my stomach. "Am I still hypnotized?"

"No," Nick said, "but he left lingering posthypnotic suggestions. He told you to be anxious and fearful."

"I'm losing myself." I swallowed hard and shook out my hands. I paced the perimeter of the room. "He has total power over my mind, my feelings, and my body. I can't fight him. I was angry and determined before the phone call, and now I'm totally weak and scared."

"He used a trigger to rapidly induce you."

"How do you know so much?" I asked Nick.

"Because while Plug studies the occult, I study conspiracies," Nick said. "Governments and secret societies have been brainwashing and hypnotizing people for generations. This isn't new, Hannah."

Plug clutched my hands and stopped my pacing. "He recited a rhyming phrase, a couplet, when you answered the phone. When you heard the words, you went right into a trance."

"What was the phrase?" I asked.

"Can't tell you," Plug said. "You could slip under again. We have to research and figure out how to reverse his influence over you."

"You need to be deprogrammed by a professional," Nick said.

"We have to go to the police," Kyla said.

"No!" I had to avoid the police at all costs.

"Hannah—"

"They'll arrest me," I said.

"We have proof—"

"We do not," I said. "We have a video of me letting a man into my room. We have a video of me with the gasoline can. We have a video of me talking on the freaking phone to someone. We can't prove any of this was John Harrison. Can we even prove he's Chelsea's father?" I grabbed Kyla's research from the table and waved it in the air.

"Hannah, even if it's not solid enough to take to the police, it's still enough to prove that you are not schizophrenic."

I dropped Kyla's papers back onto the table. I rubbed my eyes and tried to erase the image of Mom when she had to admit to me that Dad killed himself. The worry lines on her face revealed that she feared I'd do the same thing. She needed to know I wasn't mentally ill like Dad.

Plug set his hand on my shoulder. "Things will get better—"

"Does this look like she's crazy?" Nick tapped the computer screen. He'd already started another video.

Dark shadows swirled across the ceiling of my bedroom.

"That's when the book got ripped," Plug said.

"This is the one you watched?" I asked.

"I watched it Wednesday when you were in the bathroom," Plug said.

"Why didn't you tell me?"

"When was a good time? And how would it have helped?" Plug asked. I folded my arms, and we watched the recording.

I tossed back and forth in bed while shadows swirled around me. The bedcovers lifted and an unseen force thrust them against the wall. I jerked upright in bed. My eyes were wide open, but they were dark. Not green. A black mist seeped from my parted lips.

The video pixelated and flickered across the screen. We all tensed. But after a few seconds the image stabilized.

I rose and walked so smoothly, it appeared I floated an inch above the carpet. At the desk, my face lowered right into the camera lens of the computer. My eyes were brown. Not my own. Another fine mist of darkness escaped my lips. I hovered and tugged the art book in front of me, bumping the laptop in the process. The camera angle shifted slightly. I clutched several pages of the book and tore them from the binding. I let them fall to the floor. Then I ripped more pages. Again. And again.

When I finished, I drifted like a leaf back over to the edge of the bed. My spine arched backward, and my arms flung out to the sides. All at the same moment, the sheets were stripped from my mattress, dresser drawers flew open, clothes were strewn about the room, and the torn art pages swirled about as though they were in the funnel of a tornado.

A spiral of blackness shot from my mouth. Everything flying about the room fell to the floor.

The image pixelated again, and then the screen went black. The recording ended. We stood in stunned silence. No wonder Plug had neglected to tell me he'd watched this video.

"Well," Nick said, "that complicates things."

"Actually, it makes perfect sense," Plug said.

My mouth dropped open, and so did Kyla's.

"Explain," Kyla said.

"That video scared the crap out of me the first time I watched it," Plug said, "especially when a few minutes later, the demon attacked Hannah in the bathroom. This supernatural stuff can be dangerous. It can mess with our minds, mess with our memories, and mess with our realities. I researched it even more and found a connection between hypnotism and demons."

"And?" Kyla waved her hand in the air.

"Hannah, when the hypnotist unlocked your mind," Plug said, "he opened it up to his suggestions—his influence—and he also opened it up to the influence of incorporeal beings."

"Incorporeal?" Nick asked.

"Demons. Ghosts. Spirits," Kyla said.

"So the black mist I've seen isn't the Angel of Death?" I asked.

"It could be. Sometimes. But not always," Plug said. "That darkness can be any malevolent spirit." Plug twisted a ring on his finger. "It seems we are dealing with two problems here: the hypnotist and the spirits."

"Hey," Nick said, "at least you're not schizophrenic."

My cell phone rang. We spun around and watched it vibrate against the table.

"Don't!" Plug snagged my wrist.

I yanked away. "Stop making decisions for me." I had to regain control of my life. Somehow. Even if that only meant deciding whether or not to answer my own phone.

Plug bit down on the stitches in his lip.

I read the caller ID and answered the call. "Manny?"

"Where are you?" he asked.

My eyes watered, and my chin drifted downward, letting tears fall to my chest. He'd been an absolute jerk yesterday, but I would never deliberately harm his family.

"I've been so worried," I said.

Plug snatched a piece of paper and scribbled:

Don't tell him where we are!

I faced the wall. "Manny, are you and your family okay?"

"We're fine," he said, "but Hannah, the police think you set fire to our house—"

"I would never." But my shoes were filthy, and I reeked of gasoline.

"Tell me where you are," he said.

"I thought you never wanted to see me again," I said and replayed yesterday's fight in my mind. I kicked some of the dried mud from the edge of my shoe. It crumbled onto the concrete. "Are you still there?" I asked.

"Yes," Manny said. "I'm sorry about yesterday." His tone of voice had changed.

"Really?" I asked, confused. I didn't know who to believe or trust anymore. I couldn't even trust my own instincts. But I needed Manny to understand what had happened, that I wasn't crazy.

"Manny, that hypnotist from the fair has been behind all of this."

"Hannah, I need to know where you are."

"Did you hear me?" I asked.

"Yes. I want to help you, but I need to know where you are first," he said.

"I'm with—"

Plug clutched my shoulder and spun me around. "Don't tell him."

"Who are you with?" Manny asked.

"I'm trying to help you," Plug said.

What was I supposed to do? Who was I supposed to trust? I'd made so many mistakes already this week. I just wanted to make amends for all of it.

"I'm sorry," I said and stared straight at Plug. I meant it for both him and Manny. I did not want to rekindle anything with Manny after the way he'd treated me yesterday, but I needed to see him for myself to know that he was unharmed in the fire. I couldn't stand the thought of anyone else being hurt because of me.

"I'm at the Eclectic Tattoo Gallery, downtown," I said.

Plug punched the wall and bloodied his knuckles. Kyla scooped up her papers from the table and thrust them into her bag. Nick slammed the laptop shut.

"I'm coming over," Manny said. "Wait for me."

"I'll be here, but come to the back alley. I'll wait outside for you," I said.

"I'll get there as fast as I can," Manny said and disconnected.

I shoved the phone into my pocket.

"What were you thinking?" Kyla yelled at me. "We're trying to help you, and you told Manny where we are."

"I need to see he's okay." My eyes burned, and more tears spilled.

"Couldn't you tell he was okay from the phone call?" Nick asked.

"I need to see him in person and tell him what's happened," I said.

Nick tugged his knit cap onto his head and tucked the laptop under his arm.

"Wait, there are still more videos to watch," I said.

"I'll make backup files," Nick said and headed out.

"Hannah, the police are with Manny," Kyla said. "They probably instructed his every word." She closed the space between us, and the scorn in her eyes made me wince. "You're the one who didn't want to go to the police with the information we have. And you're right. We don't have any real proof of anything, but they have your prints on the gas can, the sweatshirt in your closet, an eyewitness, and now, they're coming here to arrest you. Manny's leading the way." She hoisted the strap of her bag over her shoulder and followed Nick toward the back.

"He wouldn't do that," I said and wiped away my tears.

"He already has," Nick shouted back to us and kept walking.

"You can leave," I said, "but I'm waiting for Manny."

Kyla turned back toward us. "Plug, we'll be at my house if you want to join us."

Plug rubbed his jaw and grimaced.

"Wait!" I hollered after Nick. "We need to show Manny the videos."

"Let Nick take it to make backup files," Plug said.

"Manny wouldn't lie to me," I said.

"If the police convinced him you started the fire," Plug said, "or if your mom convinced him you're schizophrenic, he would think he's helping you by leading the police here." He shrugged and moved to the kitchen sink. He rinsed the blood from his knuckles and dried his hands on a clean towel. I leaned against the wall and waited for him.

"I will never understand why you want to be with Manny," Plug said. "What has he done to help you through this?"

"I don't want to be with him," I said.

"Really?" Plug faced me. "Because you keep turning back to him."

My mind worked over the details of the past week as I searched for an answer. Manny and I kissed for the first time at the fair. Jordan died. Lily just regained consciousness. Demons stalked me. Plug and I kissed. And the hypnotist had manipulated me. I recalled how Manny said in the hospital that he didn't want us to change and how he said at his house that I was confused and needed help. But Manny hadn't helped me at all.

I had to save myself from this mess I'd fallen into.

"After they arrest you," Plug said, "they'll check you into a psychiatric facility for mandatory evaluation. They'll medicate you and keep you there. I won't be able to help you."

Plug and I stood on opposite sides of the kitchen and stared at each other.

After a minute of silence, Plug moved toward the back door and flipped off lights as he went. I didn't want to be left in the dark, so I kept right on his heels.

"What do you suggest we do?" I asked.

"Leave before he gets here."

"No. I need to explain to him what's been going on."

We stepped out into the alley, and Plug locked the back door to the studio's warehouse. He leaned against the El Camino, hooked his thumbs into his jeans, and waited.

Manny wasn't bringing the cops. I was certain. He wanted to see I was okay.

An engine revved, and I recognized Manny's family SUV when it turned into the alley. Plug reached for my fingers, but I pulled away. I didn't want Manny to see Plug touching me. I didn't want to be the cause of another fight. Manny parked, but he remained seated and lowered his head. I walked toward him, and he shut off the engine. I opened his door, and he gazed at me. His cheek was bandaged, and his right hand was wrapped in gauze.

"Are you okay?" I asked.

"Yes."

He fidgeted with the collar of his shirt. It wasn't his usual polo shirt. Instead, it was an oversized dark blue police department T-shirt. He adjusted a loose edge of cotton gauze on his wrist, and then he stepped out of the SUV.

"Is your chest still taped?" I reached out to him, but he backed away from me. "Are your ribs worse?"

"No," he said and blushed. I'd never seen him lie before, but I knew how he acted when he spoke the truth, and this wasn't it. Manny glanced down the alleyway and ripped a piece of gauze bandaging from his wrist.

"Hannah, did you set fire to my house?" Manny let the white piece of cotton fall to the asphalt.

"It's complicated," I said.

"No. It's not," Manny said. "You either did or didn't. Just tell me."

I opened my mouth, but I struggled to start my explanation.

"Hannah," Manny said, "why are you even here?"

Plug stepped next to me. "Why are you here?" Plug asked Manny.

Manny thrust a finger toward Plug's face, but Plug stood his ground.

"Back off, Eugene," Manny said. "I came to talk to Hannah." Plug narrowed his eyes at Manny. Manny looked away first and jerked his head toward me. "He's ruined you, Hannah. You reek, as if you haven't showered in days. Plus, you smell like smoke and gasoline. I bet Eugene convinced you to start it—"

"He hasn't done anything to me. He's tried to help—"

"No, Hannah. He hasn't. Your mom has tried to help you. Your doctor wants to help you. You need to let them help you—"

"We have evidence," I said, "that shows the hypnotist from the fair has been behind everything."

"You think the hypnotist set fire to my house?" Manny choked out an awkward laugh. "The police say they have evidence against you. They say you started the fire." He raked his fingers through his thick hair. "Hannah, do you have any idea how terrifying it was to have all the smoke detectors blaring and know that the house was on fire?"

Yes, I did know, but when it happened to me, it was apparently all in my mind. I suffered no real injuries. I had no bandages like Manny had now. But whatever I did to the Santos house, it was the result of a posthypnotic suggestion. I had to make Manny understand that.

"It was the hypnotist," I said and reached for Manny, but he pulled away. "He's Chelsea's father, and she's taunted me all week—"

"You're losing it, Hannah," Manny said. "Can't you hear how ridiculous you sound? Chelsea's your friend, and she didn't even know that hypnotist at the fair. Eugene is trying to turn you against me and isolate you."

"Hannah, that's crap." Plug set his hand on my shoulder. "I've tried to help you. I love you."

"You can't love her," Manny said.

"I love her," Plug said, "and unlike you, I've stood by her when she needed it most."

"I'm here now." Manny kicked a pebble on the ground, and then he focused on me. "And I've loved you longer." Tears welled in Manny's eyes. "Let us get you the help you need."

"Us?" Plug asked.

I checked up and down the alley to see if anyone else was there.

"Who's us?" Plug asked again. Then he lunged forward and seized Manny's T-shirt. Plug yanked it up and exposed black wires and a small black box taped to Manny's waist.

"Why would you be wearing a wire?" I asked.

"You set fire to my house!" Manny yelled. "The police said your recorded confession plus Chelsea's testimony—"

"Chelsea was the eyewitness?" I asked.

Plug shoved Manny hard. He stumbled backward and clutched his ribs but then regained his footing. He charged forward and tackled Plug to the ground. Plug struck Manny in the throat with his right hand and smashed his left elbow into Manny's face. Plug wrenched him sideways and rolled on top. Manny poked his fingers into Plug's swollen eye, but Plug batted his arm away. Then Plug landed punches over and over again to Manny's face. Plug held nothing back this time. A siren screamed at the end of the alley behind Manny's SUV.

"Plug!" I screamed.

He jumped off Manny as two police officers stepped out of the cruiser.

We ran to the El Camino.

"Stop!" one of the officers yelled, but we kept moving.

Plug shoved the car into reverse and nearly ran over Manny in the process. Then Plug accelerated down to the other end of the alley. We had almost escaped when another police cruiser skidded into view. Plug pressed the pedal to the floor and slammed into the front fender of the cruiser. The tires of the El Camino spun. We were wedged between the bumper of the cop car and the corner of the brick building. Plug gunned the engine. The tires smoked. Metal scraped against metal on Plug's side. Bricks snapped the mirror from the car on my side. The El Camino broke free and blasted down the street. A loud thud echoed behind us.

I gawked back at them. The cruiser jerked forward and then stalled. Two other officers staggered to the sidewalk's edge. One lifted a radio from his shoulder harness and spoke into it.

"They're going to follow us," I said.

Plug drove faster and ran a stop sign as he turned north onto Eighth Street. He barreled past smaller, older homes in the north end of Boise and headed toward the foothills.

"Grab my phone," Plug said. "Call Kyla and tell her we're coming."

⊨ • ⊨

Plug whipped into a newer, upscale neighborhood in the foothills and skidded around a corner. With one hand I gripped the belt across my chest, and with the other I dug my nails into the uphol-stered seat. The tires fought for traction on the asphalt as Plug took another corner too fast. Then he suddenly slowed and pulled into the driveway of a two-story house with manicured landscaping and a pillared porch. The garage door was up, and Plug drove straight in. Kyla waited at the interior door and pressed a button to close the garage behind us. Plug killed the engine and leaned his head against the steering wheel.

My hands remained in a death grip, and my heart pounded against my ribs.

"What are you two waiting for?" Kyla asked. "Come inside."

Neither of us moved.

Kyla walked between her Mini Cooper and the El Camino and drew her fingers along the side of Plug's prized possession.

"What happened?" She tried to open Plug's door, but it was jammed. She tugged harder. The hinges screeched, and the door opened halfway. Plug squeezed through and stepped around her.

228

"Oh, Plug! Your face," Kyla said. "Let me get something for it." She hustled past him and into the house. Plug paced the garage like a kenneled wolf. I kept my distance.

A piece of metal fell from the car onto the tiled modular floor of the garage.

"Can it be repaired?" I knew how important the classic vehicle was to him, and restoring it would be a daunting task with the mutilated paint, dented body, and missing parts.

"Doesn't matter," he said.

I approached him, and he stopped pacing. "I'm so sorry," I whispered.

"Cars are replaceable."

But the El Camino had been their oasis in a sea of chaos, as Kyla had called it when they'd invited me to join them for lunch.

I chewed on my cheek. Manny said Plug had ruined me, but Plug's face proved I was the one who'd ruined him. His lip was torn, his eye had swollen shut, and his hands were covered in blood. Neither he nor his car could be replaced as easily as we'd replaced the art book. I was destroying everything in my path.

"Come on," I said. "Let's go inside and see if we can figure a way out of this."

We met Kyla at the kitchen counter. She had the contents of a first-aid kit spread out on the polished granite. Near sliding glass doors, Nick sat at an oak dining table with my laptop in front of him. He did a quick double-take when he saw Plug and popped out of his chair to come over to us.

"Dude." Nick grabbed Plug by the shoulders and examined his face.

"Manny wore a wire and brought the cops," Plug said.

Nick huffed, and the pit in my stomach grew.

"Wired?" Nick said. "It's not like Hannah's a violent criminal."

"I've assaulted Chelsea twice, and I killed Jordan. So technically—"

"Jordan's death was not your fault," Kyla said. She passed Plug an ice pack for his eye and began to wipe his knuckles with antiseptic. "And Chelsea has been provoking you."

"They wanted to record her confession to the arson," Plug said.

"Did you confess?" Nick asked.

I shook my head.

"There's another video you need to see," Nick said.

"You watched without us?" I asked.

"We were making backups." Nick moved over to the table.

"It's bad," Kyla said without lifting her head. She continued to clean Plug's hands, and Nick avoided eye contact with me. Kyla finished with Plug and washed up.

I turned to Plug. "Have you seen it already?"

"No," he said. "I had only watched the one where you tore the book."

I sank into the cushioned dining chair. "Hit play," I said, but Nick waited for Plug to join us. Plug held the ice pack to his eye and took the seat next to me. Blood and dirt stained his new T-shirt. With his free hand, Plug weaved his fingers with mine.

Nick started the video.

I hopped up from the chair and left my bedroom, which was a mess with the bedcovers and dirty clothes all over the floor. Less than a few minutes later, it sounded like the bedroom door had slammed shut. A man stepped into view of the laptop. He set the pink elephant on the unmade bed. Then he stepped out of view again.

Nick reached out and tapped the mute button on the computer. "The hypnotist uses the same trigger phrase to hypnotize you. It's perfectly audible in this recording." The silent video showed me stepping back into the room and standing in front of my bed. Nick waited a few more seconds before increasing the volume.

John Harrison leaned in close to me and said, "Open your mind and allow your subconscious to hear me. I want only goodness for you. Open your mind and let my voice in. Experience this peace."

My shoulders drooped, and my chin drifted downward.

"Swallow this pill," he said and set it in my hand. I did as he told me. Then the hypnotist spoke rapidly with a cadence to his words. "Imagine that you are more terrified than you have ever been in your entire life. The elephant has come back to haunt you. The accident was your fault. You killed Jordan."

"No," I said.

"Yes, listen to my voice, believe what I say. Imagine that the world is changing around you. Imagine your room perfectly clean. Your bed neatly made. Unlock your mind to the terrifying possibilities. Pick up the elephant and know that it is real. Feel how soft it is, but imagine yourself ripping it to shreds."

I snatched the elephant and screamed. My arms flailed as though I was tearing it apart, but I didn't actually pull any pieces from the stuffed animal.

"Imagine the smell of the car accident. The smoke. The putrid stench of death," he said.

I coughed and threw the elephant across the room.

"Imagine being in the fire again, but this time your house is on fire. The smoke detectors are beeping. What are you going to do? How will you escape? Play out the events in your mind."

I ran out of view of the computer, and the hypnotist followed me. Doors slammed off camera.

Nick reached out and fast-forwarded the recording. "Nothing happens onscreen for quite a while, but when you come back into the room . . ." He clicked pause and locked eyes with Kyla.

"I'm not sure you want to watch this, Hannah." A tear slipped down Kyla's cheek. "It's horrible." She covered her mouth. Nick hung his head.

"How can it be any worse than what we've already seen?" I said, and as soon as the words left my lips, I felt stupid. Of course it could be worse. Nausea welled in my gut, and I doubted my ability to handle the truth.

"And he calls you Beth in the video," Kyla said almost as a side note.

"My mom's name?" I stared at Kyla.

"Did he rape Hannah?" Plug whispered the awful possibility.

Nick rubbed his forehead. "He kept his clothes on."

Images from the bathroom incident flashed through my mind. The demon could have been manipulating a memory of something Harrison had actually done to me.

"Hit play," I said and steeled myself for the worst.

Plug set the ice pack on the table and wrapped his hands around mine. "Hannah, you don't have to—"

I jerked away. "Yes, I do. How can I fight a monster I can't see? Recover from a trauma I can't remember?"

"None of this is your doing," Kyla said. "You weren't a willing participant."

"Does the video capture his face?" Plug asked. "Is there enough evidence to show the police who this guy is and what he's done to Hannah?"

"His back is always to the computer," Nick said. "Not once does the video capture his face."

"Hit play," I said. I'd had enough. I yearned for my life back. I had to regain access to my own mind and make my own freaking decisions. I needed to see what I was up against.

My phone rang.

"Are you kidding me?" I said and plucked the phone from my pocket.

"Don't answer it!" everyone yelled.

"Because I'm an idiot," I said. I checked the caller ID. "It's my mom. I have to—"

"Put it on speaker," Plug said.

I did and set the phone on the table.

"Hello?"

"Hannah! Are you okay?" Mom asked.

"No, Mom—"

"Hannah, I spoke with Dr. James—"

"Mom, I'm not schizophrenic. I have proof."

"Okay, honey, but Dr. James said that you may be experiencing an elaborate hallucination. Tell me where you are. Let me come and get you."

"No," I said. "Mom, listen, I have proof that the hypnotist has been behind everything that has happened. It's John Harrison. He's Chelsea's dad. He's done horrible things—"

"You're cutting out, Hannah," Mom said. "I'm in the hotel parking garage now. Reception isn't great here. Tell me where you are so I can come and get—"

Everyone in the kitchen shook their heads, silently pleading with me not to tell her. But before I could, Mom shrieked into the phone.

"Mom?" I said. "Mom!" Silence. The call was ended. I grabbed the phone to dial her back.

Someone pounded on the front door and rang the bell. Our heads jerked in that direction.

"Police!" A man yelled from the front porch. "Open up!"

Plug snatched my phone and pocketed it. He grabbed my wrist and tugged me out of the chair. I took one step and peeked out the sliding glass door.

"They're in the backyard," I said.

Nick and Kyla moved toward the sliding door and locked it. Nick snatched the flash drive off the table. Plug grabbed the laptop.

"How are we getting out of this one?" Nick asked.

"The more you help me," I said, "the more trouble—"

"I have an idea," Kyla said. "You two go upstairs. Nick and I will hold off the police." She pulled her keys from her pocket and gave them to Plug. "In case you need my car. Now go before they see you."

Plug pulled me out of the room, past a tall display case, and down a short hallway to the stairs. The police pounded on the front door again. Plug and I crouched at the top of the stairs and listened as Kyla opened the door.

"They'll find us," I whispered.

Plug brought his finger to his lips and glared at me with his one good eye.

"Is Hannah O'Leary here?" an officer asked.

"No," Kyla said.

"May we come in and ask you a few questions?"

"No."

"Let us have a look around your house, and then we'll leave."

"No," Nick said.

"Who are you?" the officer asked Nick.

"I know my rights," Kyla said, "and unless you have a warrant, you do not have the right to force your way inside my home."

"You're both truant. We have every right to question you."

"Then take us to the station for questioning," Nick said.

They stepped outside, and the front door closed behind them. I heard their muffled voices through the door, but I couldn't make out what they said.

Plug and I crept into a bedroom facing the front street. We peered out through the edge of the curtains. One police officer milled about on the front lawn scanning the house, and another officer directed Nick and Kyla to the back seat of his cruiser.

"Will they be okay?" I whispered. A total of four police officers returned to two cruisers and drove away.

"They'll be fine," Plug said. "Kyla's dad is a private investigator. He'll—"

"He's a PI?"

"That's how she found the information on the hypnotist. She used her dad's computer search engines."

"How'd the police get here so fast?" I asked. "Did they trace my mom's call or track down Kyla because you're friends?"

"No idea." Plug pulled my cell from his pocket and flipped it over. "Your phone probably has GPS tracking." He popped it open and started to remove the battery.

"Wait. I need to call my mom back."

Plug hesitated, but then he returned the phone to me. I dialed Mom's cell. It went straight to voice mail.

"Mom, call me. I need to know you're okay." I stared at the phone. Plug slipped it from my grasp and removed the battery.

"Harrison did something to her," I said.

"She said there was bad reception."

"She screamed!" I said.

Plug twisted a ring. "Maybe she's with the police, and somehow she was startled, or they had to disconnect the call."

I shook my head. My gut told me she was in trouble.

"We need to leave," I said.

"The police might still be watching the house."

"We can't stay here," I said. "Someone from Kyla's family will show up. Or the police could come back with a warrant."

"Kyla only lives with her dad," Plug said. "I'm sure he'll go to the police station for Kyla before he comes here."

I plopped down on the edge of Kyla's bed. Pages from her sketchbook were tacked to the walls of the bedroom. Magazines featuring the latest trends in hairstyles were stacked on her nightstand.

"Where's her mom?" I asked.

"She walked out when Kyla was two. They've not heard from her since," Plug said.

"You'd think with their resources they could find her."

"Maybe they don't want to find her," Plug said. "Kyla doesn't really talk about it, but she has a hard time trusting people because of it."

The contempt on Kyla's face in the warehouse when I'd told Manny where we were made more sense now. She had befriended me, and I let her down. Now, she'd sacrificed herself to the police in order to continue helping me.

"I haven't done anything to earn her friendship or her trust," I said.

"I have, and she knows how important you are to me." Plug lifted my hand and kissed my knuckles. His broken stitches brushed my skin. "I meant what I said in the alley, Hannah." He knelt in front of me and cupped my face. "I love you."

He waited for me to respond, but Manny's words from the alleyway replayed in my mind, and I'd never forget the pleading in his eyes when he said he'd loved me longer. How could he say that and still lie to me?

Because he believed I was schizophrenic.

Or he wanted to help the police catch the arsonist.

Plug stroked my fingers, and tingles ran along my skin. I craved more, but I was confused. What suggestions had Harrison planted in my mind? After years of wanting to wait to be intimate with someone, it was senseless for me to throw myself at Manny and Plug the way I had this last week. But now that I knew those large, hairy hands belonged to the hypnotist, maybe he'd planted physical cravings in my mind—lingering instructions. I'd become his toy. My heart sank. I couldn't breathe. What was real anymore?

I pushed Plug away. He sat back on his heels and waited.

I clutched my knees and tried to catch my breath. Maybe this was all a delusion. Mom said I was in the middle of an elaborate hallucination. Maybe I'd already been checked into a psychiatric facility. None of this was real. There was no hypnotist. No demons. No Chelsea. And no Plug.

I sank to the floor and curled into the fetal position.

"I don't know if you're real," I whispered.

Plug reached for my hands, but I tightened them into fists and pulled them into my chest.

"I'm real," Plug said. "The way I feel about you is real."

I stared across the beige carpet. Little uneven fibers extended up from the floor like a field of bleached grass. An ant emerged from the blades and explored. I reached out and pounded it to death with my fist.

Then I leaned against the bed and wiped a tear from my face.

"Hannah?" Plug said.

"Ants have plagued me for days," I said.

Plug scooted closer to me. "Harrison uses ants in his hypnotic trigger."

I locked eyes with him. "I can't remember."

"Maybe it's too traumatic for your brain," Plug said. "I'm not sure."

"I'm becoming just like my dad, and I'm hurting everyone around me." I rubbed my cheeks and cried.

"Hannah," Plug said, "You're not hurting anyone."

"Have you seen yourself in the mirror?"

Plug grabbed my hands, and I let him this time. "Hannah, forgive your dad for killing himself. And for having schizophrenia. You are not him." He tightened his grasp. "We will find a solution."

"How?"

"For starters, a shower and clean clothes will help refresh you."

"No way. The shower seems to be a favorite haunting place for the malevolent spirits." I closed my eyes and buried my face in my knees. "I can't get into a shower."

"Don't make me force you," a man's deep voice said.

I jerked my head up and yanked away from Plug.

He raised his eyebrows.

"What did you say?" I asked.

"A shower and clean clothes will help refresh you."

I rubbed my face. It wasn't Plug's voice that had threatened me.

"Hannah," Plug said, "you don't have to do anything you don't want to."

He rose and extended a hand down to me. I accepted it and stood.

"I'll change," I said.

I opened a dresser drawer and found underwear and socks. Another drawer had folded jeans and shorts. I checked the sizes. Kyla and I were nearly the same. My fingers hovered over the shorts. I was tired of wearing so many layers in this stifling summer heat, but I grabbed a pair of jeans instead.

Plug lifted out a couple of shirts from the closet, and I chose one. He hung the other one back up.

"Out," I said and pointed to the door.

"I'll be in the hall if you need me," he said.

The back of Kyla's door had a full-length mirror. I dropped everything, leaned in, and pressed my forehead to the mirror.

A knock on the door startled me, and I shrieked.

"It's just me," Plug said.

I opened the door, and Plug gave me a paper grocery sack.

"For your dirty clothes and shoes. We shouldn't leave them here."

I took the sack, closed the door, and then scrutinized my unkempt appearance in the mirror.

"No visitors during your first forty-eight hours," a man's voice said behind me. I didn't bother to turn around. I saw from the reflection that I was alone in the room.

"You can do this," I whispered to myself.

I focused on my features. Plug had said green eyes belonged to strong, courageous women. If he was right, I could do this. I could manage my own thoughts. My hair was greasy at the roots, darkness circled my eyes, and dirt lurked beneath my fingernails. I yanked the zipper of the hoodie, pulled the fabric off my shoulders, and dropped it to the floor. I reached behind me, unfastened the bra, and slipped it off. I shoved the bra and hoodie into the sack. I angled away from the mirror and kept my mind focused on the next task. I pulled the pink shirt over my head, kicked off the tennis shoes, and unzipped my jeans.

Deep breath.

I hooked my thumbs into the waistband of the yoga pants and tugged them off at the same time with the jeans. I shoved them into the paper sack and caught a glimpse in the mirror.

"Everything goes in the bag," the deep voice said.

"I'm alone." I chewed on my lip. The voices had to be the freaking spirits taunting me. I did not want to be their plaything anymore. I would not let them win.

Don't cry.

Don't look in the mirror.

Don't be weak.

I still remembered the hairy hands of the hypnotist on my body and the reflection in my bathroom mirror at home. I hadn't been naked since then.

I fought the panic and faced the wall. I tugged off my socks and shoved them into the bag. I rubbed my eyelids to block the images flooding my mind.

The hypnotist had been in my bedroom. He showed me the naked sculpture in the art book. His bulky fingers wedged the tiger-eye stone into the gutter of the book, marking the page. His voice compared the sculpture to my body . . . but not mine . . . he called me Beth. He traced the line of muscles from my shoulders to my waist—just as he had with Rodin's sculpture in the art book. Heat spread throughout my body. I wanted to scream, but the cadence of the hypnotist's voice told me to relax and feel peace. The thoughts were contradictory. My mind gave in to him when I wanted to fight back and defend myself. A moan escaped his lips while I screamed inside. His laughter reverberated off the walls. I clawed at his hands and dug my nails into his flesh.

"Stop!" I yelled.

Plug pounded the door. "I'm coming in!" he yelled, but I had wedged myself against the door, lost in my own horror. He shoved the door and pushed me backward with it.

"Hannah!" Plug reached around to me. He pushed more and had enough space to squeeze through. He snatched the lavender comforter from Kyla's bed and draped it around me. And then he rocked me in his arms.

"I remembered."

"What?" he asked.

I grabbed the paper sack and threw up.

Plug plucked a clean sock off the floor and wiped my lips.

"I remembered what happened Tuesday—the video we were about to watch with Kyla and Nick. I remembered what happened."

Plug stroked my head.

A tear slipped down my cheek. "He's changed me, forever."

"Don't accept the version he's created. You can reclaim yourself. Or reinvent yourself."

"I hope so." I let Plug hold me for a few more minutes in silence. The clean fragrance from Kyla's comforter masked my body odor. I breathed deeply and considered our next move.

"If we go to the police," I said, "they'll admit me for psychiatric evaluation."

"Yup," Plug said.

"If we go to my mom—"

"Same thing. She's bought what Dr. James is selling."

"We can't go back to the tattoo studio."

"The police are probably watching it," Plug said.

"We could search Chelsea's apartment," I said.

"She should still be at school."

"We could find evidence against Harrison," I said.

"What if he's there?"

"We lure him away first." I said. "Let's finish here and be ready to leave, but turn my phone back on and wait for him to call. He's called how many times already today? He'll call again. He'll ask me where I am. I'll tell him, and he'll come here for me. But we'll be gone."

"No." Plug got to his feet. "A million things could go wrong with that plan."

"What's the worst that will happen?" I asked. "He tells me to do something I don't want to do. If that happens, end the call and remove the cell's battery."

"And how am I supposed to get you out of the trance if I hang up on the hypnotist?"

"You've heard him multiple times—how he counts backward to pull me out."

"It's not something an average Joe can just mess with," Plug said. "There's the tone of voice, the rhythm, the word choices, the pauses—"

"You can do it."

"No, Hannah," Plug said. "You've seen me pick locks. Does that make you capable of doing the same thing? Watching is not learning the intricacies of the skill." He leaned in closer to me. "I could screw up your mind."

"It's already screwed up." I smiled, but he frowned. "You might not even need to do anything. But we need solid evidence against him." I clutched the comforter around my neck and stood next to him. "Please, Plug, help me do this."

He pressed his forehead to mine. "How much time do you need to get ready?"

"Two minutes."

"Okay." He wrapped his arms around me, and I never wanted him to let go. But he did, and he stepped out into the hall. I left the door ajar and threw the comforter back on Kyla's bed. I glared at the clean bra.

"You can do this, Hannah O'Leary," I said. "Master Gira will not win."

I fastened the bra around me and slipped the straps over my shoulders. I stepped into the underwear and pulled it up. I reached for the jeans but paused. I had to do more than just stand up to the hypnotist. I needed to defeat him. In order to do that, I had to make my own choices.

I moved to the dresser and selected Kyla's cutest pair of plaid shorts and stepped into them. I chose a different top from her closet, a sleeveless pale green blouse with a fringed collar. I slipped my feet into a pair of rhinestone flip-flops and swung the door open.

Plug's eyes widened.

"I'm not done, yet." I walked down the hall to the bathroom and rummaged through the drawers for a washcloth. I wiped my face and my armpits, found some deodorant and used that, too. I even brushed out my hair and pulled it back into a fresh ponytail. Not perfect, but at least I smelled better.

"Now I'm ready," I said to Plug in the hallway.

"Yes, you are," he said. We walked down the stairs and paused in front of the ornate display case. Plug lifted my hand, and on my palm he wrote Kyla's street address. "So you can tell the hypnotist where you are."

We peeked out the windows for any sign of police, but spotted no one.

Plug snapped the battery back into my phone and turned it on.

"I'll be in the garage, but if you need me, yell," Plug said. "Hopefully, you'll be able to tell him you're alone. If he doesn't call within fifteen minutes, we're leaving anyhow. I don't know how the GPS tracking works, and I don't want to be trapped here if the cops show up again."

"Agreed." But we didn't have to wait. The phone rang before we reached the kitchen.

"It's him," Plug said. "Convince yourself that you're alone."

"Got it." My heart beat faster. He gave me the phone. Then he stepped into the garage and left me by myself in the kitchen.

⇥ • ⇤

Plug threw me over his shoulder, and I beat my fists against his back.

"Put me down!" I tore at his shirt and scratched at his skin.

"Everything's going to be fine," Plug said and hauled me from the kitchen to the garage. I screamed louder and kicked harder.

Plug set me down next to Kyla's Mini Cooper and covered my mouth.

"Stop, Hannah."

I kicked him in the shin and bit his hand. He pinned me alongside Kyla's car.

"Hannah!" He glanced away, but kept his grip on my mouth. When he faced me, his lip was bleeding. "I don't want to hurt you," he said, "but I'll gag and tie you if I have to."

He removed his hand, and I let out a little hiss. His body weight pressed against mine, and his forehead was coated with perspiration. Plug reached behind me, and then he shifted my stance with his legs so he could open the car door.

"Get in," he said.

"I can't leave," I said.

"Get in the car!"

He pushed me toward the seat, but I clutched the frame and braced myself.

"Please, Hannah. If you've ever trusted me, do this, now."

My chest tightened. "I don't trust you. Leave without me." My gaze darted around the garage and toward the interior door to the house. I had to get past Plug. He was stronger than me, but I needed to stay at Kyla's house. I needed to wait . . . for something.

Plug cupped my face. I twisted my head away from him.

"Hannah, you're stronger than this. Have faith in yourself. Trust yourself and fight him."

"Who?" I jerked my head back in the other direction, but Plug kept his hands on my cheeks.

"The hypnotist. Use your mind. Act for yourself. What is the last thing you remember?"

My thoughts were jumbled. I couldn't remember. Why did Plug throw me over his shoulder? I went back further. Upstairs. I had changed my clothes.

"We walked down the staircase. My phone rang"—I gasped and let go of the car. Plug stepped back and gave me space. "Oh no. What happened? I can't remember anything the hypnotist said."

"He told you to stay here and wait for him." Plug's hands found mine. "He left you in the trance. I tried to wake you up from it, but nothing I said worked. I don't know how to unlock your mind, Hannah. I need your help. You've been fighting me for the past ten minutes. We have to get out of here. He will show up any second. Please, Hannah, get in the car and let me walk around to the driver's side."

I sat down, but instinct told me to jump and run. I waited for Plug to sit in the driver's seat. He started the engine and pushed the button on the garage door opener that was clipped to the visor. Plug watched in the rearview mirror as the garage door rolled up, and I bolted from the car. I ran for the house door and slammed it behind me. I flipped the lock and paced the kitchen.

Plug pounded on the door.

Then he stopped.

Everything was quiet, and I froze. I was a fool. Plug was an expert at picking locks. He threw the door open and lunged toward me. I ran for the stairs, but he tackled me at the base.

"Hannah, I don't want to hurt you, but we can't stay here. That man has sunk his claws deep into your mind." He loosened his grasp on me, and I rolled over to face him. A tear ran down his face, and blood trailed down his chin. "Please, Hannah, I love you. But I need you to fight this guy. He told you not to trust your friends. He told you to wait here for him. He left you in a hypnotic trance. I don't know how to get you to wake up. Please let me take you away before he gets here. I can't stand the idea of him touching you. It rips out my insides. Wake up, Hannah. Use the guided imagery Rose taught us. Take back your mind. Please, Hannah."

My stomach twisted. Every fiber of my body told me to distrust Plug. But that was absurd. Plug had been by my side throughout this horrible journey. He'd never hurt me. But what if I was wrong? What if my feelings toward Plug weren't real? Maybe my attraction to him was merely a planted suggestion. How was I supposed to tell the difference?

"I'm so confused," I whispered.

Plug caressed my cheek. "That's a step in the right direction. Fight, Hannah, fight for your own free will."

"Yes, Hannah," a deep voice said, "fight for your own free will. That will be entertaining."

The voice wasn't a demon or my imagination this time.

Master Gira—John Harrison—stood behind Plug.

My heart beat in my throat, and I struggled to take a breath. This couldn't be happening. I had been unsure in the hotel lounge, but now I knew beyond any doubt this was the same man I'd met on the stage at the fair.

"Go to your safe place in your mind," Plug whispered. Then he hopped up and positioned himself between me and the hypnotist.

Harrison puffed out his chest. The same glimmer in his eyes. The same bushy eyebrows. The same hands. I gagged and twisted to the side to wretch, but produced only dry heaves. The sour flavor of bile still filled my mouth. Pressure throbbed inside my ears.

Plug's feet moved. He shifted his weight to his back leg and kicked with his front. He landed a blow to Harrison's chest and smashed him into the display case. Broken glass flew everywhere and clattered against the wall. Harrison snatched a large shard and flung it at Plug. It sliced Plug's wrist as he tried to dodge out of the way. Harrison leaped and swung with another piece of glass, but Plug blocked him with his forearm. Plug struck Harrison in

246

the neck, sending him down. Harrison tried to shake it off and lift himself up, but he slipped on glass and fell back to the floor.

Plug glanced at me and pulled out his phone.

"Plug!" I shot forward to help, but I was too slow. Harrison came at Plug on his blind side, his swollen eye useless. Harrison clubbed Plug with a bronze sculpture from the display case. Plug collapsed, his phone cast aside. Harrison hammered his skull over and over.

"No!" I grabbed Harrison's arm, but he flung me away like a waif.

Plug lay limp on the floor. Blood glistened along his hairline and oozed onto the beige carpet. I reached for the phone—the display showed that he'd dialed 9-1- before he dropped it. Harrison stepped on my hand. The rubber tread of his powder-blue sneakers pressed my fingers deep into the soft fibers of the carpet. He picked up the phone and shattered it against the wall.

"Welcome to my Mystical Madness!" Harrison swung his arm wide and dropped the sculpture. It whacked my bare knee and thudded to the floor.

Harrison reached down and clutched my wrist. I yanked away, but he was stronger. He locked eyes with me and hauled me to my feet. His jeans brushed my exposed legs.

"Who seems foolish now?" he asked.

My chin quivered. I squinted and tried to think, but the room was spinning. The lights grew brighter, and my ears buzzed.

Harrison pushed me against the wall. He still held my wrist with one hand, and with the other he stroked my naked arm. Goose bumps erupted along my skin. I focused on the blacks of his pupils. I had to get away from him. I tried to shrug out from beneath his grip, but he slammed me back to the wall and wedged his forearm against my throat.

"You said you were alone." His rancid cigarette breath hit me in the face.

"I. Was." Each word hurt as he pushed harder. I strained my eyes to get a glimpse of Plug. He hadn't moved. The puddle of blood on the carpet had grown. Shapes and silhouettes crept along the base of the wall. They grew and began to churn near him.

"Plug!"

"He's dead," Harrison said.

Harrison stroked my face. Those large, hairy hands that I'd feared in my delusions touched me. I wanted to curl up into a ball and cry, but I had to save myself, and I needed to get help for Plug.

I gasped for a breath and then choked out more words. "Why. Are you. Doing this?"

Harrison drew his fingertip along my lips. "You should still be in a hypnotic state from our phone conversation." He narrowed his eyes at me.

"I never. Did anything. To you."

Darkness swirled at the edges of my vision. I closed my eyes and struggled for air. Harrison caressed my eyelids, and I jerked them open. The sun must have gone behind a cloud, because the house grew darker. I pushed against Harrison with all my might, and I dug my fingernails into the side of his face. But then he wrenched my arm behind my back.

"You are my greatest victory," he said. "I've achieved more with you than I ever dreamed possible. I've stirred your inner conflicts and heightened your emotions." He pressed his body against mine. "You know . . . you look like your mother did back in New Jersey. The same jawline. The same lips." He drew the tip of his nose along my cheek and inhaled deeply.

"If you'd given me a chance, Beth," he said, "we could've been together all these years." He leaned in, his lips next to mine.

"I'm not Beth," I whispered.

He pulled back, and his fingers moved to my neck. "You're right. Beth told me to leave her alone and threatened to call the police. Said she was married, but I knew she was unhappy with your father. She stayed with him even though he was such an arrogant man. He took more than Beth from me; he took my future. He lied to the Dean of Students and had me kicked out of Princeton. But it wasn't long after that . . . I showed him I was the master."

His grip tightened around my neck.

"Beth should've come to me after he died." Harrison tilted his head and leaned closer to me. "Instead, you left town, Beth. Changed your last name. Changed your appearance. That made it harder, but four years and five private detectives later, I found you. I suppose that gave me time to devise the perfect revenge with Chelsea. And I'm here now. Killing your husband didn't work out, but maybe killing your daughter will."

I tried to swallow, tried to breathe, but he tightened his grip. My mind raced, analyzing everything he'd said.

He loosened his grasp, and I gulped for air.

"With Chelsea?" I asked.

"Yes." Harrison laughed. "She's performed flawlessly, invading your life and taunting you . . . laying the groundwork to make everyone believe you'd gone stark raving mad."

Images flashed through my mind of Chelsea at the fair, in the broadcasting room, and at Clandestine Coffee.

"The breaker box at the warehouse?" I asked.

"And so much more," he whispered.

"The pink elephant?"

He smiled and dug his fingers deeper into my neck. I needed to keep him talking. I needed to figure a way out of this.

"You've been here. At least a year," I said, but he pushed against my windpipe. "Why wait. So long?"

"I told you. Perfect plans take time." Harrison smirked. "Your father's demise took years of stalking, and planning, and practicing my craft—"

"My father?" Nausea flooded through me. Tears raced down my face, and I glared at Harrison. "You hypnotized him? Made him think he was crazy? Made him think he'd done horrible things?" The weight of the truth sank down on me.

Harrison grinned. "But he was nowhere near as fun as you have been."

The light bulb above us burst, like the one in the warehouse had, casting us deeper into the shadows. Darkness filled my soul, and rage seeped through every pore. I kicked and flailed, because I wanted him dead.

"My dad killed himself because he believed he was crazy!" I screamed.

"So will you." He shoved me against the wall. "When I'm finished, you'll believe you killed this boy, and you'll hate yourself for hurting everyone around you. You won't be able to end your life fast enough."

"Have you hurt my mom?" I hit him again, but he laughed at my fruitless efforts.

"Don't worry," he said. "She's tied up right now, but she'll be waiting center stage for the final act when we arrive."

He jerked my left hand up.

"No."

He touched my fingertips.

He lowered his voice and spoke in a rapid monotone.

"From the tips of your fingers I want you to relax all your muscles." His touch moved from my hand to my wrist.

"No!" He did this to me the first time we met on the stage, but I still couldn't react fast enough to fight his words.

"As you relax I want you to feel an overwhelming sense of peace and goodness. I want only an immense sense of calm for you."

It was a lie, but my mind remained in his clutch. I tried to picture my safe place—the cabin, the flowers—but my anger painted everything with crimson red. I wanted John Harrison's blood. He needed to pay for all of this, but my mind was bewitched by his monotone phrases.

"Let go of your worries and relax. When I count to three you will slip into that deep resting place of serenity and comfort. One. Two. Three. Sleep!" He snapped, and my legs gave out from beneath me.

I fell to the floor.

My head bounced on the soft carpet, and my face landed inches from Plug's. The metallic aroma of his blood overcame my senses. I was conscious, but I couldn't move. My eyes were open, but I couldn't see a way out of this mess.

Harrison walked away from me toward the kitchen.

Swirls of smoke danced around Plug's head. I moved my lips to yell and wake Plug, but my words were inaudible. The mist twirled above Plug, as if brushstrokes appeared on a canvas. A dark vertical cloud began to take shape.

"No," I whispered. A black feather drifted down and settled in the pool of Plug's blood. In the space above him, a shape formed out of the darkness. Featherless wings extended from the backside of a hooded robe. Bare-bone arms with claws reached toward Plug. This was not a hallucination. The buoyant beast loomed over Plug, and I pictured Plug's chalk drawing of the screaming skulls. Plug looked nothing like the victims he'd drawn. His muscles were relaxed. His eyelids were closed. Except for the pool of blood beneath his head, I would have assumed he was sleeping. He couldn't die. Not today. Not because of me.

"Wake up, Plug," I whispered.

Footsteps moved across the kitchen floor.

The house remained dim, but the dark spirit faded away. In addition to Chelsea and Harrison toying with me, evil spirits continued to taunt me as well. And I had to fight against them all.

Harrison stepped next to me and set down two red gasoline cans. With gloved hands, he lifted me and sat me alongside the wall. He pressed my fingers around the handles of each can. Then he pulled out a cloth and wiped the things he had touched earlier, like the sculpture and the large shard of glass with Plug's blood on it.

"Hannah," he said, "stand up and walk with me."

I didn't want to, but my body surrendered to his command. I walked with Harrison, past Plug, past the broken display case, through the kitchen, and out to the garage. My plaid shorts snagged on a protruding piece of metal from Plug's damaged El Camino. I pulled the fabric free and continued walking with Harrison out through the open front of the garage.

Harrison's sedan was parked in the driveway. He opened the door to the back seat.

"Sit and stay put. Do you understand?" he asked.

"Yes," I said.

I sank onto the vinyl.

Harrison slammed the door and went back inside the garage, closing the big door behind him. He didn't even bother to tie me up. He was confident I was under his influence, which I seemed to be, despite my efforts to fight. But I refused to give up.

I closed my eyes and worked to descend to that safe place in my mind—my cabin surrounded by cottonwoods, maples, and junipers. I needed to lock away Harrison's suggestions, and then I would fight my way out of this. But a thick blanket of fog covered everything from the elevator to the grassy hill, and a wisp of black smoke extended from the roof into the foggy sky. It twisted and jerked like a cobra about to strike. I froze. This was supposed to be my safe place, but the black mist shot toward me, swirled around my feet, and coiled up my legs.

"You cannot win," a deep demonic voice said. "You're not strong enough. You're not smart enough. You're not—"

"At least I have a body!" I yelled. "You have nothing."

"A body you cannot control is worse than nothing at all!" the demon roared.

I covered my ears. I knew he was right, but I had to find a way to help Plug. I had to somehow regain command of my body and get away from Harrison.

I steeled my nerves and chanted, "Be gone. You have no power here."

The smoke receded a few feet. I chanted again, and it withdrew to the chimney of the cabin, but its laughter echoed in the hollows of the cabin.

It bellowed back to me, "You're too weak to defeat me."

I staggered and faltered, but eventually I found the ornate lock box on the porch of the cabin. I wrote Harrison's hypnotic words on the small tablet, tore off the sheet, set it in the box, and secured the lid.

Then I remembered more of Harrison's words from earlier. He had said, *Yes, Hannah, fight for your own free will. That will be entertaining.*

I grabbed the tablet, and I wrote those words in large black letters. I tore the sheet off, and I posted it to the front door of the cabin. I would fight. He'd given the command, and I would use it to my advantage.

"You're not strong enough."

"Be gone!" I yelled.

The fog thinned. My thoughts became clearer. I leaned against the wall of the cabin, and a memory resurfaced. The hypnotist had called me by name on the stage in the arena. He knew who I was. He lured me behind the food truck at the fair. That's when he planted the trigger phrase in my mind and told me to overreact to every little thing. That was also when he told me to always answer my phone when I saw his number on caller ID.

I sank against the cabin's porch and tried to catch my breath. The dark mists began to swirl at my feet. I hadn't defeated the demon. I didn't know how. And I couldn't defeat Harrison, because I didn't know how. I was losing this battle.

But I still had to ascend from this place in my mind and try to save Plug. I stood and set my hand on the sheet I'd posted to the cabin's door. The hypnotist had given me permission to fight for my own free will, and that little crack in the chains that bound me had to be the key for me to escape him. I emerged from my meditation.

I opened my eyes and pulled in a long, slow breath.

I was still slumped in the back seat of Harrison's sedan, but my mind was more alert than it had been in days. I needed to move, but my limbs remained immobile. Maybe the demon was right. I wasn't strong enough. But then the tips of my fingers and the tips of my toes began to prickle as sensation began to return. I scrunched up my toes and moved one finger at a time.

A week ago, I only thought about starting my senior year of high school and preparing to leave for Princeton. I wanted to date Manny. I wanted everyone to get along and have fun.

Now, I only wanted to save the people I loved and reclaim my free will.

Harrison came out through the front door. He closed it behind him and wiped the knob clean. He slid into the driver's seat of the sedan. Without a word, he shifted into reverse and drove out of the neighborhood. I couldn't turn my head to see if Kyla's house was on fire, but I knew he'd started it. He smelled like gasoline and smoke.

⊶ • ⊷

Harrison drove toward downtown. I rotated my wrists and bent my elbows. Each mile we traveled put Plug that much closer to death, if he was even still alive. I inched my hand toward the door. My heart beat faster, but I steadied my breathing. Up ahead I saw a busy intersection.

We stopped at the red light.

I bent my elbow and lifted my fingers to the handle. I kept my gaze away from the rearview mirror. Harrison could not know I was alert.

The light changed, and Harrison accelerated. I had to escape before the car's speed increased too much. With stilted movements, I reached for the handle, unlocked the door, and flung it wide open. Before Harrison could react, I grabbed the frame and launched myself out into the road. The asphalt caught me with unforgiving hands.

The driver behind us slammed on his brakes that squealed as he honked. A minivan in the next lane swerved to avoid plowing over me.

Harrison leaned out of his window and squinted at me, but he shook his head at the gathering commotion and drove away. The back door of the sedan swung shut as Harrison sped down the street.

Tremors traveled throughout my body. I'd done it. I'd escaped. The driver from behind ran to me and helped me stand. My legs wobbled. I tightened my grip on his arm and watched Harrison make a left at the next intersection.

"Are you okay?" the man asked.

Road rash blanketed my bare legs and arms, but otherwise I seemed intact. No fractures. No major injuries. Cars honked and drove past. I had to find Mom. I had to help Plug.

"Can I use your phone?" My voice was too faint, and he leaned in closer to me.

"What?" he yelled over the traffic noise.

I cleared my throat and tried again. "Your phone?"

He pulled his cell from his pocket and offered it to me. I dialed 911 and told the operator about the fire at Kyla's house. I read to her the address that Plug had written on the palm of my hand.

"Hurry!" I said. "Eugene Polaski is unconscious inside the house."

The man next to me paled. "What's going on?" he asked.

I dialed Mom's cell. I hoped Harrison had lied about having her. I hoped she was fine and with the police. She had to be okay.

"We need to get out of the road," the man said. I turned my back to him and waited for Mom to answer. Cars continued to honk.

"Hello, Hannah," Harrison said.

My knees went weak, and I nearly dropped the phone, but the man behind me steadied me and looped his arm beneath mine.

"You can stand in the road all day," Harrison said, "but I'm coming back for you. If you contact the police, I will kill your mother today."

I ended the call and screamed at the top of my lungs until my throat ached. The man who'd been helping me took a step back and gaped at me. This couldn't be real. Harrison couldn't have Mom. It couldn't be true. I chewed on my cheek and tried to concentrate. I dialed my home phone number and dashed across the busy street, dodging cars as I went.

"Hello?" a woman's voice said.

"Who's this?" I asked.

"Hey!" the driver yelled. "Give me back my phone." He started to come after me, but then he retraced his steps to his abandoned car in the middle of the road.

Sirens howled in the distance.

I stepped onto the sidewalk and paused, out of breath.

"I'm a police officer," the woman on my home phone said. "Is this Hannah? We've been—"

"Is my mom there?" I asked.

"No, but Hannah—"

I hung up. I refused to accept the idea that Harrison had Mom. I scanned the area to get my bearings. Mom's hotel was a few blocks away. I tried to remember the phone number. I dialed information instead. They connected me, and the hotel operator answered.

"May I speak with the general manager, Beth O'Leary?"

"I'm sorry, she's unavailable this afternoon," the operator said. "May I take a message?"

I dropped the phone on the concrete, kicked off my flip-flops, and started running. Harrison had Mom, and I had to find her before it was too late.

About a block before the hotel, I stopped on the sidewalk. A police cruiser was parked under the canopy. I assessed my options. On the left side of the road were office buildings. On my right was a church. Mrs. Santos's face came to mind. She believed with absolute faith. *A prayer can help. If you have faith, God will bring good things to you, but you have to invite him in,* she had said.

I needed all the help I could get. I stepped up to the alcove of the church, closed my eyes, and offered a silent prayer, pleading for God to listen and to help me. The sun-heated concrete began to burn my feet, and the road rash along my legs throbbed with pain.

I opened my eyes just as Harrison turned onto the street. I leaned backward into the shade of the church's overhang and hid from view. Harrison sped past me and pulled under the hotel's canopy, right next to the police cruiser. Harrison tossed his keys to the valet, and then he entered the hotel. The police weren't searching for the hypnotist. They were searching for me.

The door behind me opened, and I stumbled backward. A pastor grasped my arm to balance me.

"Would you like to come inside?" he asked.

"I just need to sit for a minute," I said. I needed to think. With the police at the entrance and with Harrison lurking somewhere inside, I had to find a different way into the hotel.

"You're injured." The pastor motioned toward my bruises and wounds.

"I'm okay." I sank into an oversized chair in the foyer and leaned forward. I needed to catch my breath and figure out a solution.

The pastor sat in the chair next to me and waited in silence. After a few minutes, he suddenly said, "You must open your heart to truly open your mind. Let the good light illuminate your path so you'll no longer walk in darkness at noonday. He speaks with a soft voice and will guide you with inspiration."

I lifted my head. He spoke in riddles like Mrs. Santos had. I missed her comforting hugs and warm smile. It broke my heart that she thought I would intentionally set fire to her house.

The pastor set his hand on mine. "Your sorrow brings Satan joy. He attempts to tie strings to your mind and body so he can manipulate you like a puppet. Take action, fight against the evil, and it will lose its energy. You have the power to dismiss Satan and his evil spirits. Have faith in your own abilities and listen to the still, small voice."

He squeezed my hand, and I wept.

"I will get you a glass of water." He rose and walked down the hall, but I didn't wait for him to return.

I wiped my face and headed back out onto the street. I had an idea.

I stayed out of the sight of the police officers and darted down into the parking garage. I ran to the spot in back where Mom usually parked. Her red Toyota Prius was there. I checked doors, locked. But my foot snagged on a soft lump hidden partially beneath her car. I reached down and tugged out Mom's purse.

Harrison must've grabbed her here. On the phone, Mom had said she was about to leave. She was here when she shrieked on the phone.

I had to find her.

I rummaged through her purse and found her keys. I unlocked the car door and sank into the back seat. I lay on my side and tried to compose myself. I could drive back to Kyla's house and help Plug, but I'd already called 911 and reported the fire. They should be there helping him. There was nothing more I could do to save him. But I had a strong feeling my mom was somewhere nearby. Harrison was here. She had to be, too.

I searched Mom's purse again and found her master key card to the hotel. That would help. I sat up and scanned the parking garage. I was alone. I ran to the freight elevator and rode it to the fourth floor. I knew from experience, fewer rooms were rented on this floor. People either wanted the top floors for a better view or they wanted the lower floors to avoid the elevators. I stepped into the vestibule and peered in both directions down the hallway. No one. I moved over to the house phone and pressed zero. The hotel operator answered.

"Do you have vacancies tonight?" I asked.

"Yes, we do."

"I want to reserve a specific suite. Can you tell me which ones are available?"

"The White Clouds, Tetons, Cascades—"

"Tetons," I said.

"The name for the reservation?" she asked.

"Jane Smith." That was too obvious. I should've thought of a more realistic name.

"And what credit card would you like to use to hold the reservation?"

I cradled the phone between my shoulder and my ear and dug through Mom's purse. I found her wallet and pinched out her American Express card. I read the number to the operator. The operator read back the details. No problem. As a hotel manager's daughter, I already knew they wouldn't run Mom's card until tomorrow at the earliest. I needed them to hold the room and not check anyone else into it so I could have a place to hide and formulate a plan. A master key would get me into the room, but a reservation would keep other people out. And I needed a guarantee that I'd be alone and safe until I knew what to do.

"One more question," I said to the operator. "Has John Harrison checked in yet?"

"Yes, would you like me to connect you?"

"No, thank you," I said and hung up the phone. I also knew from experience it was pointless to ask the operator what room Harrison was in. They weren't allowed to give out that information. I had to be smarter than he was.

I rode the freight elevator to the top floor and hoped no one would be lurking in the halls to question my appearance. I ran through the empty hall to the door of the Tetons suite and slid Mom's master key card into the slot. The door opened. I slipped inside, closed the door, and sank to the cool marble entry.

The bottoms of my feet were solid black from running on the concrete and asphalt. I forced myself to stand, and I cringed when I put my full weight on my feet. Now that the adrenaline was fading, pain shot up from the soles of my feet to the joints of my hips. I stumbled across the plush white carpet and sat at the side desk. I fumbled through the drawers for a phone book. Once I found it, I turned to the yellow pages and began dialing hospitals. I asked each one if Eugene Polaski had been admitted. Nothing. I couldn't call Kyla or Nick, because I didn't know their numbers. Besides, they were probably still at the police station.

The sun was setting. Darkness began to creep from the walls of the room toward me. I was being sucked into an emotional black hole. How could I help Plug or my mom if I couldn't help myself? I switched on the desk lamp. A small light glowed over the desktop. It was ineffective against the looming malevolence. I had to find a way to lock the doors of my mind and soul so that nothing could break through ever again.

I rubbed my temples and tried to slow my breathing. I pictured my safe place. Colorful flowers filled the rolling hills and a grassy patch waited for me beneath the cottonwoods.

"It won't work."

I jerked open my eyes to see who'd spoken, but I was alone. An ant dropped from the ceiling onto my arm. And then another fell.

Don't look up, I told myself.

I closed my eyes and wiped my sweaty palms on my thighs. I imagined my field of flowers. My trees. My breeze. I directed my thoughts. Plug had given me keys. Rose had given me keys. The pastor had given me keys. It was all related—hypnosis, meditation, guided imagery, and prayer. They all connected the mind, body, and soul. The difference was in the intent. Good or evil. Positive or negative. Hope or despair. I would use all of these keys I'd gathered together to close the door and lock out the demons.

I imagined my cabin at the top of the hill and ran to it, but as I neared it, strands of black smoke snaked from the windows. Inside, the space seemed empty at first, but mists of blackness danced along the walls and the floors. I yelled, "You have no power here! Get out!"

A broom materialized in my hands, and I swept the dark shapes and mists out the front door. I swept every crack and crevice and corner of the cabin. I swept it clean. I slammed the door closed. They would have no more access to my mind. Ever again.

"It's not enough," a soft voice whispered in my mind. The voice reassured me and urged me to do more.

I examined the empty cabin. I had swept it clean, but it remained dark. I needed to replace the previous evil with something better. I imagined sunlight beaming in through the dirty windows. I polished the windows until they sparkled. Then I set up a wooden art easel in front of the largest window as I'd seen at Clandestine Coffee. Then I added a stool in front of the easel . . . a white stool with bright paint colors splattered all over it. I'd be able to sit there and paint the flowers blooming in the field. I created a table next to it and furnished it with the art supplies I'd been introduced to this past week. The charcoal, the watercolors, the pencils, the brushes, and so much more.

I covered the barren floor with an Egyptian woven rug. I hung artwork on the walls by Picasso and Monet—bright colors and happy images. I set an overstuffed corduroy armchair in the corner with a fresh Italian soda next to it. My breathing slowed. I felt at peace. This cabin—my mind—had been invaded by the darkness, but I'd now banished the demons. Now the space housed my nascent creativity. When I had only swept the space clean, it was still unfinished. I had to fill the empty space with better things.

I stored every detail in my memory. I intended to revisit here and paint the landscape and drink the Italian soda. I stepped out onto the porch and locked the door to my place of serenity and comfort. Only I had the ability to unlock my mind. No one would ever enter without my invitation. I moved along the meadow. I heard birds in the grove of junipers, oaks, maples, and cottonwoods. The trees stood strong and stable, and I would too.

I felt the breeze on my face. I focused on the colors of the flowers. I counted and touched the petals. One, for red geranium. Two, for purple violets. Three, for yellow daffodils. Deep breath. White irises. I returned to the elevator to lift myself back to the real world. Another deep breath. I watched the display in the elevator tick off the floors, and I rose to the main level.

I felt peaceful when I opened my eyes.

On the desktop, my hand rested near a brochure advertising the amenities of the hotel. I flipped it open and took a sharp breath. I knew where Mom was.

I glanced at the time on the wall clock, midnight. I'd meditated for hours.

BOOK FOUR

Belief

An enduring belief in light rises above the darkness of night.

SATURDAY
AUGUST 31

I ran to the door and flung it open—startling a couple in the hallway. They gawked at me, and I swung the door shut. I leaned against it and listened to them chuckle on the other side.

I needed a plan to beat Harrison at his insane game. If I was too reckless, I risked suffering the same fate as my father. If I was too cautious, Mom could die.

My blackened footprints marked the plush carpet of the suite. I was filthy, and road rash covered my legs and arms. My clothes were ripped. And I stunk. I no longer cared what other people thought about me, but now, more than ever, I needed to blend in and be inconspicuous so I could sneak through the hotel and rescue Mom. A shower would give me time to devise a strategy. In the bathroom, I stripped off my clothes and hopped into the shower. I let the water blast against my neck and chest. When the spray hit my week-old seat belt bruise, it no longer stung, but the fresh road rash pulsated with pain. I wanted to scream, and then I realized I could. I was alone. The suite was huge. Chances of anyone hearing me were miniscule. I turned toward the cascade of water and yelled as it flushed the debris from my wounds. The release invigorated my mind, and ideas for a plan came to me.

An ant scampered along the small shelf next to the complimentary shampoo. I was confident this little guy was real. I once read that if an ant was separated from its original colony, no other colony would accept it. The new ants would attack it and leave it to die alone. I lifted my finger to the outcropping and let the ant crawl onto my skin. I opened the shower door and squatted down to free the ant. It scurried away across the tiles.

I finished showering, dried off, and tossed the towel to the side.

Floor-to-ceiling mirrors covered the far wall. Yesterday, I would have freaked, but now I stepped over to the mirror and leaned toward it.

Green eyes.

I blinked.

Still green.

No panic welled inside me. I was confident the evil spirits were finally gone. But I still feared losing the people I loved. I had no idea if Plug was alive or dead, but I was certain I could still help Mom.

I examined my wounds. They weren't as extensive as they felt. My left knee, thigh, and forearm had taken the brunt of the fall, but they appeared clean. So, I slipped my clothes on and tried to avoid rubbing the road rash. The tear in the side of my shorts was pretty noticeable, but I had no way to fix it. I let my hair hang loose around my shoulders to dry.

I darted through the halls, which were less crowded than at midday, but with more than 500 rooms, two restaurants, and three lounges, a lot of people still lurked about just after midnight. Even though I was freshly showered, I still received strange glances. I evaded as many people as possible, because I needed to get to Mom's office and use her computer.

The manager-on-duty and security personnel could be anywhere in the hotel, but I chanced it and swiped Mom's master key card to gain access to the back offices. The outer room was empty. I weaved through the staff desks, and once in Mom's private office, I closed the door behind me and let out a breath.

My gaze landed on an armoire in the corner. Inside it, I discovered clothes fresh from the dry cleaner and a plastic box labeled FIRST-AID KIT. I tore off my grimy outfit and opened the box. To my disappointment, it only contained a small assortment of Band-Aids and a half-used tube of Neosporin. I tossed it aside and changed into clean slacks and a shirt. Mom was taller, and I tripped over the hems of her pant legs. I attempted to fold them, but the fabric slipped out. I snatched the stapler from the desktop and tacked them in place.

I sat at her desk, tugged the computer keyboard closer, and typed the password: Hannah. I'd told Mom to use a better password, but she ignored me.

I typed into Google: How do you not get hypnotized?

Fifteen million websites came up in less than one second.

Meditation and self-hypnosis were keys. I skimmed through the tips and tricks for self-hypnosis—almost identical to the guided imagery Rose had taught in art. The main difference was to plant a posthypnotic suggestion. I closed the Internet browser and racked my brain. I needed an idea that would be impervious to Harrison.

A small icon on Mom's computer monitor labeled SECURITY SURVEILLANCE caught my eye. I clicked it, and the screen populated with six videos across and five down. I scanned the images, but then they refreshed with different views of the hotel.

This time I caught a glimpse of the renovated lounge. Propped center stage was a large wingback chair with its rear to the camera. I squinted, but the images changed. My instincts told me Mom was in that chair. I clicked around the screen, trying to figure out how to return to the previous images. Nothing worked. I pounded my fist against the desktop and shoved the keyboard away.

Harrison said she'd be waiting center stage for the final act. He probably assumed he was being cryptic, but he didn't realize I'd been in the lounge when Mom humiliated him in front of Kevin and Mr. Holloday. I was certain Harrison planned to disgrace her in the same place.

I picked up the phone to call the police. My hand shook. Harrison had told me to avoid contact with the police at all costs. I'd turn myself in if it would save Mom, but what if I was wrong and she wasn't even in the hotel? What if Harrison followed through on his threat and killed her because I called the authorities? I slammed the phone down and tugged at my hair.

Nick had said that Harrison used a rhyming phrase as my hypnotic trigger. My own posthypnotic suggestion should rhyme. I scooted back in Mom's chair and prepared to meditate. But then my eyes went wide. I needed some sort of alarm to wake me up in case the meditation took too long. I needed to hurry. I had to get to Mom.

I scrounged through the top drawer of Mom's desk and found a stop-watch. That would work. I set the alarm for twenty minutes, but hopefully, I'd finish sooner. I leaned back in the chair and began.

I ran to the safe place in my mind. The door of the cabin flew open before me. Inside, I snatched a sketchpad and propped it on the art easel. I perched on the stool in front of it and with a black marker I brainstormed ideas on the pad:

I am confident. I am assured. I will do whatever is necessary to save my mom and myself, especially when fighting against John Harrison or any other demons that might enter my life. My mind is strong enough, and it cannot be penetrated by anyone but me. I set the rules of my own life. I am mentally tough enough to fight Harrison and win. I will unite my words, thoughts, and soul. By claiming my own inner strength and power of free choice, I will be safe from evil spirits. I will triumph against John Harrison. It is my life. My body. My mind. My soul.

I read the words over and then tore off the page and set it on the table next to the easel. I'd spent the past week hoping people like Dr. James, Mrs. Santos, Mom, Manny, and even Plug would figure out how to help me, when the solution had been within me all along.

Fiddling with the chalks, I reflected on the meanings Rose had taught us. Red represented anger, but it also represented passion and courage. I selected the crimson chalk, and on the clean sketchpad I drew the outline of a large red heart. Inside it I wrote:

> *I control my mind, body, and spirit.*
> *Nobody can come anywhere near it.*
> *Using any means necessary I'll rescue my mother.*
> *Because I am in control, none other.*

I memorized it, believed it, and accepted it. I folded the pages and tucked them into my shirt. These messages would stay with me when I left this place. I moved across the wooden porch and onto the grass. I repeated my mantra—my own posthypnotic suggestion—as I glided through the field of flowers. The doors to the elevator opened with a soft ding. I stepped inside, and with a new calm assurance, I rode the elevator in my mind and watched the numbers count me out of my meditative state. A beep sounded each time the digits changed.

I breathed in slowly, opened my eyes, and rubbed my hands on Mom's slacks. The alarm on the stopwatch beeped. I reached out and silenced it.

Impulsively, I dumped out the contents of Mom's purse. Among other things, a pocketknife and a can of pepper spray clattered to the desktop. I tossed the knife back into the empty purse along with Mom's key card.

I stood and held the pepper spray at arm's length. I needed to know how it worked. I held my breath and shot a quick spray. The liquid came out in a stream and hit the wall. There was no chemical cloud. My eyes didn't burn. My skin felt fine. I took a breath, and the odor made me gag. I clutched Mom's purse and darted out of her office.

In the outer room, I fumbled through the desk drawers and searched for useful items. I found a gray crocheted scarf, duct tape, a heavy-duty staple gun, wet wipes, and a long, sharp letter opener. I added them all to the purse.

Any means necessary.

I was ready.

I lifted the phone and pressed zero.

"Please connect me to John Harrison's room," I said to the hotel operator.

"Hello?" Harrison's voice sent chills through my body, and I repeated my mantra in my head.

I control my mind, body, and spirit.
Nobody can come anywhere near it.
Using any means necessary I'll rescue my mother.
Because I am in control, none other.

"Where is my mom?" I asked.

"Hannah, I wondered how long it would take you to find me," Harrison said.

I took a deep breath.

"Ants on the ground," Harrison said, "ants on your feet, ants on your arm put you right to sleep."

His rhyme was worse than mine. I had never remembered the trigger phrase from the many times he'd manipulated me. I felt liberated hearing it now.

"Are you alone?" Harrison asked.

"Yes." I tried to use a blank monotone as I'd seen myself do in the videos.

"Where are you?"

"The hotel's back offices."

"Hannah, are you holding the phone with your right hand or your left?" he asked.

I puzzled at the question.

"My right," I said.

"Why did you hesitate?" he asked.

This was going to be tricky. "I'm tired. It's been a long day."

"Hannah, I want nothing but serenity and comfort for you. Do you understand?"

"Yes," I said.

"Hannah, the tips of your fingers are beginning to warm. Can you sense it?"

"Yes." But I told myself the opposite. My fingers were cold.

"Your left hand is heating up more than your right. Touch it to your cheek. Can you feel the warmth?"

"Yes." I pressed it against my cheek, still cold. What was he trying to accomplish? Why didn't he just tell me where to meet him? Why was he wasting time?

"Hannah, your left hand is so hot the skin is beginning to perspire. The flesh is turning from pink to red. Is it painful?"

"Yes." I tightened my fingers into a fist and repeated my own mantra in my mind. I was in control of my mind, body, and spirit. Nobody—not even Harrison—could come near it.

"The pain is worsening. Imagine you stuck your left hand into the burning flames of a roaring campfire. The pain is excruciating."

I groaned and played along.

"Yes, Hannah, it's burning. Your flesh is falling away."

I gritted my teeth and tried to figure out what he wanted me to say.

"Make it stop," I whispered.

"I can," he said. "Do you believe me?"

"Yes."

"Are you willing to do anything I tell you?" he asked.

"Yes." Because I need to find you—you sorry excuse for a freaking human being. I imagined stabbing the long-bladed letter opener through his chest like a stake through a vampire's heart.

"I can make it stop, but only if you agree to kill your mother."

My mouth dropped open.

"Hannah, the bones of your fingers are exposed to the flames—"

"Stop!"

"Do you agree?"

"Yes!"

"Hannah, the fire has died and a cool breeze lessens the pain. Your flesh rapidly heals, and soon your hand will be whole again. The pain is gone. Does it feel better?"

"Yes," I said.

"Experience only peace now. Everything is fine as long as you do as I tell you. Do you understand?"

"Yes."

"Come to the fourth-floor lounge. Do you know which one?" he asked.

"Yes," I said.

"Come through the main entrance. Don't let anyone see you or stop you. Come right away."

"Okay."

"And Hannah," he said, "if you defy my instructions, your hand will light on fire, and you will experience excruciating pain. Do you understand?"

"Yes," I said.

"Goodbye, Hannah. I'll see you soon."

I slammed the phone down. The skin on my left hand was pinker than my right. My chin quivered. The fire was an illusion. I steadied my breathing and hoisted the purse's strap over my shoulder.

The hallway outside the offices was empty. I ran through the back halls to the freight elevator so there'd be less chance of anyone seeing me or stopping me. I pressed the call button and paced back and forth waiting. Finally, the doors opened and I dashed inside. I pounded the number four button, but the doors stayed open. I poked it again, and the doors closed, slowly. The numbers ticked by slowly, and I slapped the wall.

"Hurry up!"

The elevator dinged, and the doors opened to the fourth floor. I bolted out into the hallway and darted around a corner.

And smacked right into Mr. Holloday.

"Whoa!" Mr. Holloday grabbed my shoulder. "Hannah?"

I thrust my left hand into the purse and wrapped my fingers around the can of pepper spray. Mr. Holloday was a nice guy, but I had to get to Mom.

"The police have been searching for you," he said in slow, measured words.

"Please, let me go," I whispered. I had to get to the lounge. Harrison was waiting, and Mr. Holloday was delaying me. My hand heated up and began to sweat inside the purse. I blew out a breath.

"Come with me," he said.

I let him turn me by the shoulders, and then in one quick motion, I shrugged out from his grasp, moved a few steps away, and shot the pepper spray into his face.

He swiped the liquid from his cheeks.

Then it kicked in.

He yelled and rubbed his face.

I bolted the other direction and resisted the urge to touch my own face. Tears streamed down my cheeks from being close to the spray, but I fought through it. I rounded a corner and raced down the hallway toward the lounge. The employee entrance was straight ahead.

Harrison expected me to come through the front entrance.

I swiped Mom's key card and nudged the door open with my foot. I returned the card to the purse and clutched the pepper spray. The small backroom of the lounge had wall-to-wall lockers for the employees, and it was dark. The door closed behind me, and I let my eyes adjust.

Movement across the room caught my eye. I tried to focus, but someone flipped on the lights and blinded me.

But I shot the pepper spray in that direction anyhow.

Chelsea shrieked.

I gave her another shot of pepper spray and tackled her to the ground. She swatted at me, but then the pain of the spray became too much for her. I covered her mouth and stifled her scream. She scratched at her face and clenched her eyes closed. Snot ran from her nose, and she struggled to breathe. I lifted my hand from her mouth, hoping she wouldn't yell. She gasped for breath and cried.

My own eyes stung from the lingering chemical in the air, but I refused to rub my face. I straddled her waist and snatched the duct tape from the purse. Using my teeth and hands, I tore off a long piece of tape and slapped it across her lips. She tried to rip it off, but I grabbed her wrists and twisted her onto her stomach. I sat on her butt, and she kicked me in the back with her heels. I wrapped the duct tape around her wrists several times. Then I taped her ankles together. I rolled her over. Her eyes were still scrunched closed. Her face was red and swollen.

She struggled to breathe through her nose. I ripped the duct tape from her mouth, and she took in a huge breath. And another. Then she lay there and cried.

I loathed the way Chelsea had weaseled into my anchor chair on the morning broadcast and excluded me from my own friends on the student council. I could let go of those things, but I could never forgive her for going along with her father's plans to hurt my mom.

In my head, I knew Chelsea was more of a victim of Harrison than I was, and in my heart, I doubted her ability to overcome the damage he had inflicted on her.

My eyes burned. I dug through the purse and found the wet wipes. I scrubbed my hands and then my face. My vision was cloudy, but at least I hadn't been shot directly in the face.

I returned my supplies to the purse and moved over to the door to peer into the darkened kitchen. On the other side was the lounge. Light streamed in beneath the connecting door. I was about to cross into the kitchen when a cell phone vibrated against the hard floor behind me. I stepped back and closed the door.

Chelsea squirmed, and her phone buzzed again. I searched her pockets. I searched the floor around her. Finally, I found it a few inches away.

Two recent texts were from Harrison: Anything happening? Any sign of her?

I texted him back: Nothing. All quiet.

I tossed the phone into the purse. Then I stepped into the dark kitchen and tiptoed across it. I pressed my ear to the door of the lounge and listened. A few muffled noises made it clear someone was in there. I inched the door open and let my eyes adjust to the brightness. The spotlights were aimed at the wingback chair on the stage.

Mom sat in the chair.

Rope restrained her hands in her lap, and more rope lashed her ankles to the wooden feet of the chair. A white cloth gagged her mouth and stretched around to the back of her head. Her always tidy hair was disheveled. Her always perfect makeup ran beneath her eyes. She turned her head toward me, and her eyes locked on me. Her eyebrows rose, and she shook her head wildly.

Every fiber of my being wanted to race over and free her, but I needed to figure out where Harrison was first. I fought the panic welling within me and scanned the perimeter of the lounge for him. Tables filled one side of the room. The stage took up a large portion of the other side, and the brass bar filled the remaining space. No Harrison.

I studied the area again and focused on the darker places and the edges that lurked in shadows. Maybe he hid behind the bar, crouched down as predator waiting to strike. I checked the mirrors for reflections, for movement of any sort. Nothing. But the hair on the back of my neck stood up.

And then Harrison grabbed me from behind.

His bulky hand covered my mouth and muffled my screams. His other hand dug into the road rash on my forearm. My vision blurred with the pain. He dragged me into the lounge and threw me onto the hardwood stage at my mom's feet.

Harrison paced and mumbled to himself. Then he stopped and faced me. His pupils dilated until the blackness overtook the pigment of his irises.

I repeated my mantra in my mind. I would save my mom by any means necessary. I scooted up into a sitting position and leaned against Mom's legs. She was trembling.

Harrison came closer, cocked his arm backward, and slapped me across the face with his open palm. The force of the blow threw me against the floor. Mom fought against her restraints, her screams stifled by the gag.

"I don't know how you're resisting the hypnosis," Harrison said. "You may be strong-willed like your father, but the fact is I don't need your compliance."

He wrapped his huge hands around Mom's neck and squeezed. Her eyes widened, and her body tensed.

I was strong-willed just like my father. The father I never really got to know because Harrison ruined him. The father Harrison's insanity had taken away from me. I would stop him from taking my mother also.

I dug into the purse for the letter opener, and then I spiked it into Harrison's calf. The metal sliced right through his jeans and lodged into his flesh. Blood spread in a circular pattern, darkening the light blue denim. He howled like a wounded animal and recoiled. He twisted and yanked it free. Blood dripped from the edge of the metal onto the floor. He lowered his chin, licked his lips, and glared at me. Utter madness radiated from him.

He was going to kill me.

I clutched the purse and sprinted for the other side of the lounge. I foraged through it for the pepper spray but found the heavy-duty staple gun. I spun and chucked it at him, but he batted it away. My meager efforts were nothing against him.

He came at me with the letter opener raised high.

I thrust my hand into the purse again and caught hold of the pepper spray.

I yanked it free and shot at him.

His upper lip peeled back, and he bared his teeth like a rabid canine. The letter opener clattered to the floor. Harrison covered his eyes and yowled in pain. He used his shirt to wipe his face, and he spit onto the carpet trying to clear his sinuses.

I dropped the pepper spray and bolted back to the stage. My eyes had swollen, and I struggled to see, but I reached for the pocketknife. I popped the blade open and cut the ropes on Mom's wrists. She snatched the knife from me and finished freeing herself. Snot ran from my nose, and I struggled to breathe.

Mom reached behind her head to untie the gag, and without any warning, Harrison lurched forward and stabbed the letter opener into the meat of Mom's upper thigh. The gag fell, and she screamed. Her fingers went rigid, and her arms shook.

Harrison grabbed me by the hair and threw me backward like a toy. A clump of my hair fell from Harrison's grasp and drifted to the floor. I was inconsequential. My head hit the hardwood, and everything darkened.

> *I control my mind, body, and spirit.*
> *Nobody can come anywhere near it.*
> *Using any means necessary I'll rescue my mother.*
> *Because I am in control, none other.*

Mom's screams abruptly stopped.

I lifted myself up in time to see Harrison press the pocketknife to Mom's neck. Her skin moved with the edge of the blade. She still sat in the chair, clutching the armrests. The letter opener protruded from the muscle of her thigh. Harrison whispered something in her ear and yanked at her hair with his free hand. Perspiration beaded along Mom's forehead.

"I never loved you," Mom said to Harrison. "I changed my name and moved across the country to get away from your stalking. You were a delusional idiot back at Princeton, and you are still—"

"Shut up!" Harrison yelled at her. "I was smart enough back then to manipulate your husband, and you, into thinking he was schizophrenic. I was smart enough to convince him to kill himself." Mom's eyes widened in horror. "And I'm smart enough now to do the same thing to your daughter. She will never—"

Mom kneed him in the balls, but he was relentless. He only grimaced and kept the knife to her throat. If she struggled against him more, the blade would cut her. There was nothing else she could do.

"You killed my husband?" she whispered. Mom's eyebrows creased and her face flushed crimson.

Harrison nodded. "And now I will kill you and your daughter."

"You've been manipulating Hannah the same way?" Seeing the pain in Mom's eyes knocked the wind out of me.

Harrison let go of her hair and stroked her cheek.

Mom caught my eye and yelled, "Hannah! Run!"

Harrison angled his head and glared at me with the beady demon eyes I'd seen in the car accident.

He was evil incarnate.

His lips curled upward into a sinister smile. Snot oozed from his nose. His eyelids were pink and swollen. But none of that stopped him.

He wrenched Mom's head to the side and pressed the blade into the side of her neck. Blood trickled down her skin in tiny beads at first, but then they formed a long train racing down her neck.

Rage boiled up from depths I'd never felt before. I screamed at the top of my lungs and flew across the stage, slamming my body into Harrison's. He was bigger than me, but I knocked him to the floor. The chair tipped to the side, and Mom fell free. The pocketknife skidded across the stage, and I ran for it. Harrison grabbed my ankle and jerked me down to his level. I thrust out my hand and barely grasped the end of the knife before Harrison pulled me toward him. I whipped around, moving with the momentum, and flailed my arm forward. My fingers tightened around the casing of the pocketknife, and I stabbed it into his neck.

His eyes went wide.

I jerked out the knife, and blood spurted and arced away from him. His body flopped backward to the floor. What had I done?

My gaze darted from Harrison to the knife. His blood covered the blade. I loosened my grasp, and I noticed for the first time that Dad's name was engraved in the casing. The knife had been my father's. And my mother had kept it all these years.

It fell from my hand and clattered to the floor.

Harrison's back arched and his mouth opened, as if he was silently screaming out in horror. A black mist surged from his gaping mouth. It spiraled upward, growing in size. For a brief moment the mist took the shape of decaying flesh and rotting talons as I'd seen in the bathroom mirror at home. I was not hallucinating. Not then and not now. Harrison had been possessed by this demon, and they'd acted together. But then I remembered what Kyla had said about Harrison getting kicked out of Princeton for messing with demonic rituals. Had Harrison commanded the evil spirits or had they commanded him? And for how long? The man who knew the answers lay dead in front of me. He had committed atrocities that I could barely fathom. But in some small way had I taken a step down the same path? I'd opened my mind to outside influences, and because of that my fingers had ripped Chelsea's shirt; my hands had set fire to the Santos home; my distraction had killed Jordan. Of course, I could claim innocence and say the devil made me do it, but a part of me had wanted revenge against Chelsea; a part of me had envied the Santos family; and another part of me had wanted to be rid of Jordan.

The demon returned to its blackened mist form and swirled toward me. I stared it down and refused to flinch or turn away. It hesitated. Then it spun upward and dissipated along the ceiling.

Maybe it realized my mind was closed to its games. I'd reclaimed my power.

The room brightened as though someone had turned up the lights.

I sat in shock for a brief moment. Then I snapped out of it and scrambled over to Mom.

She had her hands wrapped around her neck, but blood seeped between her fingers. Her cheeks were wet with tears. She said nothing, but her eyes begged me to help her. I tugged the crocheted scarf from the purse and pressed it to Mom's neck. Her body relaxed, and she closed her eyes.

"Mom!"

Her eyes fluttered opened. I grabbed her hands and pushed them against her wound.

"Keep pressure. I have to call for help."

Her fingers tensed.

"Do you understand?" I pleaded with her, and my tears fell onto her blood-soaked skin. I needed her to help.

She pressed her hands against the scarf, which was changing from gray to red.

I dug Chelsea's phone from the purse and dialed 911. Then I darted over to the house phone behind the bar and dialed zero. Both operators answered at the same time.

"I need help!" I said. "John Harrison cut my mom's throat. Beth O'Leary. He stabbed her thigh. Please. Send the paramedics. We're in the lounge on the fourth floor of the Main Street Hotel." I dropped the house phone and ran back over to my mom. I switched the cell phone to speaker and set it next to me. I wrapped my hands around Mom's to help stop the bleeding, but she went limp beneath me.

"No, Mom!" More tears flooded down my face and mingled with her blood. I'd been so mad at her for lying about Dad and how he died, but she didn't even know the truth herself until now. "Mom, you can't die." She moved us across the country, not to get away from the memories of Dad, but to get away from Harrison. She was trying to protect us.

She struggled to open her eyes halfway, but then blood dripped from her mouth. My heart sank.

"Mom, I love you. Please, hold on. Help is coming." I leaned forward and pressed my forehead to hers.

In the background the 911 operator asked questions, but none of it made any sense.

I lifted my head when Mr. Holloday burst through the main entrance of the lounge with a security guard on his heels. Mr. Holloday ran behind the bar and yanked out towels from beneath the counter. He darted over to us and knelt next to Mom, applying the towels to her neck. His face was red and swollen from the pepper spray.

The security guard checked Harrison, who lay motionless in a pool of his own blood.

Mr. Holloday pressed two fingers to the side of Mom's neck searching for her pulse. "Does she have other injuries—"

Chelsea let out an earth-shattering scream from the locker room.

Mr. Holloday twisted toward the sound. "Someone else is here?"

The security guard moved toward the kitchen.

"Harrison's daughter is in the locker room," I said. "She helped kidnap Mom."

Mr. Holloday glared at Harrison's body. "He looks familiar."

"He auditioned Thursday," I said. "Mom told him to leave."

Mr. Holloday's eyes narrowed, but he kept pressure on Mom's wound.

‹⠂ • ⠐›

Two EMTs helped my mom, and I sat on the edge of the stage, staring at my blood-covered hands. What were the chances Mom would survive her neck injury when Harrison died from his own neck wound?

A police photographer snapped pictures of my injuries: my face, bruised and bloodied; my head, scalped bald in one spot; my hands, covered in Mom's blood. A woman in a CSI jacket scraped under my fingernails and caught the bits in tiny bags. When she finished, an EMT cleaned and bandaged my facial wounds and then the road rash on my forearm. I told him more was along my left thigh. He cut the side of my slacks and spread ointment over the wounds before wrapping my leg in clean cotton gauze.

"Hannah, I'm Detective Samuelson," a man said. I peered up and recognized the detective from Manny's house.

"I remember."

I reached into Mom's purse for the wet wipes and left pink fingerprints on everything I touched. I yanked out a wipe and scrubbed my skin and my torn, chipped fingernails.

The EMT stopped me. "Let me do that." He used a moist cloth to wipe my hands and checked for any remaining wounds. He applied ointment and bandages to the cuts on my hands.

"You have friends who really care about you," Detective Samuelson said.

"Who are you talking about?" I asked. Certainly not Chelsea. Right then, officers escorted her through the lounge with her hands in cuffs. She had moved here last fall and had infiltrated our group. We'd accepted her, and all along she'd been doing the bidding of Harrison, laying the groundwork to make me look crazy out of my mind.

She mumbled incessantly to no one in particular. As she passed Harrison's body, she asked, "Can I go home now?"

Detective Samuelson perched next to me on the stage and set his hand on top of mine. "Hannah, Eugene is fine. Firefighters got to him in time. He's at the hospital waiting for you. He told me everything."

My head dropped in relief. "I thought he was dead," I said. My chest heaved, and I gasped for air.

Detective Samuelson wrapped his arm around me. I sobbed into his shoulder. I had hoped Plug would be saved, but I hadn't allowed myself to believe it. Just like I couldn't let myself believe Mom would be okay.

"I assure you, Eugene is very much alive," Detective Samuelson said.

In that moment, I knew for certain, my feelings for Plug were real. Out from under the influence of the hypnotist or the demons, I still cared about Plug, and I needed to see him.

"Kyla and Nick are in the hotel lobby, waiting to come up here if that is what you want," the detective said.

I brushed away my tears and nodded.

He motioned to the officer standing nearby. "Let Kyla and Nick come up."

Detective Samuelson squeezed my hands. "Your friends fought hard for you. They told us everything that's happened, and they showed us the videos with Harrison manipulating you. We've been trying to catch up to you, Hannah. We want to help you."

I glanced at Harrison's body. The CSI people were taking pictures and collecting evidence.

"Hotel security caught it all on video," Detective Samuelson said. "Well, most of it. The video pixelated out a few times. Some sort of glitch in the system. But there's enough to prove self-defense."

"Did the video show the spirit leaving Harrison's body?" I asked.

Detective Samuelson raised his eyebrows. "Spirit? I don't know. That's not my area of expertise."

The EMTs lifted Mom onto a gurney. Detective Samuelson gently took my hand and helped me up. We walked over to Mom.

She reached out for me. She was alive. And alert.

I wrapped my hands around hers.

Beneath the oxygen mask, Mom tried to speak. I leaned in closer.

"I'm so proud of you," she whispered.

I pressed my cheek against hers. "I love you so much, Mom," I whispered in her ear.

"We need to get her to the hospital," an EMT said.

Reluctantly, I let go of Mom. I kissed her on the forehead and tucked her hand in next to her side.

The EMT adjusted the oxygen mask on Mom's mouth and nose. "The knife didn't sever any major arteries in her neck," he said, "but she may need surgery to repair the damage. And the thigh laceration needs to be stitched up, but it will heal. Would you like to ride in the ambulance with her?"

"Yes." I walked with them toward the lounge doors and cried silently.

Kyla and Nick exploded through the entrance before we reached it. Kyla threw her arms around me.

"Are you all right?" she asked and held me tighter. Her indigo hair buried my face.

"Of course not," Nick said and wrapped his arms around both of us. "But she will be. If she can take down Tall-Tree-Chelsea and her Devil-of-a-Dad, Hannah can do anything."

They held me even tighter.

"Hannah," Detective Samuelson said, "if you want to ride with your mom in the ambulance, we need to go."

Kyla and Nick drew back, but they each held onto my hands. I nodded at the detective.

"Meet me at the hospital?" I asked Kyla and Nick.

"Of course," she said. "We'll do whatever you want."

❧ • ❦

Lights flashed beneath the awning of the Main Street Hotel. A throng of reporters shouted questions and thrust their microphones in my face. Mr. Holloday and Detective Samuelson shielded me with their arms as I followed Mom's gurney to the ambulance. The aromas of blood and pepper spray still clung to the inside of my nose, and my stomach churned.

"Hannah!" the reporters shouted in chorus.

"Did you love your mom?" some dumb guy asked.

"Why did you set fire to your boyfriend's house?" another one yelled.

Mr. Holloday helped me up into the colossal white ambulance.

"I'll meet you at the hospital," the detective said.

He closed the door, and I sat on the side bench. I held Mom's hand, and the ambulance crept through the crowd of onlookers that had formed in front of the hotel.

The driver flipped the sirens on and sped toward the hospital.

❧ • ❦

A team of doctors met my mom in the ambulance bay. Kyla and Nick waited there for me as well. The doctors assessed my mom and rushed her off to surgery. Kyla had the forethought to tell them we'd be waiting in Eugene Polaski's room, and a nurse assured us they would find me there after the surgery.

"How'd you beat the ambulance here?" I asked Kyla.

"You've never seen her drive," Nick said.

Kyla smiled and looped her arm through mine. "Let's go see Plug."

Before we reached his room, we ran into Mrs. Santos and Manny in the hallway. We halted about six feet apart. They each wore navy blue police department T-shirts, and it was the first time I'd ever seen Mrs. Santos without makeup. She wiped a tissue beneath her eyes, but more tears spilled down her pallid cheeks.

Manny shoved his hands in his pockets and stared at the floor. My first instinct was to kick him for not believing in me and sticking with me through the hard stuff. But then I remembered how Jordan's mom had slapped me in this very same hospital. I remembered how awful it felt. The hypnotist had left my mind open to his manipulation and to evil influences. The accident was a result of both.

I had no idea if Jordan's family could ever forgive me, but I knew that Manny couldn't forgive me for changing. He wanted our relationship to stay the same forever in a tight little box, and I'd ruined that for him. He had folded when I needed him the most. It's easy to be with someone when everything goes right, but Manny couldn't deal with my dark side when everything went wrong. And I wanted to be with someone who could.

"Hannah," Mrs. Santos said, "the police explained to us that you were not responsible for the fire."

"I'm still sorry you had to go through that," I said.

"I jumped to conclusions," Mrs. Santos said. "Protecting my children was foremost in my mind, and . . . I apologize for assuming the worst about you."

She had once thought of me like a daughter. She'd rocked me and hummed lullabies to me after the accident. But everything changed when she found me on the couch with her son.

Manny gazed up at me. "Can we go somewhere and talk?"

"No." I answered too quickly. But exhaustion clouded my mind, and I couldn't bear the idea of having a drawn-out conversation with Manny right now.

"I'm sorry." He ran his hand through his chestnut hair and frowned. He seemed to struggle to find the words, and then he suddenly pivoted and walked away.

Mrs. Santos gazed at me for a moment, and then she followed Manny.

"That went well," Nick said.

Kyla wrapped her arm around my shoulders and escorted me to Plug's room. I paused at the door. Necro was already there, huddled over Plug's bedside. Plug's grandma sat nearby with her hand resting on Plug's leg. Necro lifted his head and smiled when he saw me. Days ago I thought he was scary looking, but Harrison, in fact, had been the scariest man I'd ever seen on the face of this earth. I had been so wrong about so many things. Nick nudged me, but I was immovable. So much had happened in the past week. Was it all really over?

Necro tapped Plug's leg. "Hannah's here."

Plug turned his head toward me, and a tear rolled down his cheek. Plug's head was wrapped in bandages, and new stitches blanketed his lower lip. His rings, plugs, and trinkets had all been removed from his face and fingers. An IV tube ran from his arm to a bag dangling from a pole.

Necro came to me and took my hand. He led me to Plug's side and set my hand on top of Plug's. We said nothing. No words were necessary. I knew that Plug had been as worried about me as I had been about him. And now the comfort of touch was all either of us needed. A heart monitor beeped, and the blood pressure cuff activated. When it finished, I lowered the rail on the bed, lifted Plug's arm, and lay next to him. I wrapped my arm around his waist, and he wrapped his around my shoulders.

Necro set his hand on mine while Kyla and Nick filled him in on everything that had happened over the past week, focusing on how the hypnotist and malevolent spirits had worked in concert to torment me. They explained that Harrison's ultimate goal was to seek revenge against my mom. They made it sound so simple.

There was a tap at the door, and I recognized Detective Samuelson's voice. He moved around to the far side of the bed so we could see each other without me needing to move.

Dr. James came in behind him and stood at the end of the bed. "How are you feeling, Hannah?"

"I'm not schizophrenic and neither was my dad."

"Detective Samuelson has filled me in, and I'm here to see if I can help in any way." Dr. James worked his finger into the knot of his solid black tie and loosened it.

"I have some news," Detective Samuelson said. "When the officers took Chelsea down to the police station, they ran her prints through the system. Turns out she's not Harrison's daughter."

"What?" Kyla asked.

Detective Samuelson nodded at her. "Chelsea's name is actually Sarah, and she was abducted eighteen months ago. The police had primarily focused their search on the East Coast." He handed me Sarah's missing-person flyer.

I sat up, stunned. The flyer pictured a brunette with little makeup. The description said Sarah played cello in the youth symphony and loved to read. Nick and Kyla looked over my shoulder at the flyer.

"It doesn't even look like her," I said. Harrison had manipulated her mind, changed her appearance, and orchestrated her life. She was his pawn. Nothing more.

"Monarch slave," Nick said. "He used hypnosis not only to change a bookworm into a volleyball player but also to change her into a coconspirator."

"What will happen to her?" I asked. None of this had been her fault.

"Lots of counseling," the detective said. "Her parents in New Jersey have already been contacted, and they're on their way out here."

"Unbelievable," Kyla said.

Nick rubbed his jaw. "I'm telling you, crap like this goes down all the time. We, the citizens, just never hear about it on the daily newscast."

Necro cleared his throat. "What about Hannah? Will any charges be filed against her?"

Detective Samuelson shook his head. "Hannah, you will need some serious counseling yourself to—"

"To make sure you're deprogrammed," Nick interrupted, and then he glared at Dr. James as he continued to speak. "We'll research the options and make sure you have the best expert in the field." He turned to Detective Samuelson. "Right?"

He smiled at Nick. "I'm sure we can find someone that you, the department, and Dr. James will endorse."

"You're right, Nick," Dr. James said. "Prolonged hypnosis and mind control is outside my area of proficiency, and I regret that I wasn't able to help Hannah more. But I will do everything in my power to find the right expert to help her, and Sarah, recover fully."

"Do any of you have any other questions?" Detective Samuelson asked.

"Can I stay here?" I asked.

"Yes." Detective Samuelson reached into his pocket, pulled out a business card, and gave it to me. "Call me if you need anything, but it appears you're taken care of here. I'll be in contact with you and your mom later."

I settled back down into the small bed and felt at peace with my friends beside me.

SUNDAY

SEPTEMBER 1

I paced the perimeter of Mom's hospital room. She shifted in bed, and I paused to see if she'd wake, but she continued sleeping. I slid the window blinds to the side and let in the first rays of dawn, but even that didn't make a difference. The doctors assured me they'd repaired the damages caused by Harrison—the physical damages—but I needed Mom to be alert enough to tell me herself.

I blew out a long breath. I needed a distraction.

Next to Mom's bed, I stood at the tall rolling table and opened the lacquered wooden box of premium artist's pencils that Nick and Kyla had given me last night. Inside, there had to be at least fifty different colors. I flipped open the new sketchpad, caressed the blank white page, and imagined the possibilities.

After a moment of indecision, I selected a cranberry pencil and roughed out the edges of a geranium. I became more confident with the form and darkened the color. Then I added golden tones to highlight the petals and ashen gray to shadow the blossoms. I closed my eyes to recall more of the violets, irises, and daffodils that bloomed in the safe place of my mind.

When I opened my eyes, Lily and Mark were in the doorway. Lily sat in a wheelchair and Mark stood behind her. A pang struck my heart, because the golden silk scarf wrapped around Lily's head, concealing the bandage and hair loss, was the present I'd picked for her at the mall last Sunday.

She glanced from me to my mom and back to me again.

"Can we come in?" Lily asked.

"Of course," I said and bumped the bed table, sending my sketchpad to the floor. I bent down to retrieve it.

Mark wheeled Lily into the room and then set the brakes at the base of her chair.

"Manny told us everything," Mark said.

"Everything?" Everything from his perspective, everything he knew about, but certainly not everything that had happened over the past week. I wiped my sweaty hands on the hospital scrubs I wore.

"You look more like yourself," Lily said.

"So do you." The swelling had gone down around her eyes and lips. Her skin had regained much of its healthier color.

Lily pointed at my outfit. "You always did look brilliant in blue."

"Yeah, my choices were these scrubs or a hospital gown." I plucked at the baggy top. I'd showered—without incident—while Mom had been in surgery yesterday. It had felt great to rid myself of Harrison's blood and the stench of the pepper spray, but now sweat rolled down my back. I was nervous to talk with my old friends after all that had happened this week.

"You're here early this morning," I said and glanced at the clock on the wall. "It's still before seven."

"How could any of us sleep with all that's happened?" Mark said.

"You're right." I retied the drawstring at my waist. I had been awake since Friday. I knew I should be exhausted, but I couldn't rest until I knew for myself that Mom was going to be fine.

"So you heard about Chelsea?" I asked.

They nodded.

"Chelsea convinced us you were crazy." Mark rubbed his face. Then he shook out his arms. "My head understands she was a puppet, but my heart can't believe our whole relationship was fake."

"Are you going to see her?" I asked.

"I heard she's in the psychiatric wing with no visitors allowed," Mark said, "but I'm going to try. I just wanted to stop here first and tell you how sorry I am . . . for everything."

"Thanks, Mark. It means a lot to me."

He gave me an awkward hug, and then he headed out.

I turned to Lily, and we smiled weakly at each other. "I'm glad to see you're out of bed already."

"They changed my meds, and it made a big difference." Lily wrung her hands. "I know Jordan's gone. My heart's been ripped out forever, and there's no going back to fix any of it. A grief counselor visited me. I think that'll help."

"I'm so sorry about everything." Tears spilled from my eyes down to the tiled floor.

Lily clutched my hand and tugged me closer. "No, I'm sorry."

I knelt in front of her, and we cried together.

"I never intended for any of this—"

"Stop!" Lily said. "I begged you to go to that hypnotist show. If I hadn't—"

"Harrison would've found another way to get to me." I drew back to see her face. "This was not your fault. He targeted me and my mom from the beginning."

"And Chelsea . . ." she started, but her voice trailed off.

"There's no way either of us could've guessed what was going on with her," I said.

"I can't imagine what she's been through. Or you."

"I was manipulated by Harrison for a week," I said. "Chelsea was under his reign for eighteen months."

"I know you said Harrison would've found another way to get to you, but I still can't get over the fact that if I hadn't insisted you go onstage that night . . . Jordan would still be alive." She flushed, and tears raced down her cheeks.

"None of this is your fault, Lily."

"You're right. It's Harrison's fault." She fidgeted with the golden silk above her ears. "Oh, Hannah, I'm probably the crazy one here, but I told Manny I'd put in a good word for him. This is undoubtedly the first thing he and I have ever agreed on. It wasn't his fault and well . . ."

I wiped my face and waited for her to continue.

"He's in the hallway," she said. "He hasn't left the hospital since you got here yesterday. He wants to talk to you."

"There's nothing left to say." I didn't want to see him.

"He wants to speak to you in private," she said.

"I'm staying here with my mom."

"She's asleep, Hannah. You guys can talk right here."

My chin quivered. I wasn't sure I could deal with any more drama.

"You and Manny have been friends a long time," Lily said. "You can listen to what he has to say."

She was right. I owed him that much.

"At least do it for me," she said before I had a chance to respond.

"Okay."

Lily clapped her hands together and beamed. Her hazel eyes sparkled for the first time since before the accident, and I caught a glimpse of my friend's previous vibrancy. Recovery was possible. For all of us.

"Wheel me back out to the hall," Lily said. I did and found Mrs. Sloane waiting to take Lily back to her room. Mrs. Sloane grasped my hand.

We hugged each other tightly.

Over Mrs. Sloane's shoulder, I made eye contact with Manny, and my heart pounded. His eyes were red and swollen. Tears flowed freely over the cuts and bruises on his face. Wet spots dotted his navy police T-shirt.

Mrs. Sloane released me. I said goodbye to her and Lily. Then I returned to my mom's room. Manny followed me.

Once inside, he reached for me, but I jerked away. He wiped his cheeks with the backs of his hands.

"Hannah, please," Manny said. His brown eyes widened, and he raked his fingers through his hair. "I want us to go back to the way things were before."

"We can't." Images of the accident flashed through my mind, along with the awful smells and sensations. I had known in the single moment when I lost control of my bladder that things would never be the same for me, and I was right. I didn't want to go back to the way things were before—living in self-doubt and worrying about maintaining my composure all the time.

I'd learned this week that I was lovable no matter what happened. I fought for control of my own mind and my own happiness. I saved my mom's life. I fell in love with Plug. And I had seen Manny's true nature.

"Please, Hannah," he said.

I pinched my lips together and shook my head.

"So, it's over? Just like that?" he asked.

"You're the one who quit on me when—"

"I saw you with Eugene, and I got jealous." He took a step closer, and I held my ground. "I saw you changing, and it scared me. The idea of schizophrenia scared me. The police told me you set fire to our house."

The pain in Manny's eyes tore me apart. A week ago, we almost had it all. And being near him—the smell of his shaving cream, the curve of his lips, the memories of the Ferris wheel, and the possibilities of what could have been—overwhelmed me.

He reached for my hand, and I let him take it. He laced his smooth fingers through mine, and with his other hand, he tucked my hair behind my ear.

"I can't imagine life without you," he said and leaned in to kiss me, but I pushed against his chest.

"No," I said with a steady voice.

"How can you just stop loving me?" he asked.

I hadn't stopped, but I had changed, and my life couldn't be about what was best for Manny. He'd have to figure that out on his own. Right now, I needed to make choices for myself. And a lasting relationship required more than love. It required determination and commitment from both people.

I lowered my voice. "Whether I had schizophrenia or not, you stopped believing in me when I needed you the most."

Manny flushed, and his jaw tensed.

"You need to leave," I said.

He dropped his head and walked out of the room.

He'd been my best friend for years. I had believed we'd be together forever. I moved over to the window, pressed my forehead against the cool glass, and wept. It was over.

After a few minutes, I wiped my tears and moved back over to the tall bed table. I opened the sketchpad to a fresh page and drew a leafy vine around the perimeter, dotting it with violet blossoms. With a black pencil, I wrote in the middle of the page:

Dear Chelsea . . . Sarah . . .
    I'm so sorry for everything you've endured with Harrison. I hope you can find peace reuniting with your family. If I can do anything to help, please contact me. You're in my thoughts.
                                        Sincerely,
                                        Hannah

A tear fell from my cheek onto the page and distorted one of the blossoms I'd drawn. When Chelsea had yelled at me in the school hallway on Monday, she had said that Jordan could never go home again. Then in the hotel lounge, she had asked the officer if she could go home. More tears fell, and I mopped my face with a tissue from the side table. At least Chelsea was going home now.

I carefully tore the page from the sketchpad, folded it into thirds, and wrote Chelsea's name on the outside. Then I wrote the name Sarah, too, because I was uncertain which name the hospital had her listed under. I took it out to the nurse's station and asked them to deliver it. They said they would.

When I returned to Mom's room, her eyes were open, and she tried to clear her throat. Relief flooded through me, and I hurried to her bed. She smacked her dry lips together and licked them.

"Water?" she whispered.

I lifted the cup and angled the straw to her lips. She took a few sips, and then I set the cup on the side table next to the six-pack of Dr. Pepper that Nick and Kyla had brought me last night. I swept wayward hairs from her face, and my fingers lingered on her pale, warm skin.

She reached up and grasped my hand. "You're okay?" she whispered.

"I'm fine, Mom. How are you?"

"Sore." She touched the bandage around her neck. "You saved my life." Tears rolled down her face, and she wiped them away. "I should've told you the truth sooner—"

"Mom, even you didn't know the whole truth about Harrison and Dad, but now we do. And I know that you moved us across the country to protect us from Harrison. I know you did the best you could to keep me safe."

I stepped over to the nearby chair and picked up the brown box. I turned and set it next to Mom.

"What's this?" she asked.

Without explanation, I removed the lid and lifted out the family album. I turned to the first page and showed Mom her wedding picture. She covered her mouth and sobbed. I flipped through the pages of the album so she could see the progression of our family in the pictures. Last night I had asked Nick and Kyla to go to my house and get the box for me. At the time, I wanted to comfort myself, but now I realized I needed my family to feel whole again.

Mom gripped my hand. "Thank you for saving this," she said. I showed her the loose snapshots in the box. We reminisced and thumbed through them together.

"I love you," Mom said, "and I loved your father."

"I miss him so much."

"Me too," she said.

I brushed my tears aside and embraced her.

⤙ • ⤚

Soft morning light spilled in through the window of Plug's quiet hospital room. My entire body relaxed when he opened his eyes and smiled at me.

"You're awake," I whispered and stepped toward his bed. The aromas of antiseptics and disinfectants made me want to sneeze. I lifted my hand to my nose and actually missed the fragrance of sage.

"Where's your dad?" I asked.

"Breakfast with Grandma. They'll be back." Plug patted the spot next to him. I recalled how the hypnotist had insisted that the best seats in the house were on his stage. He was wrong. The best seat in the house was right here next to Plug. I sat and took his callused hand in mine. His knuckles were marked with cuts from his battles with Manny and Harrison.

"How are you?" I asked.

"I hurt a little." Plug grinned, as much as his stitches allowed.

"You suffered a brain injury," I said. "I'm sure you hurt more than a little."

"Only a concussion," Plug said.

"A severe concussion," I corrected him. "And a torn-up face, and—"

"Are you here to make me feel better or worse?"

"Sorry," I said. "I am so sorry. For everything."

"Stop apologizing," Plug said. "It is what it is. And I can tell you, this week has been the most exhilarating week of my life."

"It was almost the last week of your life."

"It would've been worth it."

I leaned forward and kissed the one spot on his cheek where there were no bruises or stitches.

"Think about it," Plug said, "I've spent years researching the occult, and in one week, we experienced—"

"Oh, so you only enjoyed being around me because I was haunted by malicious spirits and stalked by an evil psychopath?"

"Fringe benefits." Plug pulled me closer. "Besides, this is only the beginning for us. Who knows what the future holds. Maybe next week will be filled with witches or voodoo or—"

"Stop," I said and laughed. But he was right; this was only the beginning for us. If I hadn't participated in that hypnotism show, I wouldn't be here next to Plug now. The worst thing in my life had led me to the best thing. I gazed at Plug and considered the possibilities of the future. With him, I could let go of all my worries and feel more relaxed than ever before.

"For now," I said, "maybe we could just have a boring week of nothing but us."

"Hmm," Plug said, his eyes brightening as he touched my face. "Nothing but us? That has a lot of potential."

Praise for Margo Kelly's *Who R U Really?*

"Kelly's first novel is a suspenseful page-turner with multiple suspects, a little bit of romance, and a strong but not overbearing message."
—*Kirkus Reviews*

"Suspenseful novel that's guaranteed to give readers goose bumps—particularly as events heat up toward the end. A good choice for families to read together."
—*School Library Journal*

"*Who R U Really?* is a fantastically creepy book that is surprisingly realistic and totally engrossing . . . Once I opened it, I couldn't close it. *Who R U Really?* is a satisfyingly unique YA thriller that left me guessing up until almost the very last page . . . This book is very realistic and I really enjoyed the writing style."
—*Tempest Books*

"This was such a good book. A story that all of us should read . . . This was a great read that opened my eyes even more about the Internet."
—*Just Us Girls blog*

"Based on actual events, the story should be required reading for all teens."
—*VOYA magazine*

Praise for Margo Kelly's *Who R U Really?*

"Kelly shows us just how terrifying, dangerous, and unknown the world of online gaming can be— especially for a young teen . . . The book is well written and the story believable and engaging . . . I strongly recommend this book. It was a great read and delivered a strong, important message."
—*Idaho Statesman*

"This book is sure to spark a dialogue between parents and teens as well as tell an appealing cautionary tale to a younger audience and would be a good addition to any middle school, high school, or public library."
—*Idaho Librarian*
(A Publication of the Idaho Library Association)

"This tense thriller offers useful lessons."
—*Horn Book Guide*